Nobody had promised us that Hell would be easy

It had been the most unpleasant world in the Confederación, until Springworld was colonized. Now I figure it's a toss-up, though Hell might just have an edge.

Hell has only one important industry: training people for violence by tempering them to violence. Just about everything that moves on this rotten planet can kill you, including the Hellers. Maybe especially the Hellers. Planets that are serious about war send their future military leaders here to learn their trade. They either learn it or they die.

We were signed up for the *soft* course. They told us we probably wouldn't die.

JOE HALDEMAN &
JACK C. HALDEMAN II

THERE IS NO DARKNESS

SF
ACE BOOKS, NEW YORK

Parts of this book appeared, in rather different form, in *Asimov's SF Adventure Magazine*™, as the novellas ''Starschool'' (Spring 1979) and ''Starschool on Hell'' (Summer 1979).

THERE IS NO DARKNESS

An Ace Book

Published by arrangement with the authors

ISBN: 0-441-80564-7

First Ace Printing: February 1983

Published simultaneously in Canada

Manufactured in the United States of America

Ace Books, 200 Madison Avenue, New York, New York 10016

For Mother and Dad

Malvolio: . . . I say to you, this house is dark.
Clown: Madman, thou errest: I say, there is no
darkness but ignorance . . .
—*Twelfth Night*

PROLOGUE

THERE WAS A TIME when the dominant language on old Earth was English, a complex language directly related to Spanish but with only oblique ties to Pan-swahili.

Throughout most of the Confederación, English is the concern only of scholars, but there are still a few places where it is taught as a mother tongue: an island and part of one continent on Earth, and the sparsely populated planet Springworld.

To admit ignorance of Springworld is not particularly damning, since the young planet has almost nothing of interest beyond the fact of its archaic native language. Its name is a sarcasm: the environment is about as hostile to human life as can be found on any inhabited world. The population must be genetically engineered for giantism and strength, not only to have a fighting chance against the aggressive fauna, but simply to remain *standing* in the fierce winds that characterize its everyday weather.

The only nearby planet of any importance is Selva, which gives Springworld its sole economic contact with the rest of the Confederación. Some of the pharmaceuticals that Selva manufactures depend (for a growth medium) on Springworld's native lichen *volmer*. Since Springworld is fanatically self-sufficient, its trade with Selva has always been done on a strictly cash basis, resulting after several generations in a cash surplus of several million pesetas. With a culture that scorns luxury and prides itself on its independence, Springworld has had difficulty spending this surplus.

In A.C. 354, it did spend some, by sending a boy off to a strange school, and in return got more than it had bargained for.

Prospectus and Admission Requirements:
The Second Voyage of *Starschool**

Starschool offers a unique educational experience for young people destined to become their worlds' leaders, especially in fields associated with interplanetary commercial and political relations. During the five-year term, *Starschool* will visit sixteen Confederación planets, selected either for cultural and historical interest (such as M'walimu and Earth) or on the pragmatic basis of political importance.

The first tour of *Starschool* (A.C. 348-352) was so successful that the Regents have been able to significantly broaden the program without greatly increasing tuition costs (though these are admittedly quite high). Two new worlds have been added, Mundovidrio and Hell, giving students exposure to two extremes of scholarly activity. As most of our clients must know, Mundovidrio is the home of Instituto del Yo Esencial, where students will spend a month in the systematic exploration of states of awareness. Hell, on the other hand, has no commerce other than the hiring out of mercenaries and training other planets' military leaders. Students who are not philosophi-

---

*Starschool is an English word meaning ''Nyota'skuli'' or ''Universidad de los Astros.'' English, of course, was the language spoken by the first people to go to another world in search of knowledge.

cally opposed to it will be given the opportunity of taking a short (and arduous) course in military leadership.

Entrance requirements for *Starschool* are necessarily flexible, with applicants coming from dozens of disparate cultures, but those whose formal education does not approximate the level of an urban bachillerato degree must expect to do extra academic work between planets. The *Starschool* certificate is the equivalent of an advanced degree in interplanetary affairs . . .

EARTH

Curriculum Notes—Earth

Most of what people think they know about Earth is wrong. It is quite an advanced planet technologically, not a primitive backwater. Although currently in a period of economic decline, Earth still has abundant resources, both material and human, and though it may never regain the primacy it had in the early years of the Confederación, it is in no sense on a dead-end street. Aside from its obvious value to historians, archeologists, and linguists, Earth maintains a lively commerce in the exchange of medical techniques, and its entertainment industry is second only to that of Nairobi'pya.

Since all of the Confederación's first-order cultures are directly descended from Terran subgroups—geographical, ethnic, or political—every traveler can find some part of Earth that holds particular historical interest. Communication difficulties have been very much exaggerated in the past. It is true that Earth hosts more than two hundred languages, and thousands of dialects, but even the smallest village will have people who understand Spanish or Pan-swahili.

You must bring to Earth an open mind and a spirit of adventure . . .

1

I WAS OBVIOUSLY supposed to be impressed: loincloth, beads, two meters of hard black Maasai'pyan. Mr. B'oosa walked up to me with two quarterstaffs over his shoulder: hollow shafts of aluminum not quite as long as he was tall. He was a lot shorter than me.

"Mr. Bok," he said. "A friendly challenge?" The expression on his face was not friendly.

"Busy. Sir." I was trying to get some useful exercise out of a weight machine built for people half my size.

"The challenge doesn't interest you?"

I sighed and let the weights rattle back to home position. "I can't fight you, Mr. B'oosa. I outweigh you by fifty kilos . . . and besides—"

"Besides, you're a hardy Springworld pioneer? And I'm just a rich man's son?"

"*And* a head shorter than me *and* five or six years older. Homicide doesn't attract me, thank you sir."

"Oh, but that's exactly the point." He tapped the floor with the two quarterstaffs. "With these, the match will be more than fair."

It would be fun to take him down. But when you're a giant among pygmies, you learn to hold your temper or be branded a bully.

A small crowd was gathering around us. It was between

classes and *Starschool*'s high-gravity gym was packed with students getting in shape for planetfall.

"Come on, Carl; never the wrong time to teach a *ricon* a lesson." That was Garcia Odoñez, another scholarship student. I think he was studying to be a bad example. "You aren't afraid, are you?"

I just looked at him; what I hoped was a withering glance.

"Have you ever used one?" B'oosa held a staff out to me. I tested it. It twisted easily and I smoothed it back into shape, more or less.

"No sir." I could tie the damned thing around his neck.

"A Springer fights fairly or not at all." I tried to hand it back to him but he wouldn't take it.

"An impressive display of brute strength, Carl." He flipped his staff easily from hand to hand. "But strength counts for nothing with the quarterstaff. The request stands."

"Perhaps you could tell me why—why you're challenging me out of nowhere—and I might go along with it. I can't see that I have any quarrel with you." No real quarrel with him personally. But he was a *ricon* and the *ricones* had not made life pleasant the past year.

"You misunderstand. This is not a personal thing . . . I just want to settle a wager. One of my colleagues" —colleagues!—"Mr. Mengistu believes I can best him at the quarterstaff mainly because of longer reach and greater strength. I contend that skill alone determines the winner. If I can beat you, he agrees, size and strength mean little."

"How much are you betting on this little contest?"

He shrugged. "Five thousand."

My father once made P4000 on a crop several years ago. Bad weather had driven the price up. The harvest cost him two fingers and almost killed him.

"All right. But be ready to lose more than a few pesas. Teeth, for instance."

"I doubt it. Where would you like to have the match?"

"Anywhere it'll be easy to clean up the blood. Right here, if these people will clear away."

The crowd shuffled back, making a rough circle four or

five meters in diameter. Didn't look like much room to me, but B'oosa nodded and stepped to the other side of the circle.

I'd never used a quarterstaff—Springers don't have time to learn how to beat on each other with sticks—but I had seen a few matches at the public combats on Selva, during the month while I was waiting for *Starschool* to pick me up. It didn't look all that difficult. You use the staff for both offense and defense, trying to block and attack at the same time.

I swung the staff in a fast arc, getting the feel of it. It made a sound like a spear whipping through the air. The circle widened a bit. "If this were more solid you'd be a dead man. Sir."

"It isn't and, no, I wouldn't be. Take your guard."

"My 'guard'?"

"Take your guard. Prepare to defend yourself. Like this." He spread his feet and held the staff at a slight angle, protecting his body. I did recognize the position and copied it. I had more body to protect, though.

"Are there any rules?" I asked.

"It's ungentlemanly to aim for the eyes. If you knock out a person's eye you must be careful not to step on it."

His own eyes looked calm and suddenly very old. His whole manner changed as he began to advance crabwise toward me, somehow gracefully. Relaxed yet tense, like an animal stalking.

My reflexes had to be better than his; he was a city man and I grew up on a planet full of fast hungry predators. His confidence got to me, though. I decided it would be safest not to play around. Get in there fast and first.

I tried to copy his slow shuffle. Go for the groin? Hell, I didn't want to *kill* him. Solar plexus; that would put him down. I stood my ground and waited for him to come into range.

It seemed to all happen in a fraction of a second. He suddenly danced in and rapped the knuckles of both my hands, so hard I dropped the pole. Reached down to pick it up and he banged me a good backhand to the top of my skull. I shook my head to clear the dizziness, scooped up the staff and drove straight for his solar plexus. He tapped it aside easily with one end of his staff and the other end whistled around to the side of my head—

I woke up lying in my bunk with a coldpack strapped over my left temple. I sat up and, man, fireballs started to tear my head apart.

"Are you all right, Carl?" It was Alegria, a pretty little girl from Selva.

"Sure, just fine. Great. Nothing like a little workout." I swung my feet down to the floor and blocked out the light with one hand. "How long have I been out?"

"All night and half the morning. You came out of it before we got you to the infirmary"—yeah, I could remember that, barely—"but the medic gave you a pill and you were out again, so we carted you back down here. You weigh a ton."

"One hundred-sixty-two kilograms, anyhow." It's not true that I'm sensitive about my weight. People are always exaggerating.

"In case you're interested, you don't have a concussion or anything."

"Feels like I've got concussions to spare. Be glad to share 'em with that little son—"

"Hush, Carl. The Dean thinks it was an accident."

"Accident? Why should I cover up for that *ricon*—"

"Think straight, you big farmer. We aren't covering for *him!*"

Of course . . . giant Springer bully picking on . . . oh, Christ. I leaned back on the pillow. Gently.

"You missed three classes, last night and today. I put your assignments on the table there."

"Thanks, Alegria, you're sweet." A pity she wasn't a meter taller. I felt her hand on my forehead and opened my eyes again, just a squint.

"Want me to get you some wake-up pills? You've got to get your classwork done before we get to Earth." Otherwise they keep you in quarantine until you catch up academically. "You don't want to miss part of the tour."

Far as I was concerned, Earth could go to Hell. "How long before we get there?"

"Less than three days and you've got four days' work. Pills?"

"Just some analgesics."

"On the table, next to your books." The bed creaked a little when she got up and I heard the door slide open. "Study hard, Carl." Then she was gone. I took the headache pills, then lay on the bunk another ten minutes, feeling miserable, before I got up and looked at the books. All of them Earth history, geophysics, customs and so on—not exactly a joy to read even if they'd been in English. But of course, most of them were Spanish and Pan-swahili, both of which I should know better than I do.

My head was still aching when they parked *Starschool* in orbit next to Earth's Customs Satellite. All spindly and spiderlike, the starship-university is great for punching holes through space, but it isn't equipped for landing on planets at all. The lightest gravity would cause crushing torques, tear it apart. We always orbit planets and shuttle down. But first we have to go through the *cinta roja*. "Red tape," you figure it out.

First a team of Earthie doctors came aboard *Starschool* and poked and prodded us to make sure we weren't bringing any nasty alien bugs down to their precious planet. Then we had to fill out a lot of forms. I got writer's cramp from signing my name so many times. Finally we transferred over to the Customs Satellite and stood for a long time in two lines. The line I was in was for everybody who weighed over seventy-five kilograms. It was a short line.

The Dean, Dr. M'bisa, walked over. He was arguing with a little Earthie in a light blue uniform.

"We signed a contract, Mr. Pope-Smythe, a *legal* contract that said *nothing* about this idiotic tax! It guaranteed all of our expenses while—"

"Please, Professor. I didn't say there was anything wrong with your contract. But that's strictly between you and Earth Tours, Limited. None of our business at all.

Perhaps you can get them to reimburse you ... but there's no way any of your students can be allowed to make planetfall until every overweight person has paid the Extraweight Alien Tax.''

"You know as well as I do that Earth Tours will never—"

"Again, Professor, that's *your* problem. My problem is that all of these people have to pay the Extraweight before I can go to lunch. The tax probably isn't covered in your contract because it wasn't in effect until last Avril—but you still have to pay it; the Alianza's laws don't make exceptions for agreements between private, profit-making organizations. Besides, the tax isn't that much—only ten or twenty pesas for all but a couple of these people.''

"And for them?''

"Well, it goes up quite a bit for those over ninety kilos. How much do you weigh, son?'' He was talking to me.

"One hundred-sixty-two kilograms.'' All of it muscle, too, goddammit.

"That much? Oh, dear. Let me see.'' He riffled through the tables in the back of a pamphlet. "That would come to P16,800.''

The Dean exploded. "That's outrageous!''

"It's the law.'' Mr. Pope-Smythe shrugged and held the pamphlet out for him to see.

"Oh, I believe you.'' He waved the book away. Then he snatched it back and checked the figures.

"Dr. M'bisa,'' I said, "I don't want to go to Earth that badly. Not P17,000 worth.'' P17,000! A small fortune on Springworld. My father's biggest crop had brought P4000. "Besides, I don't have a tenth that much.''

"It's not your decision, Carl.'' He looked sour. "Nor your money. That's what the General Fund is for, unforeseen emergencies.''

"But it's more than half my tuition!''

"I well know that. Your planet is getting a real bargain.''

People weren't going to like this. The General Fund was also used to add unplanned side trips, and to make certain purchases for scholarship students. Without it, only *ricónes* could afford souvenirs from places like Nuovo Colombia. "It's too big a bite. It's not worth it."

"Perhaps not," he snapped, then continued, more mildly. "You have no choice in the matter, and neither have I. The Hartford Corporation signed an agreement with your government detailing the benefits you would receive from *Starschool*. You may elect not to land on Hell or Thelugi. You will at least set foot on every other planet. If you don't, your government could sue Hartford for breach of contract."

"I'm willing to take the responsibility."

"How good of you. Unfortunately you cannot. The Regents of *Starschool* stand *in loco parentis* to you until your twenty-first birthday. Until then, you have only limited legal responsibility for your own actions."

He put his hand on my arm. "As you say, it *is* a big bite. But we do have to make allowances for foreign customs, foreign laws, even when they're unreasonable. People will understand."

Somehow it sounded all right when the Dean said it. But after everybody got weighed, all but one of the others was under ninety kilos. Their *total* tax was P1130, not even a tenth of mine. The only other one over ninety was Mr. B'oosa, who had to pay P1900. He just whipped out his checkbook and paid it himself. Hell, why not? He had five thousand extra for knocking me flat the other day.

The total tax took over half of what was left in the student expense fund. That made me one real popular fellow, having accounted for more than nine-tenths of it.

Piling insult on insult, they organized us alphabetically for the Tour, in groups of three. I had to share rooms with good old Mr. B'oosa and another *ricón* by name of Francisco Bolivar. I could tell it was going to be a long Tour.

But even before we got on the shuttle down to Earth's only spaceport, Chimbarazo Interplanetario, I had figured out a plan. A simple plan.

I hoped.

By the same genetic engineering that made me a giant,

all Earthies were midgets—nobody weighed more than forty kilograms.

Somewhere on this beat-up planet there had to be a job—a high-paying job—that called for a man, a boy if you want to get technical about it, who weighed more than four Earthies and stood two and a half meters tall. I swore I would earn back that P16,800, every pesa of it. And get off everybody's list.

II

CHIMBARAZO INTERPLANETARIO was just another space-port. It was big, but who's ever seen a small one? We had a half-hour to kill before getting on the Tour flyer, so I found the nearest newsprojector, slid a demipesa into the slot and pushed the button marked "English."

"Section, please," the machine said.

"Let me have the wannads section," I said.

"Wannads? Query? We have no wannads section."

What did they call wannads on Earth? Wish I'd hit the books a little harder those last three days. "How about jobs?"

"How about jobs?" it echoed. Goddamn dumb machine.

"Do you have a 'jobs' section?"

"Jobs? Query? We have no jobs section."

Employment. "Do you have an 'employment' section?"

"Yes, we have an employment section." *Click.* "Your time has expired. Please deposit two demipesas."

"But I already paid, you stupid—"

Click.

I gave up and slipped it another two demis. A list of jobs came on the screen. Turning a knob, I started to scan them.

It didn't look very promising.

16

EMPLOYMENT OPPORTUNITIES
Chimbarazo-Macro-BA Area

ABSTRACOTYPIST, senior, 30K, gd wrk cond, 314-90343-098367.
ACETOGRAPHER, degr only, 12K, 547-23902-859 430.
ACTOR, sal var, feelie-sens, exp only, no minors, 254-34290-534265.
AEROSPACE ENG, PhD only, 38K, cisplan envir spec pref, Lun office, 452-78335-973489.

. . . and so on. Didn't even know what half of them meant. I must have scanned a hundred before one caught my eye:

GLADIATORS, prizes to 20K, taxfree, esp vibro-club. 8 indiv, 75 team openings. Some animal work. 738-49380-720843.

I wrote down the number and ran to the flyer, just barely making it in time. The Dean scowled at me as I strapped myself in, feeling guilty for taking up a whole row of three seats. On our way to the art museum in Macro-Buenosaires, I studied the city map and found a large arena, not far from the museum. As soon as the Tour landed, I slipped away. So much for culture; I had work to do.

I'd seen a couple of gladiatorial matches before; not on Springworld, of course, but places like Selva and Nurodesia. They don't have to fight their planets so much, so they fight each other in the arena. On Earth it turned out to be quite different, and even more popular.

I bought the cheapest ticket and found my way to a bleacher area. Everybody was cheering and yelling at once; a solid roar like thundersurf. Hard to see what they were so excited about. Two men were slugging it out down in the arena, but from the bleachers you could hardly tell what they were doing. I rented a scope from a robot vendor.

Don't think either of them were Earthies. One was tall and black like B'oosa, probably a Maasai'pyan. The other was tan and shorter, but seemed to have a weight advantage. They were fighting with short clubs, each with his left hand taped behind his back. It *was* exciting, and looked kind of hard; lots of fancy footwork and dodging back and forth.

After a few minutes the short guy hit the tall one a solid blow to the throat, knocking him down. A white-suited man ran out and looked at the one who had fallen. Then he made some signals to the crowd, waving his arms in wide circles. When the black guy tried to get back up, he pushed him back down again, not too gently. The crowd was going insane. It was pretty obvious the guy in white was some kind of a referee, and he'd just declared the short guy to be the winner. A couple of boys with a stretcher came out and tried to carry the loser away. He pushed them aside and limped off by himself, rubbing his throat.

I turned to the man sitting next to me and tapped him on the shoulder. He looked at me and jumped, *really* jumped—must have had his eyes fastened on the fight the whole time and not noticed a giant sitting next to him.

"Pardon me for surprising you," I said in bad Spanish, "but I am a stranger here and am in need of some information."

"You certainly are a stranger," he said with a laugh. "Don't think I have ever seen anyone stranger." I think that was a pun in Spanish. "What would you like to know?"

"How much did that little fellow just win?"

"Little?" He looked me up and down, shook his head. "I guess he is, to you. He just took the heavyweight club—vibroclub—championship of Macro-BA. Twenty-five thousand pesas."

"Sounds like easy money."

He laughed again. "No, sir. For every one who even gets within reach of the championship, many dozens go *perdid*."

"*Perdid?* What's that?"

"A gladiator who can't fight anymore. Sometimes because he's wounded too badly and has to retire. Sometimes because the fear grabs his heart and he can't face the ring. Sometimes because he's dead."

"They let people die?" Oh boy, they hadn't said anything about *this* in the textbooks.

"Not 'let,' sir. All gladiators are supposed to be friends, and who would kill a friend? But nevertheless, it happens. It is considered bad; bad form." He turned back to watch the ring.

A man in formal clothes handed the winner a piece of paper, probably a check. He held it up high and strutted around the arena. The crowd roared, about half of them cheering and the rest booing or hissing.

"Where's that guy from? He looks too big to be an Earth . . . Earthman."

"He's from Hell. Most of the heavyweights are. Mean bastards. Get some heavyweights from Maasai'pya—like his last opponent—and some from Perrin or Selva, occasionally Dimian. Never saw one as big as you, though. You a Springer?"

"Yeah. Would I fight in their class?"

He laughed again. "There isn't any heavier. You have fights on Springworld?"

"No. Never saw one until I went to Selva."

"Then don't even think about it, friend. Go up against a Heller and you'd be *perdid* in three seconds. They're trained from birth to maim and kill."

"Springworld's no vacation spot. I think I could take one on."

He shrugged. "Don't set too much store in your size and strength, sir. The big ones fall, too. Training is everything."

I remembered how B'oosa had knocked me senseless. "I suppose you're right. But I could learn. Where would one go to learn more about the fights?"

"Well, there's an information office beneath the box seats over there. But if you really want to see what's what, go to the Plaza de Gladiatores. That's where the fighters are.''

''Far from here?''

''No, it's inside the city. About two hundred kilometers north.''

I watched one more match, a quarterstaff duel—really felt for the guy who lost—then took the underground express to the Plaza de Gladiatores. It was a large square, very pretty in the afternoon sunshine, full of trees and bright flowers. All around the edge of the square were taverns full of people, many crowded around outside tables talking loudly under the awnings. Bands of musicians roamed from tavern to tavern, strumming on guitars and tooting horns, trying to drown each other out. Sounded pretty confusing at first, but after I got into the swing of things it seemed to fit together nicely.

I walked to the nearest tavern and went inside. Practically had to bend over double to get through the low door. People were talking and laughing loudly, but they stopped when I crawled through the entrance. By the time I found a table they had rightly sized me up as a tourist and were loudly ignoring me again.

The chair was too tiny and too low, so I dusted off a piece of floor and sat down.

I ordered *cerveza preparada*—beer with lime—and when it came, two men walked over to my table. I was having some trouble figuring out which of the crowd were tourists and which were gladiators, but at least one of these guys had to be a fighter. One was obviously an Earthie, short and slim but muscular, wearing a white jump-suit so tight it looked like he'd just been dipped in a vat of plastic and left to dry. The other, the fighter, was a little too tall and heavy to be an Earthie. His face was horribly scarred, three puckered lines going from his forehead to chin. Most of his nose was missing and the scars pulled down his eyelids to give him a permanent wide-eyed stare. He spoke first, in English.

"Mind if me and my friend join ya?" He didn't wait for an answer, just hooked his foot around a chair, pulled it out noisily and sat down. His friend did the same, but without all the commotion.

"How did you know I could speak English?"

"Shize, big as you are, you gotta be a Springer. Springers talk English, don't they?"

Never met a Springer who "talked" English the way he did. We usually save cuss words for special occasions. But I nodded and asked where he was from.

"New Britain. That's a place on Hell. My friend here's an Earthie—where'd you say you're from, Angelo?"

"Mexico," he said in Spanish, pronouncing the "x" as an "h." "But also I speak English."

"Both of you gladiators?"

"*I'm* a gladiator," the Heller roared. "Little Angelo here, he's just getting started."

"How do you go about getting started?" I asked Angelo.

He took a sip from the mug of spiced wine he was holding. "First there are many years of schooling. Then you have, what you would say, an apprenticeship; where you fight the animals. If you are good at fighting the animals, you may have luck and be asked to join a team. That is as far as I have gotten; I just joined the Mexico D.F.—in English, uh, you would call it Meck-sico City—quarterstaff team."

"Then, if you're gonna be a *real* gladiator," the Heller butted in, "the crowd's gotta notice you. You gotta stand out. Then ya get offers for two-man matches, an' that's where the real money is."

"How much real money?"

"Smallest prize'd be about five grand, goes up from there. Biggest has to be the Earth Championship, quarter of a million. No tax, either; every pesa free and clear. Any other job, Welfare tax takes ninety-five dightin' pesas from every hundred you earn."

"It is a just tax," said Angelo. "Fair to all."

"Bullshize!" he snorted. "I don't see how you can sit

there and take it. Less'n a million workin' people takin' care of billions of lazy dighters.''

"It works, *amigo,* it works."

"Sure it does—as long as the guys payin' taxes keep on pluggin' away. What if they all up an' quit? Place'd fall apart. Wouldn't have no offworlders comin' in to take over their jobs." He turned to me, grinned. " 'Cept for gladiators. Always be lots of us comin' in for that, long as it keeps payin' them tax-free pesas."

"What about me?"

"You? What about you?"

"I could use some of those tax-free pesas myself. Be a gladiator."

The Heller cackled, then laughed loud and drained his beer mug. He banged it on the table twice. "Sorry, Goliath, wrong ballgame. Angelo was talkin' a lot of bullshize, but one thing he said was right. If you ain't studied for years, you ain't got a chance in the ring. Be *perdid* in a couple seconds."

"Probably not just wounded," Angelo added, shaking his head. "Dead."

"Damn right. Fighter'd be a fool to give you a chance to get hold of him. Bet you could break a man like he was a stick."

I probably could. "So why do you think I'd get killed right away? Maybe I wouldn't give my opponent the chance. I'm in pretty good shape."

The bartender brought over a pitcher and filled up the Heller's beer mug and mine. He took a sip, held it and studied me over the rim of the mug. "Look, you Springers do arm wrestlin'?"

"You mean 'elbows on the table'?"

"Right." He planted his elbow in front of me, forearm straight up. Muscular, but kind of puny next to a Springer's. "Now I'll bet you this round of beer that I can pin your arm before you can pin mine."

Easy money.

"That's a bet." I put my elbow next to his and he curled his hand around my wrist. I was getting settled to push when his left hand lashed out and I felt the point of a dagger digging into my throat.

"Now you can either go down real gentle or I can cut your throat and just let your arm drop on its own." The bartender stood behind the Heller, grinning. Angelo was smiling gently, looking away. The Heller just stared at me, his expression as cold as the steel of the dagger against my throat. I'd been had.

"You win." I let him pin my arm and tossed the bartender a pesa.

The Heller put the dagger back in its hip-pocket sheath. He leaned back in his chair, grinned. "You look like a pretty smart fella. Get the idea?"

"Yeah. No rules."

"Well, they got rules, but they ain't that strict about enforcin' them, if you know what I mean. And fighters learn lotsa tricks."

I squeezed the last drop of lime into the beer and drank a little. It was bitter and warm. "Still, I may have to do it."

"No dightin' way. They wouldn't let you. Easier ways to commit suicide, anyway."

"But I need money, and fast. Sounds like nobody but gladiators can make any on Earth."

"How much do you need, Springer?" Angelo asked.

"Almost 17,000 pesas. I've got a little over a month to find it."

"There might be a way . . ."

"What?" Anything.

"Most places have animal fights—you don't have to be a real gladiator and they pay four, five hundred pesas. Tax free."

"Shize, Angelo, you want to get him killed?"

He shook his head and looked straight at me. "You're almost as big as a bull. You could fight the bulls in Mexico."

"What's a bull?"

"It's a big dightin' animal with horns a mile wide. It'd eatcha for breakfast."

"It also has teeth, then?"

"No, *amigo,* he was joking. Bulls don't bite people. But they can be ferocious animals and their horns are sharp. Still, it would be less dangerous than fighting the gladiators." He scribbled something on a slip of paper and handed it to me.

"Go to the *Plaza de Toros* in Guadalajara and talk to this man. He may be able to arrange some fights for you."

I finished the beer and went back to the underground express. Maybe I should have gone straight to Guadalajara, but I wanted to think about it a little and get a good night's rest. And find out something about bulls.

III

THE TOUR WAS spending the night in the Hotel de la Bahia, a huge old hotel on the harbor, in the middle of downtown Macro-BA. I got my room number from the clerk and took a lifter to the 167th floor. My roommates B'oosa and Bolivar were already there.

"Ah, the peasant returns," said Bolivar. He was standing in front of a mirror, combing his beard. B'oosa was draped over a little couch, reading a tape. He grunted, didn't look up.

"So how was the museum?" I asked.

"Lots of pictures. Fossils. Cultural relics of all sorts. Worth seeing. Where were you all day?"

"Out hunting a job."

"Job-hunting? What do you want with a job?"

"Have to pay back the Extraweight Alien Tax."

"Hell, why bother?" Bolivar slumped into an over-stuffed chair. "Nobody else is going to—and you can't help having been born a big ugly monster."

"It's important. To me."

"Besides, what kind of a job can you get on this crazy planet? They're socialized from top to bottom—nobody gets to keep a tenth of what they earn." He grinned. "Except criminals, I guess. You going to—"

"And gladiators," I said.

"Ridiculous," B'oosa rumbled. "Don't you know they *kill* gladiators here? Ignorant savages. You're going to risk your life just because a few of the other peasants are mad at you?"

"As I say, Mr. B'oosa, it's important."

"It's ridiculous." He went back to his tape.

"Mr. B'oosa's right, Carl. It'd be suicide for you to go up against a professional fighter. Didn't he knock *any* sense into that thick head of yours?"

"I won't be fighting *men,* Francisco." Didn't have to call Bolivar "Mister" until he turned twenty-one. "I can make enough money going up against animals."

"They fight animals here? What kind?"

"Somebody mentioned bulls."

"Bull whats?"

"I don't know. Just bulls, I guess."

"A bull is a male cow," B'oosa said without looking up.

"That's great," I said. "What's a cow?"

Francisco shrugged his shoulders. B'oosa didn't say anything.

"One way to find out." I fished in my pouch for the piece of paper the Mexican had given me. It had a name and a number. I punched it up on the phone.

A girl's face filled the screen. *"Buenas noches. Plaza de Toros de Guadalajara."*

Hauled out my creaky Spanish again. We always used Pan-swahili around B'oosa. "I'd like to speak to Mr. Mendez, please."

"Just a moment, please." She disappeared and came back in a couple of seconds. "Whom shall I say is calling?"

"I'm Carl Bok, of Springworld."

"I see, yes. What is it you wish to talk to Mr. Mendez about?"

"I'd like to arrange to fight a bull."

"Just a moment, please." A holding pattern appeared on the screen and then dissolved to show a dark man in a business cape, a thick cigar protruding from beneath his bushy moustache. He spoke in heavily accented English.

"Señor Bok. I am taken to understand that you are from Springworld and you wish to fight the bulls."

"That's right."

"Have you ever fought the bulls before?"

"Señor Mendez, I've never even *seen* a bull. But I need money."

He laughed. "One might admire your courage, but . . ." He reached to his right and brought a shiny black ceramic figure into view. "This is how a bull looks, Señor Bok. But very big, sometimes five hundred kilograms. And very, very dangerous."

"I'm not exactly a midget, myself. How are these bulls fought?"

"Señor, there are two ways of fighting the bulls. One is the *corrida,* which is . . . very hard to explain, but you could not do this. It is a special way of fighting the bull, which takes many years of difficult training. And the bull always dies. Sometimes the 'matador,' which is what we call this special kind of gladiator, sometimes he dies, too. But not often. It is not an easy profession to master."

He was absently stroking the ceramic bull. An ash fell from his cigar.

"And the second way?"

"The other kind of fighting the bulls requires less knowledge, less experience. But it is far more dangerous. The bull does not always die, does not usually die. Thus he becomes used to fighting with men. As we say, he becomes 'wise.' And the men die almost as often as the bulls. Almost every night a man dies. It is sad, but the *turistas* seem to like this better than the *corrida.* And there is never a shortage of boys, foolish boys, who want to face the bulls. Except certain bulls, who learn too much. Even the boys are afraid of them."

"What kind of weapons are allowed?"

"There are three classes, Señor Bok. All may use a cape—this is to distract the bull in its charge. One class may use an *estoquita,* what you would call a short sword, or a long knife. This pays P200. The second class may use a club, not a vibroclub; this pays P400. The third class uses only the cape, and pays P750.''

"And this third has to kill the bull with his bare hands?"

"Oh, no, Señor. In any of the classes it is sufficient to merely stun the bull, to bring him to his knees.''

"When is the soonest I could fight?"

He flipped through the pages of a little book. "Señor Bok, the *only* opening I have in the next two weeks is tomorrow night, at 7:30. But this bull, you don't want to fight him.''

"Why? Is he one of the wise ones?"

"*Si,* very wise. He is called *La Muerte Vieja,* The Old Death. He has won every time he has faced a man, twelve matches. Even the foolish boys, with more courage than brains, know better than to fight this bull. That is why he has no opponent. Twelve matches . . .''

"Well, he'll lose the thirteenth. Put me down for the third class. Just the cape.''

"Señor! You don't know . . .''

"I'm very big, Señor Mendez. More than twice as big as an Earthman.''

"But less than half the size of *Muerte Vieja.* You are untrained. You are placing yourself in grave danger.''

"We'll see, Señor. I'll come by your office tomorrow.''

"Very well. The *turistas* will love the blood.'' He shook his head sadly. "*Buenas noches,* Señor Bok. And good luck.''

"*Buenas noches.*'' The screen faded.

"You're insane,'' Francisco said quietly. "Totally insane.''

"No he isn't,'' B'oosa said. "Not totally. You don't know much about Springworld, do you, Pancho?''

B'oosa could get away with calling him Pancho. "Just that it's full of stupid giants and it's not important enough to be a stop on the Tour. Why?''

"You tell him, Carl.'' B'oosa went back to his tapes.

"What should I know about your fabulous world?"

"I wouldn't know where to begin. Look at me.'' I walked to his chair, towered over him. "I'm a giant because only giants could survive on Springworld. With the possible exception of Hell, it's the harshest planet ever colonized. Take those hurricanes on your planet, magnify the force of those winds by a factor of four. They sweep across Springworld six or seven times a year, leveling damn near everything in sight. All our permanent structures are underground. Between the storms we cultivate and harvest the volmer plants, a kind of a lichen that grows in the crevasses of rock formations. And while we're doing this we have to watch out for the quakes, the twisters and animals you wouldn't believe.''

''Try me.''

''We've got lots of native animals, Francisco, and a few others that have slipped in and adapted themselves. Almost all of them are big and mean. This bull sounds like he's about the size of my pet razorlizard. But my pet has teeth, spines, and claws . . . and I tamed him myself.''

''I see. But I doubt that your cuddly pet was fully grown when you trained him. I doubt that he had fought twelve men before you came along with your leash.''

''True enough. He was small—not much bigger than you—when I caught him. With my bare hands, I might add. I have confidence.''

''I hope it's warranted.'' He shook his head. ''Anyhow, we'll see tomorrow.''

''We? Are you coming along?''

''Of course. Somebody has to bring back the pieces.''

IV

WE GOT TO the Plaza de Toros early. I signed a contract full
of fine print, absolving everybody in sight from the responsibility of safety to my body, and went down to the
"gladiator's box," a set of front-row seats.

They hadn't started the knock-down, drag-out bullfights
yet, but were still doing *corridas*. It was a fascinating
spectacle, exciting but sad. Sometimes very delicate and
graceful, sometimes brutal.

Señor Mendez said that the *corrida* had been fought for
over two thousand years with very little change. It did
have a pagan, primitive feel to it. Nowadays, especially on
Springworld and Hell, death is rarely such a long drawn-
out affair.

Everybody was dressed in fancy costumes for the *corrida* (normal gladiators fight naked, the way they did on
Selva) and they marched through a complicated ritual before each bull was killed.

When they first let the bull into the ring, a bunch of men
riding large animals called horses would make the bull
charge and try to stab him with a spear while he was trying
to get at the horse. The spears (called pics) only went in a
few centimeters and served to tire the bull and make him
mad.

Eventually the matador came out—unarmed—and made

the bull charge his cape, a big red piece of stiff cloth that
he held out away from his body. The closer the matador let
the bull come to his body, the louder the crowd cheered.
That was the best part, as far as I was concerned. That
little guy had to be some kind of brave. I watched a
half-dozen of them and, somehow, nobody got hurt. I
could see why Señor Mendez had said it took so many
years of training.

The last part was the most dangerous. It was also the
saddest. This was the so-called moment of truth, where the
matador kills the bull. He hides a sword behind his cape
and when the bull charges the cape (or the matador; by this
time he might have figured it out) he whips the sword out
and stabs the bull. Sometimes he has to do it several times
before the bull finally lies down and dies. I'd never believed the death of an animal could affect me so much—
I've killed thousands protecting myself and the crops on
Springworld—but by the last *corrida* I had decided I wasn't
going to kill Muerte Vieja. No way.

A dark young man sat down next to me. *"Buenos
dias."*

"Good day," I said in Spanish. "Are you fighting
today?" Stupid question. He was sitting in the gladiator's
box as naked as I was.

"Of course." He couldn't stop staring at me. "The first
bull, Hermano de la Oscuridad. You?"

"The second. Muerte Vieja."

"Jesus Christ—how did Mendez talk you into that?"

"He didn't. Actually, he tried to talk me out of it."

He shrugged. "Well, you're big enough. I suppose if
anybody can take Muerte V., you can. Where's your
estoquita?"

"I'm not using one."

"Ai! You're out of your head! A club just isn't—"

"No," I said. "Just the cape."

He let out his breath in a whistle and shook his head.
"Señor, I'm afraid you have more *cojones* than brains."

"Who doesn't?" I was feeling a little giddy, a small
case of stage fright, I guess. "A man with more than one

brain would look very strange." He laughed a kind of a squeaky giggle. I think he was as nervous as I was. "Seriously, I don't expect too much trouble. I grew up on a planet full of large animals, most of them wild. I learned to handle them at an early age."

"Still . . . what planet was that?"

"Springworld."

"Never heard of it. Is everybody on Springworld as large as you?"

"Most are bigger."

He whistled again. "Maybe you can take him, then. May the luck be with you."

We sat back and watched the *corrida* for a while. They were dragging a dead bull out. The matador was walking around the ring, bowing to applause.

The stands were starting to fill up. Must have been the *turistas,* come to see the real thing. Us.

"Do you know why they call him 'the Old Death'? Why he got his name?" the man said.

"I assume he's killed people."

"A lot of bulls kill fighters. But only Muerte Vieja has killed six. Half of those who have fought him. Of the ones who have lived . . . well, they no longer face the ring."

I could guess why.

"Have you ever seen him fight?" I asked.

"Yes. Four times." He scratched the stubble on his chin. "The last three times, the fighters died on his horns. Now nobody will fight him, not even the young foolish ones. Nobody but you." The tone of his voice indicated that wasn't exactly a compliment.

For some reason it hadn't occurred to me to be scared. Suddenly I was very aware of the sand drifting in the arena, the smell of blood, the rough wood of the bench I was sitting on. All of a sudden it wasn't a game anymore, it was *real* and my throat went dry; cold sweat broke out on my forehead and palms.

"Would you like some advice? I've probably fought more bulls than you have." I couldn't tell whether he was being sarcastic or not. I didn't even care.

"Sure. Sounds like I can use all the help I can get."

"First, forget about the cape. Muerte V. knows all about capes, he is a very wise bull. He'll ignore it and charge for your body. Best to have both hands free."

I was glad to hear that. I'd planned to wrestle him the way we wrestle young razorlizards. The cape would just get in the way.

"Second, always stay to his right. He tries to hook with his left horn, and he's half blind in his right eye."

"He hooks with his left because he can't see well with his right?"

"No, señor, all bulls favor one horn or the other. I wish to God that the man who struck his eye had hit the left—that would probably have been the end of Muerte V., before he could earn his name. Five good men would still be alive."

"Five?"

"Yes. The man who clubbed the bull's eye was impaled on his left horn when he did it. It went in the groin and came out just below the navel. He was dead before they could get him out of the ring. He was the last to fight him with only a club. He was also a friend of mine, a brave man who had fought many bulls."

I shuddered. What had I gotten myself into? "Anything else I should know?"

"Hmmm . . . señor, Muerte V. is old, quite old for a fighting bull. You might be able to outlast him by making him charge from far away. Do this many times. Dodge each charge and run in the opposite direction. By the time he can stop and turn, he will have a long way to charge again. Don't try anything stylish or brave. Just keep running from him, you might wear him out. The *turistas* won't like it, but better to be hissed than dead."

"I get paid the same whether I get cheered or not."

"Exactly. Though I wish . . . I wish you had an *estoquita*. Perhaps with your long arms you could find an opening and kill the beast. He's a noble bull, and it's always sad to see a brave one die—but he may kill another six before he's too old to fight. And only boys will go against him, desperate boys, beginners. Too many more will die in the sand.''

It was late afternoon and getting dark, shadows spread across the arena. Suddenly overhead lights crackled on and a loudspeaker blared, in English: "Ladies and gentlemen, the gladiatorial combat will begin in about fifteen minutes. The first pair is Octavio Ramirez, veteran of fourteen fights, against the bull Hermano de la Oscuridad—Brother of Darkness—seeing his third fighter. Cape only.'' Then the announcer repeated it in Spanish, then Pan-swahili.

"You're not using a weapon either.''

"No, but Hermano isn't Muerte V. I'm quite confident.''

We talked about bullfighting—both kinds; Octavio wanted to be a matador some day—until a trumpet blared over the loudspeaker, signaling that the fight was about to begin. A door opened and Hermano galloped out into the ring. He was smaller than the bulls killed in the *corrida;* Octavio told me that was usually the case.

The men on horses (called picadores) were on the field when the bull came out. But this time both horses and men were sheathed in light plastic armor rather than the gaudy costumes. Octavio watched with great concentration as the bull charged the horses. This way, he said, you could predict how he would act when you faced him alone in the ring.

The picadores "pic'ed" the bull about a dozen times, then rode out of the ring. Octavio jumped over the wall onto the sand.

"Wish me luck, Carl.''

"*Buena suerte,* Octavio . . .'' He waved a hand and walked out to meet the bull.

The referee watched very closely. He had a high-powered rifle loaded with sleep-darts—if Octavio were injured badly (signifying the end of the match), he could knock out the bull with one dart, and the medics could come take Octavio to safety. Unfortunately, often the dart wouldn't take effect immediately—or the fighter would be injured so badly it wouldn't make any difference. But Octavio didn't look scared.

He stopped about twenty feet from the bull and whipped the cape at him. Hermano had been watching Octavio without too much interest until he saw the cape. Then he started walking toward him and, about halfway, broke into a run.

Octavio stood his ground and let the bull pass inches away from his body, guiding the beast with a slow, graceful sweep of the cape. I'd learned the move was called a "veronica," a classic maneuver over a thousand years old. The crowd cheered as the bull slipped past. Hermano slowed so quickly that he actually skidded, then turned around and charged again. Octavio was waiting, and lured him by with another veronica. He repeated this several times, then Hermano seemed to get disgusted and just walked away. He leaned up against the ring wall, looking tired or maybe just bored.

Octavio got in front of him and whipped the cape. The bull just looked at him. He came closer and whipped again. Nothing. Closer still—and suddenly Hermano leaped at him. Octavio put the cape out, but the bull wasn't interested and went directly for the fighter. He saw what was happening, threw the cape into the bull's face and leaped aside. I saw the referee bring the rifle to his shoulder and take aim.

But the bull missed, and went a good twelve meters before it stopped and tossed the cape away with a shake of his head. Now Octavio had to fight without the cape. I figured it probably wouldn't make too much difference; the bull was obviously "wise." Octavio moved toward the center of the ring and Hermano watched him go, his huge head swiveling slowly.

Suddenly the bull charged. Octavio set his feet and crouched forward, waiting. When the bull was only a few feet away, he jumped, touching the bull's shoulders with his feet, and did a double somersault over Hermano's back. He landed on his feet and whirled around. The bull charged on, tossing his head. Eventually he stopped and looked from side to side, puzzled. The crowd roared with laughter.

Octavio shouted and the bull looked around. He started to circle the fighter slowly, then charged again. The same stunt, and the bull was mystified again.

Octavio "jumped" the bull five times. You could tell Hermano was getting tired; it took him longer to come back after each charge. Maybe Octavio was getting tired, too. On the sixth charge he must have jumped too soon; he landed on the bull's head instead of his shoulders, and Hermano tossed him straight into the air. He landed on his stomach and lay still.

Hermano skidded in a tight circle and charged back, his horns low. The rifle cracked, but the bull charged on, then stumbled, then fell in a heap not two meters from Octavio.

The crowd gasped and then cheered.

"Ladies and gentlemen," the loudspeaker said, "although Señor Ramirez was beaten by the bull Hermano, and thus is not eligible for the regular prize, the judges have agreed to award him a special purse of five hundred pesas, for extraordinary valor and skill."

The *turistas* cheered, but looking at Octavio stretched out on the sand suddenly I didn't feel that my P750 was that much money after all.

"The next match, ladies and gentlemen, will be a special treat—for the first time in Guadalajara, perhaps in all the world, one of the giant supermen of Springworld will fight a bull, with only the cape—and not just any bull, ladies and gentlemen, but the famous and terrible Muerte Vieja!"

Cheers. But I didn't feel like a "giant superman." I just felt scared.

"And so, in fifteen minutes, Carl Bok of Springworld, in his first fight, against Muerte Vieja, seeing his thirteenth fighter. One hundred-sixty-two kilos of human brawn and wit against four hundred-fifty kilos of wise bull. Bets may be placed with the robot vendors."

I wondered what the odds were. But I wasn't sure I wanted to find out.

V

THE MEDICS CARRIED Octavio away and an electric tractor hauled off the sleeping bull. From hidden nozzles in the sand, water sprayed in a fine mist to settle the dust. After a few minutes, the picadores came out.

Then the trumpet again and Muerte Vieja thundered into the ring. What was it Octavio had said about these bulls being smaller? Ha! This one looked very big. And very mean. He started to charge for the nearest horse, then slowed and stopped, just out of pic'ing range. He remembered.

The picador urged his horse closer, but the huge bull kept backing out of range. Looking wily rather than frightened, he backed halfway across the arena. Another picador circled around and stabbed him from behind.

Muerte V. roared and spun around, catching the horse's armored belly with his horns. He tossed his head and lifted horse and rider nearly a meter off the ground. They seemed to hang motionless for a brief moment—and then they fell to earth with a clatter of plastic armor. The picador flew over his horse's head and plowed into the sand.

The man was trying to stand up when Muerte V. slammed into him from behind. A toss and the man was flying again, spinning end over end like a thrown rag doll.

The horse got up and limped away on three legs. Muerte V. didn't even look at him, but charged under the man and caught the picador on his horns before he could reach the ground. He tossed the man again, but by then the other picadores had the bull surrounded, so he couldn't chase after him.

They pic'ed him unmercifully while the dismounted man crawled to safety. Even with all his armor, it looked as if he'd had more than just the wind knocked out of him. Still, I'd have been glad to trade places with him.

They must have pic'ed the bull at least thirty times before they formed in a line and paraded off the ring. The board fence creaked under my weight and almost buckled as I vaulted over. I was so scared my knees were trembling, and they almost gave out when I hit the ground. By the time I got my balance, the bull had covered half the distance between us. I could feel the beat of his hooves through the ground.

I took Octavio's advice and stood as still as I could until Muerte V. was only a couple of meters away; then I leaped to my left and landed running. I felt the wind of the bull going by and then heard a loud splintering crash.

Looking over my shoulder, I could see that the bull had collided with the fence and his horns were stuck in the wood. He freed himself with a toss of his head that sent boards flying. I ran on a few steps and stopped, turned to face him. He'd already begun his charge. I got set to jump again. Once more he tilted his head and tried to hook me with his left and I jumped out of his way as he stampeded by.

I sprinted about a hundred meters—no trick at all in Earth gravity—and turned, but he wasn't coming after me. He just stood there, watching. After I stopped, he walked toward me very slowly. He came to a halt maybe ten meters away.

His breath was a sandpapery rasp and his mouth was flecked with white foam. Streaks of blood, dull brown with caked dust, ran from the pic wounds. A milky film covered his bad eye, and the lid was half-shut. One horn had broken off a few centimeters from the tip, and ended in jagged splinters rather than a point. A hoof pawed the sand and his right ear twitched constantly. Even from this distance he stank, a mixture of wet fur and bad meat.

He charged. I tensed and jumped, but this time he wasn't fooled a bit—sharp pain in my leg and I spun awkwardly around, landed on my shoulder and face. Wiped sand out of my eyes and staggered to my feet. Bright red blood pulsing out of my calf.

The referee had his rifle up but didn't shoot. Too late, I realized I should have stayed down. That might have ended the match. Muerte V. stumbled in a turn—he was tiring—and charged back.

Couldn't jump, so I waited and when he got close enough I sidestepped, grabbed a horn and twisted myself up onto his back, just like you would do to tackle a razorlizard. I clamped my long legs around his chest and rode.

I hung onto his neck while he bucked and tossed, trying to get me with those horns. He was going for the wall and I knew I'd be crushed if I didn't do something. I let go of his neck and, next time he tossed, grabbed a horn in each hand and leaned all my weight to one side. His head twisted and the horn bit into the ground, sent up a spray of sand for meters and then *crack!*

I floated through the air for what seemed like a long time, then my chest scraped along the sand for a while and I stopped, tried to scramble up, fell, got up again and looked back.

Muerte V. was lying on his side, shuddering. He gave a kick with his back legs and lay still. The crowd was whistling and stomping—I didn't know whether that was good or bad—and I limped over to the bull's body and saw what had killed him. His horn dragging through the sand had hooked a pipe buried under the surface, part of the plumbing used to water down the sand between fights. The shock of hitting it at full speed must have broken his neck.

Two medics and a man in formal clothes came into the ring. The man handed me a check—750 pesas—and said something in rapid-fire Spanish that I couldn't follow. The medics guided me off the sand, to the infirmary. The

crowd was still making a lot of noise and I was just trying
to stay upright.

They put me on a table—the beds were too small—and
started treating my leg. Octavio was stretched out on one
of the beds, still unconscious. A door opened and Francisco came in.

"Carl! Are you all right?"

"Dandy. Bleeding is my hobby."

"Don't worry, señor," one of the medics said. "You'll
be out of here in a half-hour. We've fixed a million of
these little *cornadas*."

"Did it go well, Francisco? How did I look?"

"Call me Pancho, man. Didn't you hear the loudspeaker?"

"No."

"They called it one of the greatest . . . killings they'd
seen in Guadalajara. They want you back."

"Thanks, anyhow. I think I've had my share of bulls."

"I should think so."

We both watched them work on my leg. Having sprayed
it with something that felt cold and stopped the pain, they
put on plastic clamps that held the edges of the wound
together. Then one of them mixed up a dish of plastiflesh
and painted it over the wound.

"We can take the clamps off as soon as the plastiflesh
dries, señor. It will hurt for a day or two, but by the time
the plastiflesh peels off, you'll be as good as new. Here."
He handed me a little vial of pills. "Don't take more than
four a day."

"Shouldn't I see a doctor?"

He laughed. "For a little scratch like that? No, señor,
just eat a couple of good rare steaks to put back the blood
you lost. Why pay a doctor to tell you that you'll be all
right in a week?"

"He's right, Carl," Pancho said. "Earth may not have
much to be conceited about, but it's a great place to get
sick. Even Heaven sends people here to learn medicine."

After about fifteen minutes they took off the clamps and
tried to find me a cane. They had quite a collection, but

none of them was long enough to do me any good. I just swallowed a pill and limped away.

By the time we got on the underground, the pain was almost gone. Almost.

"Well, Carl, I guess that bull finally punched some sense into you. It was a nice gesture, but . . ."

"Gesture nothing. I'm still going to pay back the fund. Every pesa."

"But you said—"

"I said I'm not going to fight any more *bulls,* and I'm not. Those animals have been bred for fighting for two thousand years, man, and they have gotten pretty tough. Just a plain animal, a wild animal, I can take. You know if they have any reptiles, like lizards? Lizards I can handle."

"That, I don't know. This planet's so crowded, I doubt they have many animals around that aren't used just for food."

"Well, Octavio—he's the little fellow that fought before I did—said they use these bulls for food after they're killed in the ring. Maybe there's all kinds of animals they do the same thing with."

"Could be. We could ask around."

"Yeah—I know just the place to go."

Pancho grinned, rubbed his hands together. "Well, don't leave me out. As I say, somebody has to go along to pick up the pieces."

VI

THE PLAZA DE GLADIATORES was much different at night. No more people than were there during the day, I guess, but they all seemed to be outdoors. Hot as it was, I couldn't blame them. All the musicians were outside, too; it was loud and festive and not too well lit. There were only a couple of light-panels; most of the illumination came from long torches burning. There was a delicious smell of meat roasting. I realized I was hungry, really starved. In front of one of the taverns they were cooking a huge slab of meat over an open pit of glowing coals. Waiters scurried in and out of the taverns, balancing large trays piled high with food. The trays were almost as big as the waiters themselves, and the food looked delicious.

"So this is where you spent the day," Pancho said. "Now I wish *I* had missed the museum, too."

We sat down at a small plastic table under a huge old tree and a waiter came over. We ordered drinks and meat— strong drinks and rare meat.

"Now what?" Pancho asked. "We just sit here until some—" He was interrupted by a heavy *thud,* followed by a low twang. A dagger had appeared in the tree between us. It looked vaguely familiar.

"Shee-*ize,* Springer! You still here?" The Heller from this afternoon came swaggering up, pulled his knife out of the tree and sat down. "Just can't soak up enough of this local color, can ya?"

I explained in a few words about the bullfight. He had heard of Muerte Vieja, but had never seen him in action.

He inspected the fresh scar on my leg. "Gonna give up the bulls for a little scratch like that? Shize, I seen guys took a horn in the gut and were back—"

"Hell no!" Pancho said, with more violence than I would've used against this customer. "Carl just wants to try some other kind of animal. The bulls—"

"Aw yeah," the Heller said with a chuckle. "I shoulda known, a big mother like you, them bulls wouldn't be no big shize. Where you goin'—Houston?"

"I don't know. That's what I came back here for, to find out what else there was to fight."

"You don't know about Houston, the Houston Sea?" We both shook our heads. "Tiburónes—great fun! You never seen a tiburón fight?"

"What is that in English? What kind of an animal?" Pancho asked. Guess they don't have them on Selva, either.

"Sharks, man, tiburónes. Great big fish, sharks; rows of teeth, big teeth. *Great* fun!"

"How much do you get for killing one?"

He laughed. "You can't kill 'em, man. They'd probably toss you in the slammer if you killed one of them. All you gotta do is stay alive. Think it's P300 a minute."

"Man . . . *eaters?*" Pancho said.

"R-i-g-h-t, man, dightin' right." He was getting excited at the idea. "They eat men. They eat fish. They eat each other. They eat anything. I heard they'll even eat a plastic two-by-four if they're hungry enough. And they're always hungry."

"How big are they?" I asked.

"Come in all sizes—little ones the size of your arm up to biggies twice *your* size. And man, they hungry all the time."

"Weapons?"

"Nothing but a dightin' vibroclub."

Didn't sound too good. On Springworld we hunt fish, swimming underwater for them—but they don't hunt us back! Nothing carnivorous in our oceans and lakes is as big as a man. Besides, I wasn't sure how well I could fight underwater.

"Hmm . . . I don't know," I said. "Know of anyplace they fight lizards?"

He roared with laughter. "Lizards? Them little green dighters? How many you want to take on at once? A thousand? A million?"

"Guess you don't."

"No man." He sobered up a little. "What, you got lizards on Springworld big enough to fight?"

"Bigger than your tiburónes. Lots of teeth, long claws."

He raised both eyebrows. "Then you got nothin' to worry about. These sharks—they really do look mean and all, but all you gotta do is touch 'em on the nose with a vibroclub and they swim away. Almost nobody ever gets bit. Almost."

I looked at Pancho. "Think I'll try it."

He shook his head. "I think you'd try it even if you didn't know how to swim. God!"

The Houston Sea was about two thousand kilometers from Guadalajara, five thousand from Chimbarazo. To save money (my money, anyhow), we took the shuttle to Guadalajara and, from there, an airbus to Houston. Didn't save too much money, though; travel's pretty cheap on Earth. Most of the public transportation is taken care of by the taxes everybody seems to pay.

It was a "tourist special" and we had plenty of time in the air to read the brouchures. The Houston Sea is a kind of natural memorial to a big turning point in human history, when the old Atomic Age nations went out with a bang and the Alianza moved in to fill the power vacuum. The Houston Sea used to be a land mass called Texas. The big port they call Houston used to be an inland town called Oklahoma City.

I liked Houston better than any of the other Earthie cities

we'd seen. For one thing, everybody spoke English. It wasn't crowded or dirty and you could smell the salt air from anywhere in the city.

The "shark shows" were handled by an organization called Underseas Entertainments, Inc. They were located in a skyscraper just offshore, an old-fashioned building half underwater. We saw our first shark while we were gliding over the water on the covered sidewalk that connected the skyscraper to land.

"There's one," said Pancho, pointing off to our left.

It was swimming along just under the surface, one fin sticking out of the water. It was gray and leathery-looking and just a little smaller than I am. Pretty big, for a fish.

"Make a good-sized dinner," I said with a nervous chuckle.

"You or it?" asked Pancho. We both stared at the fin neatly slicing the water. I didn't answer him.

Since I had phoned ahead and made an appointment, they were expecting us. A young man at the reception desk told us to go down the lift to the "minus-two" floor, two stories underwater.

Stepping out of the lift, we found ourselves facing a transparent wall. It brought us up short; we both stopped dead and stared. I didn't even try to count the number of sharks on the other side of the plastic. Most of them were about a meter long, some a little less. But there were five or six the size of the one we'd seen topside, and they all looked hungry.

The strange thing about these sharks was they were constantly moving; they never stopped, they never rested. It made them seem less like fish, more like some streamlined eating machine. On Springworld, I'd spent hours watching fish, but all the fish I'd ever seen spent a good part of their time just floating in one place with their gills waving around, like they were resting or thinking. These creatures flicked and wiggled in and out of sight continuously, as if they were constantly looking for something. Probably lunch. They had a terrible kind of beauty, a mixture of grace and meanness—the wide, unblinking eyes, the huge crescent mouth. One swam by with his mouth partly open; it was full of wicked-looking, triangular teeth.

"Quite a sight—eh, boys?" I turned, startled. It was the man I'd talked to on the 'phone; I recognized his garish blood-red tunic. Mr. DeLavore.

"You must be Mr. Bok." He grabbed my hand with his tiny one and pumped it up and down. He turned to Pancho. "And . . . ah . . ."

"Señor Bolivar," Pancho said.

"Good, good." DeLavore gave Pancho's hand the same treatment, introducing himself. "You must be Mr. Bok's partner. Won't you both please follow me."

We followed him through a door, down a corridor to another door, this one with his name on it. We passed through an empty anteroom into a plush office.

"Sit down, please, sit down." He stood behind his desk while Pancho sank into a deep easy chair. I eased myself onto the arm of one and it didn't break.

He settled behind his desk and made a steeple with his fingers, studied it for a long second. An unexpected furrow appeared in his smooth forehead and he cleared his throat.

"I'm not in the business of talking people out of joining our Shark Show team. But I have to make sure before anyone signs anything, that . . . that they know exactly what they're getting into."

"I know that it's dangerous," I said. Trying to be helpful.

"But you're from offworld. Both of you're from offworld. Have you ever seen Shark Show?" We hadn't, of course.

"I shouldn't think so. Our offworld franchise only extends to one planet outside of Earth-system. And neither of you is a Heller, obviously.

"Fighting sharks, well . . . here." He took two objects out of a drawer and laid them on his desk. Weapons. "You've seen vibroclubs before." I hadn't. It was a metallic stick about a third of a meter long with a wooden handle and a wrist strap.

"Don't use it. You have a choice, of course, but don't

use it, take my advice. The worst thing you can do to a shark is to hurt him. That makes him angry, and if you get a shark angry you just don't have a chance.'' He set the vibroclub down.

''That's for grandstanders and . . . suicides. You get paid twice as much, but you probably won't get to enjoy spending it. This is what you want to use.'' He picked up the other instrument. ''This is a billy, a shark billy.''

The shark billy was a plastic stick about a meter long, with a flat plate on one end that had lots of little nails sticking out of it.

''You use this to *push* the shark away,'' he said, demonstrating. ''The small nails don't hurt him; they're just to make the billy cling to his hide.

''I have some tapes here that show you how to use it.'' He pulled the drapes behind his desk, exposing a huge holovision cube. We saw several tapes of people using the billy. It didn't look too difficult—when a shark swims toward you, you just thrust the thing at his nose and push him away.

None of the tapes showed a person fighting alone, though; all of them were two people, back to back.

''Do you use the billy any different when you don't have a partner?'' I asked.

''Oh, if your partner's hurt, we try to pull you out immediately. There's no—''

''No, I mean if you don't *have* a partner. Fighting alone.''

''Alone?'' He looked puzzled, then astonished. Then he laughed. ''No, nobody fights alone. Never. If you left your back unprotected, you'd be hit from behind immediately. The sharks'd have your kidneys for breakfast.''

''But I'd planned—''

''Mr. DeLavore,'' Pancho interrupted, ''sometimes it takes this big boob a long time to catch on. I'm going to be his partner, of course.''

''Pancho!'' I was aghast. ''You can't risk—''

''Risk, nothing. I'm not going to let you have all the fun.''

"Well, fun . . . uh, before either of you decide, there's one more tape I've got to show you."

It started out like all the others, except that one of the fighters was a woman. They drifted down in the shark cage, a framework of close-spaced metal bars, and swam out of it when it reached camera level. Each of them was wearing a weight-belt with a freshly-killed fish attached (the sharks won't normally attack a human being; they go after the bait and the human kind of gets in the way). They swam out a short distance and took the normal back-to-back position. There were about half-a-dozen small sharks circling them. They threw away their shark billies and held hands.

"Until then," DeLavore whispered, "we hadn't known they were suicides."

Before the billies had sunk out of view, one of the small sharks shot in for the attack. He opened his mouth impossibly wide and slammed into the fish on the girl's belt. His teeth evidently sunk into her abdomen and got hung up on the leather belt. He started thrashing around, stuck, and she tried to push him away with feeble gestures. Then a huge striped shark, bigger than me, slid up from underneath them and, ignoring the people, swallowed half of the small shark and just kept on going. But the little shark had too good a grip on her and she . . . unraveled as the two fish sped upward. The people disappeared in a cloud of blood and suddenly there was nothing but sharks, dozens of them flying in from every direction. And inside the billows of blood, a dim scene of incredible ferocity; sharks twisting and worrying away at their quarry, fighting with other sharks over choice bits . . .

"Whew." The picture faded. "Things like that happen often?"

"No. Definitely not. Sharks look dangerous and, although singularities like this are horribly impressive, they're actually afraid of people, most of them. And they're cautious, anyhow, by nature." He slid the curtain back in place.

"By our statistics, an untrained man—as long as he can

swim with a tank and is reasonably careful—has less than a two percent chance of being bitten during the show.''

''That two percent is what the people watch for, though,'' Pancho said.

DeLavore reddened, shrugged his shoulders. ''That may be. We've never made a survey.''

''If you do get bitten,'' I asked, ''how badly are you likely to be injured?''

He hesitated, then looked straight at me. ''You'll die. Most likely, you'll die.''

He didn't seem to be fudging on *that* statistic.

''I don't want to mislead you as to the danger. A single shark probably won't kill you. When people normally get bitten—outside the show, that is—it's usually no worse than a lost limb or a large chunk of meat. If they manage to get by the shock, they can go to a regeneration clinic. But most of them are attacked by a single shark. There are literally hundreds of them near the camera site for Shark Show. Once you start to bleed, you'll attract the attention of every shark in the neighborhood. Even if you're right above the cage it's not likely you'll get to shelter in time. They can move very quickly, as you have seen.''

''Well, Carl?'' Pancho said.

'' 'Well' yourself. I'm in this for the money, and you—''

''You've got yourself a couple of shark fighters, Mr. DeLavore.''

Never try to figure out a Selvan.

VII

THEY FITTED US OUT with tanks and got some flippers for Pancho. I didn't get flippers; my feet were almost as big as the largest size they had. They adjusted our weight belts—I had to wear two—and gave us our billies. We decided we weren't quite crazy enough for vibroclubs.

For about thirty minutes we practiced swimming—floating, actually—in the protected pool below the ready room. It was a lot like exercising in the zero-g gym on *Starschool*. No sweat.

Then we ended up waiting in the ready room until just before seven. It was cold and damp, not at all like the plush offices. It was awkward sitting on the low wooden benches. Pancho and I spent a long time staring at a bunch of empty lockers. Finally a bored attendant came in and gave us some last-minute instructions. He was pretty scarred up and missing a couple of fingers. Guess he hadn't made it to the regeneration clinic in time.

"If you just never let 'em know you're scared, you won't have no trouble. Just keep calm and keep pushin' 'em away. Keep looking at your feet, don't forget that—look at your feet. The biggies usually attack from below. Don't even think about your back unless you feel your partner get hit—and that's the only time you hurry; get back in that cage fast. Every shark in the neighborhood'll be after

you. One at a time, you can take care of them, no matter
how big and mean. But you can't handle fifty. Got it?''

''Do we get paid for all the time we're underwater?'' I
asked, trying to seem equally bored.

''No, just from the time you leave the cage to the time
you return. With luck, though, you'll get five or ten free
minutes before the first shark gets interested.''

''What if they *never* get interested?'' Pancho asked.

He shrugged, spit on the floor. ''Ain't happened yet.''

The cage he led us to was smaller than I'd expected. I
had to squeeze into the opening and couldn't stand up
straight when I was inside. Everything on this world was
built for midgets. As they craned us over the water, Pancho
and I went over our simple strategy for the last time.

We'd stay as close to the cage as possible, keeping it
directly below our feet to keep the biggies from charging
straight up the way that one did on the suicide tape.

One tap on the back would mean ''back to the cage''
and two taps would mean ''back in a hurry.'' We didn't
figure there'd be any other kind of message of any
importance.

I braced myself for the shock of entering the water and
found that it was pleasantly warm, almost body temperature. Must have held my breath for a full minute before I
remembered to breathe through the mouthpiece. I tried to
get my body to relax a little. It wouldn't. I felt like bait on
the end of a fishing line.

We dropped past the cameramen, invisible inside their
silver bubbles, and as the cage reached the end of its
tether, we stopped with a soft bounce. No sharks around
yet. We swam out the cage door and took up our position
about two meters above. Back to back.

We floated, waiting. I could see only one of the cameramen, about twenty meters away, directly in front of me.
A broad ray of light, dim green, almost exactly the color
of the water, came from the silver bubble. That was the
holograph laser—people could sit in their living rooms
drinking beer and watch us get bitten in three dimensions.

Maybe I hadn't been paying close enough attention, but

suddenly it seemed that there were quite a few sharks circling us. They were staying some ten or fifteen meters out and didn't look particularly aggressive, but I kept a wary eye on them anyway.

Pancho moved a couple of times and I assumed he was fighting. I still wasn't worried, because these fish were only a meter or so long and didn't look like they could give you too much trouble, even bare-handed.

Suddenly, all the sharks I could see swam off in a hurry. They were instantly replaced by a herd of individuals about twice their size. We'd been warned that groups of sharks are usually sharply segregated by size and you rarely saw a big and a little one together. There was an obvious reason: the little one would soon end up inside the big brother.

They must have circled for five minutes before the first one approached. He slid to within two meters of me—one shark length!—and stopped obediently when he ran into my shark billy. He turned and swam lazily away. I started to relax a little.

We had several encounters like that. I could feel Pancho's activity against my back. It wasn't too terribly frightening, since the big sharks didn't seem to be all that interested in us. One by one, they went away to more fruitful pursuits.

I just floated there counting my money, 150 pesos every minute. Two hours' worth of air in the tanks—a fortune if they kept away.

I suppose I had about ten minutes' worth of that kind of optimism. The next group was a bunch of really tiny sharks, about half the size of the first pack. They came in closer than the others, but few of them seemed disposed to attack. Every now and then one would make a mad dash for the fish on my belt—faster than the big ones—but I always managed to push him away in time.

Suddenly Pancho pounded on my back, twice. During the split second while I was deciding whether it was an accident or a signal, I could see blood starting to diffuse through the water.

As we'd arranged, I jerked the fish from my belt and

flung it to the sharks, then swam downward with all my strength. What we hadn't arranged was that Pancho and I would arrive at the cage door at the same time. Or that it would be stuck. Without thinking, I pulled the door off its hinges and shoved Pancho inside. The sharks were really moving now and there was blood everywhere. Pancho must have been hurt pretty bad. I felt sick to my stomach, but I couldn't take the time to check him out as I backed through the narrow opening, pushing away the most aggressive sharks with my billy.

Some of the sharks had been attracted to the fish we'd thrown, but most were heading for the cage. They were hauling us up, but not nearly fast enough to suit me. I faced the open cage door with my back to Pancho, pushing wildly at the sharks trying to get inside. Most of them were small, but there were a lot of them and I knew they could kill us as easily as the big ones.

I got a momentary break as a huge shark came up from below the cage and scattered the small ones around the door. It left with several wiggling in its mouth. I hoped one of them was the one that had bitten Pancho.

In cold horror, I watched the large shark turn in a sharp circle back to the cage. It was heading right for the opening.

I braced myself and pushed him square in the nose with the billy. The force of the impact sent the cage swinging. Pancho kept trying to help but I was so big I nearly filled the cage and there was no way he could get up by the door anyway. I had my hands full. The shark was not backing up like he was supposed to do. Larger than me, he filled the door, jaws opening and closing blindly. I pushed him and I pounded him and he still kept coming.

Suddenly we surged out of the water. That damn shark was more inside than out and he just wouldn't quit. Pancho came up from somewhere behind me and, working together, we finally shoved him out. He made one hell of a splash.

I got all tangled up spitting out my mouthpiece and turning to Pancho. He wasn't bleeding.

I was.

Pancho pointed at my foot. Sure enough, that was where all the blood had been coming from—I was missing a big chunk out of my ankle. I put my hand on it and blood streamed out between my fingers. Then it started to hurt. Plenty.

"God, Carl—I'm sorry. I just couldn't reach that little dighter until—"

"Forget it." He couldn't help being only a meter and a half tall. "They'll patch this one up just like the other one. I'll be as good as new tomorrow."

Then I passed out.

They glued a new heel on with plastiflesh, all right, but this time it was a little more incapacitating: I was not supposed to put any weight on the foot for two days. Well, I was ready for a rest, anyway.

Sitting in the motorized chair made me exactly as tall as Pancho. It was a strange sensation, being able to talk to people without looking down. We walked and rolled back to Mr. DeLavore's office.

He was there with our money, but unfortunately he wasn't alone. B'oosa and the Dean were waiting with him.

"Carl," B'oosa said, "this is ridiculous."

I'd had enough. "Mr. B'oosa," I said, trying hard to hold my temper, "this may seem ridiculous to you. But you have never tried to scratch out an existence on a barren planet. You have never felt the pain of the winds wiping out an entire crop, or the futility of trading with people who take advantage of you, knowing full well there is nowhere else you can go. You could probably buy my father's farm ten times over, a *hundred* times over. There is no way you can understand what this means to me."

I rolled up to the desk. "How long did we stay, Mr. DeLavore?"

"Carl . . ." B'oosa said.

"Mr. B'oosa," I said, not looking at him, "this is my affair, and Pancho's. You have no right to interfere and no right to bring the Dean . . ."

"I asked to come," Dr. M'bisa said.

"How long?" I repeated.

Mr. DeLavore glanced at B'oosa and the Dean and licked his lips. "Eighteen and a half minutes." He handed me a check. "That gives you P2775 to split."

B'oosa laughed humorlessly. "Get bitten about twelve more times and you'll have your 17,000, Carl. If you're lucky, maybe you'll get bitten in the head and they can grow you a new brain."

"It's not that dangerous," DeLavore said, glowering. "Only one out of fifty—"

"*Normal*-sized people," M'Bisa snapped. "There's nobody on this planet large enough to protect a giant like Carl. We saw the fight. It was a cheap and dangerous stunt. And the faulty equipment—"

"Don't worry, Dr. M'Bisa," I said. "I won't be fighting the sharks again."

"Oh, really," B'oosa said. "No more sharks and no more bulls. What next? Elephants?"

I stared at him for a long second. "Depends on how much they offer."

"Carl . . ." Dr. M'Bisa looked really pained. "You can't continue this, this *absolute nonsense!* I forbid it!"

I tried to control my voice. "You can't, sir. I am a free agent. In space you can give me extra work, flunk me, whatever. When we're dirtside my time is my own. Isn't that right?"

"Yes, yes, technically. But this is *Earth!* The cradle of mankind. You're losing so much, so much to learn."

"I'm learning," I said. I stared at the check and did some rapid mental arithmetic. P14,662.50 to go. "I'm learning a lot."

VIII

I WAS SUPPOSED to stay with the class. I was supposed to stay in the wheelchair. I was supposed to start behaving myself and forget about trying to pay back the Extraweight Alien Tax. Forget it? No way.

Doing something about it, however, was a bit of a problem. B'oosa watched me all the time, like some sort of an appointed guardian. Could hardly go to the bathroom without him.

I hobbled across the hotel room to the window.

"Don't you think you should stay off that foot until it heals?" asked B'oosa, looking up from his books.

"It doesn't hurt too much," I lied.

"It's your body," he shrugged, putting his feet up on the table and going back to his books.

Francisco bounded into the room. He looked pretty peppy for a guy who was yesterday's shark bait. "Mail call," he said, as he plopped a small pack of envelopes on the table beside B'oosa's feet. Mail? Who got mail around here?

I got mail. They were all addressed to me, c/o *Starschool*. The holo of the shark fight must have attracted a lot of attention. Springers are pretty rare on Earth and it's unusual, to say the least, to find one fighting animals.

Most of them were job offers. A lot of them mentioned

bulls. I'd had enough of bulls and sharks to last me ten lifetimes. Some were from girls, wanting something called a date. They often enclosed small holos. Not bad looking, some of them; but small, small, small.

"What's all that?" asked B'oosa, picking up one of the discarded letters.

"Business," I said.

"This doesn't look like business," said B'oosa, picking up one of the holos. I blushed.

"Most of them are."

"You won't have time for any of that. We're leaving this afternoon to tour the Boswash Corridor, remember? Or have you even bothered to look at the itinerary?"

"Boswash. Humph."

"It's educational. You could use some enlightenment."

"I could use some money."

"Forget it, Carl. When will you get it through that thick Springer skull of yours that nobody blames you for the tax and nobody expects you to pay it back?"

"That's easy for you to say. Your family could probably buy my entire village."

B'oosa looked thoughtful for a second. Maybe he was counting it up. "That's most likely true," he said seriously. "But beside the point."

I gave up. He'd never understand me. He started pushing the letters around on the table. "Quaint custom," he said with a slight smile. "Mail. Actually written by the sender, not facsimiled. Quaint."

I saw a name I recognized and palmed the letter before B'oosa got a chance to get his hands on it. It was from Markos Salvadore, the Heller I'd met in the Plaza de Gladiatores. I slipped the letter into a fold on my tunic. Don't think B'oosa saw me.

"What's a Boswash Corridor?" I asked, feigning interest.

B'oosa looked startled, laid down the letter he was scanning. "Glad to see that you're showing a little healthy curiosity. Boswash is a megacity along the northeast coast of this continent. Very historical. Here, let me show you." He got up to get a book off the dresser.

While his back was turned, I flipped out the letter, opened it. All that was on the paper was a phone number. I memorized it, crumpled the paper.

"This is Boswash," said B'oosa, spreading open a book to a brightly colored map. "We'll be heading for Deecee this afternoon and tomorrow we'll go to New York. When this planet was made up of a lot of separate countries, Deecee was the capital of this particular country and New York was the largest city. There will be a lot for us to do and see in these cities."

"Sounds exciting," I lied. "When do we leave?"

"In about two hours."

"I can hardly wait."

That much was true.

*   *   *

The Deecee terminal was everything I'd hoped it would be: loud, crowded and hectic. Our tour group was swallowed by the seething mass of people. Everyone seemed to be in such a hurry. In a hurry for what, I couldn't imagine. Or care. It was perfect cover for me. B'oosa was on my right, Francisco on my left.

"Have to go to the bathroom," I said, turning the wheelchair abruptly, heading for the large doorway marked *Hombres*. They were right behind me, but stayed at the entrance.

I never slowed down. Slipped the wheelchair into one of the empty stalls and headed out the back door on foot. My heel still bothered me a little, but not too much. I had to get to a phone.

The bathroom's back door opened into a large crowded concourse just like the one I'd left. Looked around, saw a bank of phones, headed for them. Quickly. I stood out like a planet among moons. Even hunched over and hobbling, I loomed over the midget Earthies.

I crammed myself into one of the booths in back, more-or-less out of sight. Didn't know how much time I'd have before B'oosa and Francisco started looking for me, but it couldn't be very much. I hoped to be gone by then. Punched the number the Heller had given me. Must have been a long way off; took a whole handful of coins.

A face materialized out of the grayness. A hard face, scarred, with unruly black hair slicked back, a mustache. His frown broke a little when he caught my image. He almost smiled.

"Ah, Mr. Bok. So good of you to call. Allow me to introduce myself: Paul Wolfe of Wolfe and Associates. A certain mutual acquaintance said he might be able to get me in touch with you."

"You mean Markos Salvadore? The Heller?"

He nodded. "Mr. Salvadore does odd jobs for me from time to time. I find him a little coarse, but effective in his own way. He mentioned your problem to me."

"Problem?"

"He indicated you needed money and had a short time in which to obtain it. You may have noticed that this is somewhat difficult to accomplish on Earth."

"I've been finding that out the hard way."

"So I see. I don't know if you are aware of it, Mr. Bok, but you are creating something of a minor sensation here on Earth. Springers are not common on this planet and, I must admit, you put on quite a show. This is where I come in."

"Yes?"

"You see, one aspect of my business is, well, organizing shows such as the one you performed in with the sharks. But mine are special events; oneshots, we call them. They are very popular with those who watch such matches, which is to say most of the population of Earth. I can pay you well."

"How well?"

"I think the figure mentioned by our friend was in the neighborhood of P15,000. Does that sound about right?"

I nodded. It was exactly right. "What would I have to do for that?"

"Fight a polar bear to the death. Either his death or yours."

No way. I remembered the bull and how he had died. Never again.

"The money sounds fine, Mr. Wolfe, but I won't kill for it. Would it be all right if I rendered the animal unconscious instead?"

He thought for a moment, tugged at his mustache. "That would be more difficult than killing it, but I suppose that one as large as you could just possibly manage it. My public wants to see blood and they'll get it either way. The bear, of course, will be under no such restraint."

"When and where?" I asked, anxious to get moving. For P15,000 I'd wrestle a firelizard with both arms tied behind my back.

"The match will take place in Anchorage-sibirsk. Preferably tomorrow afternoon if you can manage it. I have a network slot at sixteen hundred hours. It would fit in nicely."

"I'm on my way," I said. "Uh, how do I get there?"

"Where are you now?"

"Deecee."

"Good. Take the tube from there to Seattle, then catch the shuttle up to Anchorage-sibirsk. My men will meet you there. They should have no trouble recognizing you." He leaned back in his chair.

"Don't worry about expenses. Charge them to me. I am well known here."

No doubt. Just one more thing. "These bears," I asked, "are they anything like bulls or sharks?"

He laughed. "No. Not at all. I think you'll find this particular animal a challenge."

Not exactly what I wanted to hear.

"I will see you this evening," he said. "I look forward to meeting you in person, Mr. Bok."

"Likewise," I said and he broke the connection with a wave of his hand. For P15,000 he could be as abrupt with me as he wanted.

I unfolded myself from the booth. Tight fit. I was cramped.

"Bears, huh?" A voice behind me. A familiar one. Oh no, not now. Francisco.

"What do you want bears for?" he asked, laughing.

"What I want is the P15,000."

"We'd better go now," he said.

"No, Pancho. Look, I've got to do this."

He grabbed my arm, started to pull me down the corridor.

"This way," he said. "Hurry."

"Hurry?"

"B'oosa won't be gone long. I sent him to the pharmacy to get you some medicine."

"B'oosa? Medicine?"

"I'm covering for you, you clown. Your head is as dense as your biceps. If we're going to grab the tube before B'oosa finds out we're gone, we'd better hurry."

"We?"

"Let's just say that I'm fond of animal life." He dragged me through the crowd.

IX

THE TUBE WAS boring, but fast and cheap. They strapped us into a two-person pod and slipped us on our way. Once again, I was a tight fit. It was uncomfortable, but the trip didn't last long.

There wasn't much of anything to see, either. Most of the tube was underground. When we did come up to the surface it was always in some barren, deserted place. At 1200 kilometers per hour everything slid by pretty fast.

The Seattle terminal looked just like the one in Deecee, only a little smaller. Still full of people, though. All in a hurry. We caught the shuttle to Anchorage-sibirsk without any trouble.

The shuttle was a lot slower than the tube and we got to see a good bit of the country. From what Pancho had told me, I expected everything to be meters deep in ice and snow. It wasn't that way at all. Sure there was some snow around, and ice in the mountains, but mostly there were trees. No plants on Springworld grow half as tall as the trees we saw. I was really impressed. Although there were a few houses scattered around and several small cities, the whole area seemed mostly uninhabited. This was pretty unusual for a planet as overpopulated as Earth. Someone told us that this was one of the last places on the planet where any wilderness at all existed, mostly because people didn't care to live there. It was changing, though, and fairly fast. Days were long in the summer and certain areas were covered by automated farms that grew larger each year. A lot of people to feed on this planet.

We also learned a little about bears. Most of the people we met on the shuttle had stories about them. Most of the stories were about the terrible things they did. The stories were all second hand, though. It took us a long time to find someone who had actually been face to face with one. He was a grizzled old man with one arm. We found him sitting in the observation car on the shuttle. He didn't want to talk much, but after Pancho bought him a drink, he loosened up a bit.

"Not like the old days," he said. "Not a bit. My pappy and my pappy's pappy knew how to live. Seven generations in the back country, never once took a pesa from the government. A man was a man, then. Had to be, to stay alive. Things change. Everybody wants something for nothing. Government takes care of everybody. Spoon feeds 'em, does everything for 'em 'cept change their diapers. Now in the old days . . ." His voice trailed off. He stared at the mountains in the distance. "A man was a man, that's all."

"We were wondering about bears," I said. "Polar bears. Do you know anything about them?"

The old man laughed. "Bears. Hah! I was practically weaned by bears, been around 'em all my life. Mostly they're shy, stay away from people, but not always. Watch out for females with cubs, they'll tear anything apart to protect them cubs."

"I don't think we'll run into anything like that," I said hopefully.

"Also mean if they're cornered, mean as hell. If they're threatened and caught with their back against a wall, they can be ten kinds of trouble. I know. Let me tell you, I *know*. I remember that time I was running my trap lines with my son—John it was, my second son—and out of nowhere it came . . . nowhere . . ." He drifted off again, lost in thought.

"How big are these bears?" asked Pancho.

"You." He pointed at me. "You an offworlder, right?" I nodded.

"How tall are you?"

"Two and a half meters."

"Biggest bear I ever saw was almost three meters tall, weighed more than six hundred kilos. Know that for a fact, killed him and dressed him myself. Cost me four dogs and an arm. When he reared up and came at me it was like a mountain walking tall. Took a full clip before he fell and by then, well, he'd done his damage."

"What's the best way to knock one out?" I asked.

"With a big club and ten friends," he said.

"No, I mean with my hands."

"Your hands? Don't kid me." He looked me over carefully. "Guess a fella as big as you might be able to handle one at that; a small one, maybe, if you were fast enough. You got to grab him right here." He indicated a place on the side of his neck. "Push down real hard for a few seconds. If you're in the right place and strong enough, he might go down. If you don't have it right, you're dead. You won't get no second chance."

"I hope I won't need one."

"You planning on rasslin' a bear? Boy, you got rocks for brains."

"I don't know. I think I can do it. Besides, Mr. Wolfe said—"

The old man looked like he'd been hit in the stomach. "Mr. Wolfe, you say? Mr. Paul Wolfe?"

"Yes. I talked to him and he—"

"Got no use for Wolfe and his crew," he said, getting up from his seat. "Got no use for them what does business with him." He purposely tipped his drink into Pancho's lap, eyes daring Pancho to do something about it. Everything froze for a split second.

"You see, we have—"

"*Bastards,*" he growled, turning away from us.

I started to go after him; he didn't understand. Pancho stopped me by laying a hand gently on my arm.

"Don't do it, Carl," he said. "The man's got a grudge and I think it's pretty deep. We don't want any trouble."

We sure didn't want trouble, but as Anchorage-sibirsk slid into view, I wondered just what it was we were headed for.

The men who met us at the terminal were tough-looking, but polite and all business. They took us straight to the hotel, one of those old-fashioned glass and steel things that stick way up in the air. Wouldn't last five minutes in any halfway decent storm on Springworld. They paid us for our tube and shuttle tickets, gave us a little extra for something they called walking-around money. Told us not to leave the hotel room as Mr. Wolfe would be in touch with us shortly.

One wall of the room was glass and it looked out over the sprawling city to the mountains beyond. A light snow was falling. As cities go on Earth, this one was pretty small; only about 14 million inhabitants. Even so, it was the largest city in this part of the planet and had a pretty wild reputation as a rugged, knock-down kind of place. Pancho seemed unnaturally eager to find out. Me, I just had my sights set on that P15,000.

Before long the phone chimed and Mr. Wolfe's face appeared on the screen.

"Mr. Bok," he said. "I'm glad to see that you managed to arrive safely. You brought a friend, I am told." He looked in Pancho's direction.

"His name is Francisco Bolivar. Pancho."

"You understand that Mr. Bolivar cannot help you with the bear."

"He's here to give me moral support," I said.

"Very well," said Mr. Wolfe. "I have no objection. I am free to see you now. My men will bring you up."

"Up?"

"Yes. My office is located on the top floor of this building. I own this hotel. Didn't they tell you?"

"No."

He shrugged. "It is only one of my properties. And not

the most profitable, by any means.'' Again he broke the connection abruptly. One thing was for sure; I didn't have to worry about Mr. Wolfe being good for the P15,000. Looked like he could buy planets.

We were taken by private elevator to the top floor, where we exited into a large anteroom. It was plush; thick carpets on the floor, paintings on the walls. There were several desks in the room, most of them occupied by body-guard types who just sat there, watching us, looking tough. Large desks, looked like real wood. A woman sat at one and she smiled at us.

''Good afternoon, Mr. Bok. Mr. Bolivar.'' She nodded pleasantly toward us. ''Mr. Wolfe is expecting you. Won't you go in?'' She motioned to a door behind her desk, only one of many doors leading from the room. With all these doors and people around, it's a wonder anyone ever got to see Mr. Wolfe.

I had expected to find an opulent office and I was mistaken. It was functional to the point of being stark: one desk, one phone, no books, no windows. Behind the desk sat Mr. Wolfe. He was big for an Earthie, but still quite a bit smaller than me. He didn't rise when we entered, but he did manage a kind of half smile. I figured for him that was doing pretty well.

''Mr. Bok, you're taller than I expected,'' he said. ''Do they all come that big from Springworld?''

''Most of them,'' I said. ''Some are taller.''

''You'll do fine, Mr. Bok.'' He handed me a small folder, filled with papers.

I opened it, flipped through it. Lots of fine print with parties of the first part and whomsoevers scattered all through it. A typical contract, written by lawyers so that only lawyers could understand it. I found the important parts: P15,000 for one Carl Bok of Springworld to fight to the death (or unconsciousness) one polar bear or to stay in the arena with said animal for a minimum period of one half hour.

''What if the bear doesn't feel like fighting?'' I asked

Mr. Wolfe. "It's going to be a pretty dull half hour. An expensive one for you, too."

"I wouldn't worry about that, Mr. Bok. It has yet to happen."

Pancho came over and looked at the contract over my shoulder. I don't think the legalese could have made any more sense to him than it did to me. English was a foreign language to him.

"Is Mr. Bolivar your lawyer?" asked Mr. Wolfe. I got the feeling that he was only half joking.

"Oh no," said Pancho. "I'm just a student, like Carl. We are amigos, comrades."

Mr. Wolfe handed me a pen. "It's a standard business form. You will sign all three copies." He paused. "If you please," he added as an afterthought.

I signed. For P15,000 I would have signed almost anything.

Mr. Wolfe took back the pen and the folder. "Very good, Mr. Bok," he said. "The money will be waiting for you at the end of your match. I hope you will take this evening to see a little of our town. We are quite proud of it. Justifiably so, I might add. I would, however, advise that you try to stay out of trouble. That is, any trouble that might lead to physical harm. You are my property until 1630 tomorrow and I like people to take care of my property. It is a small vice of mine."

Property? Should have read the fine print, I guess.

"I'll take care of him," said Pancho.

"You do that," he said. He looked at me. "It is good to do business with you, Mr. Bok. I am sure it will work out to our mutual benefit. Good day."

It was a second before I realized we'd been dismissed. I reached over the desk and shook Mr. Wolfe's hand. Pancho and I were escorted back to our room.

Anchorage-sibirsk is supposed to be some sort of a frontier town. How anything with a population of 14 million could be considered frontier was beyond me. Fourteen families make a crowded city on Springworld. But Pancho was eager to find out what it was like and I owed him at least that much for getting me away from B'oosa.

We started the evening out with dinner in the hotel. It was delicious; real meat and everything. When I tried to pay, they waved me aside. All taken care of by Mr. Wolfe. Whatever else is to be said about the man, he likes his property well fed.

Pancho asked at the desk what a person did for excitement in this town. The clerk said that just stepping outside was excitement enough for most people, but if we wanted to see what the city was really like we should drop by the Casino de Mabel.

We got directions and started to walk. It was chilly, but we had light jackets. Most of the city, at least the part we were headed for, was domed. Temperature there was a constant 23° C. Before we had gone more than a few steps, a surface vehicle pulled up beside us. Although it was long and sleek, it couldn't hold more than five or six people. An extravagant waste of space.

The man sitting next to the driver slid a window back. "Mr. Bok?" he asked.

"That's me," I said.

"We're to provide transportation for you." A door slid open on our side. I looked at Pancho. He went in without question. I followed him.

Soft seats, cushions. It didn't take an expert to know that we were surrounded by real leather and wood trim. There was a bar and a phone in the back seat. A glass partition separated us from the front.

"Where were you headed, Mr. Bok?" The voice was a little tinny through the speaker. The volume was gentle. Someone had given a lot of thought to this vehicle.

"The hotel clerk recommended the Casino de Mabel."

"An excellent choice, Mr. Bok. We'll be there in five minutes. Please make yourself comfortable."

A fleeting thought came to me. "Does Mr. Wolfe own that, too?" I asked.

"Of course."

It figured.

The Casino de Mabel was gaudy from the outside, but no more so than the other establishments that lined the streets. Inside was a floor show and gambling, plus the usual food and drink. The floor show was ending as we came in. They were doing something called the Can-Can. It was supposed to represent a period of time called the Gold Rush. I didn't understand any of it. Just a lot of people jumping around.

Pancho wanted to try the gaming tables. He had a little money, plus what Wolfe's men had given us. He also had a crazy idea about getting rich. I hadn't slept through the probability theory courses in math, so I wasn't tempted. All I wanted was my P15,000.

Pancho sat for a while at a table playing something called blackjack, an activity that used small plastic rectangles called cards. At least he was consistent. He consistently lost. Then he moved to a game called roulette which involved a lot of numbers and a wheel with a small ball. It looked silly. He lost there, too, but not too much. When he moved on to something called craps, played with small cubes covered with dots, I decided to leave him to his own devices for a few minutes. I needed a breath of fresh air. The air in the casino was thick with tobacco smoke. Tobacco is illegal on Earth, but evidently that particular law was not rigidly enforced in this town. The two men watching us split up, one following me, the other staying at his seat a discreet distance behind Pancho.

Outside, under the awning of the casino, the fresh air felt good, although I wished the dome wasn't overhead so that I could breathe some real air for a change. It looked black and crisp beyond the dome. My bodyguard stood about ten meters away, never crowding me and never letting me out of his sight. People walked in a continuous stream up and down the walkway.

I studied their faces as they walked by. Not as much hurrying here, but maybe it was the time of day. A good many people wore hard-set faces of quiet desperation. It bothered me a little and and—*wait!* Wasn't that . . .

He bumped into me, mumbled "Tracy's Bar," and kept on going. The Heller! I turned to follow him and was bumped by another person. I started to push him away.

"Don't follow us," the second man whispered. It was Angelo, the Heller's sidekick. "Half hour from now." They both disappeared into the crowd.

As brief as it was, the encounter had attracted unwanted attention. My bodyguard was walking toward me. I bent down, pretended to pick up something off the walkway. He came up to me. I stood up, turned to walk back into the casino. "Too crowded out here," I said. He nodded and we went back inside. He stayed four or five steps behind. He'd been well trained.

I found Pancho playing a large device called a slot machine. It only took pesas and those only one at a time. I figured he'd pretty well blown most of his money. I leaned toward him, as if to inspect the coins he had in the cup in his hand.

"Trouble," I whispered. "At least I think so." As quickly as possible I told him about meeting the Heller and Angelo.

He finished losing the coins in his cup and made a big show about wanting to go somewhere else for a beer. We headed for the door and I nodded to the two men to follow us. They would have, anyway.

We got into the vehicle and the driver pulled away from the curb.

"Tracy's Bar," I told him.

"Isn't it time to head back?" he asked.

"Tracy's Bar," I said firmly. "Or we get out and walk."

The driver changed direction and the other man talked hurriedly into a microphone. I couldn't hear what they were saying. They reached some sort of a decision and the driver cut down a side road.

"One drink," came the voice over the speaker. I didn't have to ask if Mr. Wolfe owned this place. I had a feeling he didn't.

Tracy's was dark and dirty, full of tobacco smoke. It was difficult to see more than a meter in front of you. Pancho and I stumbled to the bar, ordered two beers. The bartender brought them, took our money, rang it up.

"What do you figure's happening?" asked Pancho.

I shrugged in the darkness. He knew as much as I did. I picked up my beer and the bartender leaned forward and ran a rag across the bar in front of me.

"You're the Springer," said the bartender. It wasn't a question.

"That's right," I said. "What's—"

"Go to the bathroom," he said.

"What?"

"Start walking toward the bathroom, lunkhead." He moved his head slightly to the right and I could see a dim light above a bathroom door.

I looked into my beer and whispered to Pancho. "Head for the street. See if you can drag them away. I've got to see what the Heller wants."

Suddenly Pancho moaned and I nearly broke out laughing. I didn't know the little fellow had it in him. What an actor. He clutched his stomach and twisted toward the door, knocking people aside as he went. Both of our "friends" followed him. In the confusion I slipped back to the bathroom.

I was almost there when someone grabbed me by the arm and jerked me into a dark booth. I started to pull away and a familiar voice said, "Shize, Springer, it's me."

I relaxed. Until then I hadn't realized how tense I'd been. "What's up?" I asked him.

"You are, Springer. You are."

"I don't—"

"You don't have a chance. That's not going to be an ordinary bear tomorrow, it's one of them bio-engineered things. It'll kill you. I didn't know, I swear. Wolfe's got me over a barrel for some things I did for him a long time ago when I was young and hungry. He figured I could get you here and I did. But I didn't know he was setting you up."

"He thought he was helping you, amigo," said Angelo.

"I should have known better than to trust Wolfe," said the Heller. "All he wants is a lot of blood and you're going to provide it. If the bear kills you, so much the better, as far as he's concerned. There are laws against this kind of stuff, but in case you haven't noticed it, Wolfe *is* the law around here."

"I figured that out."

"Good for you. There's hope for you yet, Springer."

"How am I supposed to get out of this?" I asked.

"Not easy, but there's—" The Heller was cut short by the *thunk* of a knife on the table. He started to make a move, looked up and stopped. Our two bodyguards were back. Five or six men stood behind them. None of them looked happy.

"Mr. Bolivar has taken ill," said one of them. "Mr. Wolfe suggests that perhaps you would like to return to your room. You will need rest for tomorrow."

I didn't imagine I had any choice in the matter. They led me out to the vehicle. Pancho was stretched out on the back seat. He didn't look like he felt too good. I was more worried about him and what might be happening to the Heller and Angelo than I was about the bear or what they might do to me. The vehicle started moving.

"Ten minutes, Mr. Bok." The voice was as even as ever.

Pancho moaned and held his head. He started to say something, but couldn't get any words out, fell back against the seat.

We got to the hotel room and I propped Pancho in the shower, turned it on full cold. After a few minutes he came around.

"Don't know what happened, Carl. Don't think they hit me. As soon as I got to the street everything went blank. Someone put me out quick."

"I think we're in over our heads, Pancho," I said, as he dragged himself out of the shower. "These boys play rough."

As Pancho dried himself off, I walked to the door and tried to open it. I couldn't. It was locked from the outside.

"What are we going to do?" asked Pancho.

"Get some sleep," I said. "I've got a bear to fight tomorrow and you might have to pick up the pieces."

The bed was soft and too short for me. I slept on the floor.

X

A LATE BREAKFAST was delivered to our room. I requested some literature on bears and read about them for a while. The old man had been right on the nose.

Bears were dangerous.

I had no idea what a bio-engineered bear might be like, but I figured I'd find out soon enough.

I worked out a little in the hotel room, doing some exercises to loosen up. My foot seemed to have healed nicely and there was no trace of the *cornada* wound. Earth doctors *could* do wonders, as they said. I hoped Wolfe had some good ones on his payroll.

Pancho and I were taken to the stadium. It was a long ride, almost to the edge of town. I kept wondering about the Heller and what he had said. I hoped he was all right.

The stadium was open at the top, with heated stands. Looked like it could hold over 100,000 people and although it was early, it was already filling up. The sky was blue and clear overhead. I asked whether we could see the bear.

Our bodyguard shrugged and led us down a series of corridors and stairs. I could smell the animals before we saw them. Hear them, too. They made a lot of noise.

"In there," the bodyguard said, gesturing at a door. He leaned against the wall and lit a cigarette. "Take a good look."

Inside was a huge room, filled with caged animals of all descriptions, some I didn't recognize. They all had one thing in common, though—they all looked dangerous. I walked around and . . . there!

Even on all fours, it was nearly twice as tall as me. Easily went over a thousand kilos. It paced restlessly from one end of the cage to the other, taking random swipes at the bars with a huge paw as it went. Its fur was a dirty yellow-white and matted; it smelled like a thousand wet dogs. Foam dripped from its jaws.

It looked like a bad dream come alive. I wanted out. This was crazy.

When I turned from the bear, Pancho was talking with three men in the doorway. Several policemen stood out in the hall. Pancho didn't look happy at all. Two of the men were heavy-set, burly types, the third had "lawyer" written all over him. He was carrying a folder. Copy of my contract, no doubt. I joined them.

"Mr. Bok," said the lawyer, extending his hand, "I represent Mr. Wolfe."

I ignored the hand. "Then you can tell Mr. Wolfe he can fight this creature himself."

"You jest, of course. The contract—"

"I signed to fight a bear, not a monster."

"You signed to fight whatever we put you against. Not to do so would be a serious breach of contract. At my word, if I felt you were inclined to back out of our agreement, these policemen would take you into custody. The penalty for breach of contract is one year in prison for each P1000 forfeited. The judges around here are not lenient in such matters."

"And I suppose all the judges are hand-picked by our friend Mr. Wolfe."

He just grinned, the bastard. "Fifteen years in prison is a very long time, Mr. Bok. Besides, your two friends from last night, the gentleman from Hell and his small partner, will be anxious to watch you on the holo. They are special guests of Mr. Wolfe, and if you should fail to appear, it is possible they could meet with an accident. That would be tragic. I suggest you ready yourself for the match. It is almost time.''

The two heavies followed us back to the dressing room. I felt like busting a few heads, but it was hopeless. They really had us. Maybe I did have rocks for brains.

Pancho gave me a rubdown while we waited. He was somber and depressed, even more than I was. After a few minutes another guard came, this one armed with a heavy pistol on his hip. He handed me the knife I was supposed to use on the bear. It was smaller than my hand, worthless. I kept it anyway, put it in my belt. Maybe I wouldn't have to use it. Maybe I would.

''Carl?''

I turned to Pancho. He slapped me on the back, squeezed my arm. He was close to tears.

''Good luck,'' he said. ''Come back.''

''I have to come back,'' I said, forcing a cheerfulness I didn't feel. ''My wheelchair's stuck in a restroom in Deecee. Someone's got to pay the rental on it.''

We shook hands and I went out to face the bear.

The crowd roared as I walked onto the sand. Didn't all these people have anything better to do with their time than watch me get mauled? The stadium was filled. I felt dwarfed and insignificant as I walked to the middle of the arena. I was accompanied by two remote-controlled holo cameras about a meter tall that glided along beside me on stilted platforms. A referee stood on the edge of the sand. I noticed he didn't carry a rifle. Another rule bent a little. An announcer was saying something over the loudspeakers, but I couldn't make out the words through the noise of the crowd. Then they let the bear loose and the stands went wild.

It was easy to see who they were rooting for.

At first the bear just circled the arena, panting and sniffing at everything. He seemed to be confused about where he was. Maybe I had a chance, after all. I just kept away from him, stayed on the opposite side of the arena. This lasted about five minutes. Then he sat down and sniffed at the air, weaving his massive head back and forth. I had a wild feeling that he might fall asleep.

Then he smelled me.

He came toward me in a slow lope. I had to move away from the wall so I wouldn't get cornered. I faked a movement to my left and he wasn't fooled a bit. He didn't seem to be mad or anything, just curious. When he hit me I got the feeling that it was a playful slap. It sent me flying about ten meters and I landed on my side with my ears ringing. Before I could get to my knees, he was on me, rolling me around like a ball. He still seemed to be playing, not hitting very hard, but a thousand-kilo playmate was something I didn't need. I rolled out of his reach and got to my feet.

The next time he came at me, I twisted around and got on his back. That had worked once. He didn't like that too much and tried to shake me off. I held onto his thick fur with one hand and tried to find the pressure points on his neck with the other. It was impossible. His fur was too thick, I couldn't get enough pressure on the arteries. He kept pulling his head around, trying to bite me. His jaws made a horrible snapping sound, his teeth were huge, his breath stunk. He was getting mad.

He tried rolling over and I jumped free, got out of the way, fast. He could squash me with no trouble at all. I tried running away and slipped. By the time I got to my feet he was on me, rearing back on his hind legs.

I knew exactly what that old trapper had felt like. This was the first time I'd seen the bear upright and it was frightening. *Tall!* I went weak in my knees. He grabbed me easily with one huge paw. I fought it without any effect. His claws were as long as my hand. The other arm hit me hard and before I knew what was happening, he'd drawn me up to his chest. My face was buried in his smelly fur and I struggled like a wild man. I kicked and I bit and I threw my arms and legs everywhere they would reach. Nothing worked. My ears started pounding and all I could see was red. I was blacking out. I tried to get to my knife, couldn't. I bit at his fur, huge hunks of it came off in my mouth. I spit it out, bit some more. I kicked and kicked and kicked and something must have happened because I suddenly became aware of his loud roar and I was rolling end over end across the sand. This time I drew my knife. It seemed pitifully small.

He charged and I swung. No doubt about it now—he was mad. I tried for his eyes, figuring that was my only chance. I never came close. He batted my hand away and I watched the knife fly into the stands. Gone.

Then I noticed my hand; it was slashed and bloody, the tendons were showing. I must have looked too long because out of nowhere a huge paw filled with claws caught me in the chest and sent me flying. Everything below my chin was covered with blood. I shook my head. There had to be an answer. A holo camera moved in for a good shot.

Cube squares. It came to me just like that.

There are limits as to how large any given animal can grow. There is always an inhibiting factor. I'm about as large as any human can be. If they're much larger, their skeletons can't support their weight. That's why they can't grow ants as big as houses. That bear was big. *Too big*. Something had to give.

At the next charge I hit him hard and low. He wasn't expecting anything like that and he lost his balance for a second. A second was all I needed. I threw everything I had against the leg that was holding his weight. He went over with a loud crack. A broken bone. Maybe now I could hold my own. He roared in pain, stood on his hind legs.

Oh damn, a front leg. I had to break a *front* leg! I backpedaled as fast as I could. It wasn't near fast enough. He was coming and he was coming hard. Blood flecked at his mouth and his head swished back and forth as he roared and charged at me. I never had a chance. He caught me a good one along the side of my head. Everything went black for a split second and I tasted blood and suddenly there he was, hovering over me on his back two legs, ready for the kill. I was backed up against a wall, nowhere to go. A holo camera was silently circling around to get a good close-up of the bear ripping me apart. Too close.

The bear stood to his full height and pulled back his good arm. I twisted to my right and grabbed the holo camera by its base. He swung and I swung, putting everything I had behind it. I was a little faster and mashed the side of his head with the camera. He went down in a heap, legs twitching. He was out cold.

Cold meant unconscious. I'd won. It took a few seconds for that to sink in. Then I could hear the crowd through the ringing in my ears. *I'd won!* I dropped the holo camera and it automatically righted itself. Flowers and beer bottles were being thrown through the air. I didn't care about that at all. P15,000 was waiting for me at the end of the corridor. But before I'd made it off the sand, my legs gave out from under me and I guess I kind of passed out for a while.

Because when I opened my eyes, B'oosa was there. The Dean, too. Pancho was there, everything was blurry, my eyes wouldn't focus. They were arguing with somebody. I tried to sit up, couldn't. My chest was sprayed with plasti-flesh. Best I could do was to open my eyes and try to focus.

Everybody was mad; at me, at Pancho, at Mr. Wolfe, at the lawyer. Everybody seemed mad at everybody else. I felt right at home.

"About time you joined the party," said B'oosa, noticing that my eyes were open. My eyes might have been open, but my brain wasn't working too well.

"You found me," I said.

"A giant like you leaves large footprints; everyone remembers you. It was easy to trace you here. But we couldn't find out where you were staying last night. People in this city seem remarkedly close-mouthed." He glared at Mr. Wolfe, who was standing behind his lawyer and several bodyguards. "And these goons," he indicated several policemen standing around, "detained us so that we were unable to stop that ridiculous fight."

One of the policemen stepped forward. "Goons?" he said. "I resent that. We're respectable—"

"Shut up!" said B'oosa with considerable irritation in his voice. No one challenged him. They'd have been fools to try.

I tried to sit up, managed it this time. "All this doesn't matter," I said. "It's over and done. Let me get my money and leave."

"There are complications, Carl," said B'oosa. "There evidently will be no money."

"No money?"

"There is a clause in your contract," said the lawyer, "that holds you responsible for any damage you might cause during the match. It is a normal precaution we take. You signed the contract; it's valid and will hold up in any court. You're liable for damages."

"What damages?" The only damage I could see was done to me.

"The holo camera you mistreated suffered considerable stress."

"They're practically indestructible," I shouted. That's why I'd picked it up.

"Nevertheless, we have determined that it incurred damages to the sum of, shall we say, P15,000."

"That's ridiculous!" Plasti-flesh or not, I was going to tear him apart.

Pancho and B'oosa held me back. Even as mad as I was, it didn't take very much effort on their part. I'd had it. In more ways than one.

Dr. M'bisa, the Dean, came over to me. He was really upset. "Forget it, Carl," he said. It was the last decent thing he said to me for two days.

XI

I REALLY CAUGHT IT. I suppose I'd brought it on myself, but it seemed like everyone was over-reacting. I had several long talks with the Dean. At one point he handed me a petition from the students saying that they didn't hold me responsible for the tax. I noticed Pancho hadn't signed it. At least he was on my side. Seemed like he was the only one, though, and he caught a lot of trouble for going along with me.

There wasn't anything official they could do to us, though. I caught some extra schoolwork and stuff like that, but I hadn't really broken any rules, just stretched them a lot. Bad judgment was the term the Dean used, along with childish pride and stubbornness. He used these terms a lot in our little discussions. I didn't mind the schoolwork; I was mending in bed, anyway. The rest of the group was in and out: the official part of the tour on Earth was finished and there were ten days of free time before we left.

That gave me ten days and I was still P14,662.50 behind.

B'oosa chided me a lot in that detached way he has. I think he was amused at the lengths I had gone to to try and pay back the money. He also told me the Dean was probably worried about the bad publicity and loss of potential students if one of us happened to get himself killed on an unsupervised adventure.

I was lying in the hotel bed, surrounded by books, when B'oosa walked in with Pancho. The books were for effect; actually I was digging through my mail. There was a lot of it.

"Back from the great cultural centers of the universe?" I asked.

"You really ought to try it sometime, Carl," said B'oosa. "It's possible some knowledge might work its way through that thick skull of yours."

"Love to," I said. "But as you can easily see, I'm a poor invalid, confined to bed. I may never heal."

Pancho tossed a book at me. I caught it easily. With my "bad" hand.

"You don't fool me," he said. "I saw you doing deep knee bends last night after you thought we were asleep. You're just lucky the Dean hasn't sent down word to keep you tied up for the next week or so." He flopped in a chair and B'oosa walked to the bed, picked up one of the letters.

"More bears?" he asked.

"No," I shuddered. "But just about everything else. What's a lion?"

B'oosa set the letter he was holding back down on the bed. "Are you sure that you don't have any Maasai'pyan blood in you?" he asked.

"No, I . . ." Then I realized he was joking. "Why?"

"You remind me a little of my brother. Of course he was not quite so tall as you, and somewhat darker. But you had some things in common, when he was your age."

"Like what?"

"Stubbornness. A certain tendency toward self-destruction. Do you know the word '*eunoto*'?"

"No."

"In English you might say 'rite of passage,' but the translation would not be accurate.

"Our planet was colonized by people from the Maasai tribe, from Earth. They were a very . . . conservative people, on Earth, almost anti-technological, preserving traditions whose origins are lost in prehistory. The ones on Earth still do.''

''Your people rebelled?''

He nodded slowly. ''That's right; that's why we call our planet New Maasai, Maasai'pya. In breaking off from the old ways, my ancestors cold-bloodedly evaluated the body of Maasai tradition and updated it point by point, changing the culture to one compatible with the new interstellar community.

''One tradition we maintained—though in a radically altered form—was eunoto. On Earth, this was four days of tightly controlled ritual, marking the passage of a young man from the warrior class to the elder class. These 'elders' were only seventeen or eighteen years old, which reflected the reality that the warrior class was a hopeless anachronism. It had been centuries since they had had anyone to fight.

''Yet the notion of a ritual period marking the passage from irresponsible youth to responsible adult—*kivulana* to *mwenyeji*—was worth preserving. The details are unimportant, but the essence of it is that for one year a young person is neither child nor citizen. He decides for himself when his eunoto year will be, sometime between the onset of puberty and the age of twenty. There is a separate body of law for eunoto, which encourages physical testing, even recklessness. Murder is not allowed, but assault is, under conditions of dueling.

''My brother and I did not learn to use the quarterstaff in a gymnasium. We learned in the jungle and in the street; we had to fight anyone who desired combat, and under certain conditions we did have to issue challenges.''

''And if you didn't fight or challenge?''

''You went back to kivulana. Not only was that a disgrace, but it meant you had to begin eunoto over again. Some people never do finish eunoto; they are objects of pity and scorn.''

I could tell there was a big moral coming. ''So what did your brother do?''

He laughed ruefully. ''It was rather bizarre. On the last

day of his eunoto, another boy delivered to him a truly blood-curdling insult. It was a set-up. When the insult was delivered, by a third party, the boy was on the other side of the world, and wouldn't be back for several days.

"A rational person would have shrugged it off. What my brother did was set himself up for a duel and then refuse to fight. So he got his revenge, but at too great a price."

"Another year of vacation?"

"Oh, it is that. A boy's dream, in fact, or a girl's: the government subsidizes your travel to anywhere in the world." He got a faraway look. "Climb mountains, swim rivers, swagger your way through waterfronts and bazaars—do as you wish for a year. Test yourself, find the boundaries of your ability. You learn much about life, but after a year you should have learned enough: humility, restraint, a sense of purpose. A person who deliberately sends himself back is marked for the rest of his life. He has declared himself unable or unwilling to grow."

"And he gets another year of helling around at the taxpayers' expense," I said.

"That is part of it," B'oosa admitted. "But do you see that this is what you are doing? You made the gesture, and that was not a bad thing. But persisting beyond reason *is* bad. Is childish. What will your parents, your planet, think if you get yourself killed here? What will they think of *Starschool*?"

"My parents," I said slowly, "my planet . . . would expect me to pay my own debts."

"As I would!" he said with surprising force. "Debts that you yourself incurred. But this is not something for which anyone holds you responsible. Everyone aboard *Starschool* sees this cynical tax for what it is—everybody but you."

Pancho had been silent through this whole discussion, leafing through the mail. B'oosa looked to him for confirmation. He shrugged. "*Un hombre hace lo necesario.*"

"Every planet must have that proverb," B'oosa said. " 'A man has to do what a man has to do.' Real life admits options. A year of eunoto would teach you that. You both should dye your skin black and go to Maasai'pya.''

"Perhaps eunoto is where one finds it," Pancho said.

B'oosa rolled his eyes toward the ceiling. "*Boys!*"

"It's something I have to get through."

He started pacing. "If you keep fighting monsters for free, and dealing with people like that Wolfe, all you'll get is dead. I would miss having you around to entertain me."

"How can I tell the good offers from the bad? I get so many. Look." I held up a handful of envelopes.

"Most of these have clauses you wouldn't like. They are all trying to take advantage of your temporary novelty value. And your lack of legal training, I might add. If I had seen your contract with Mr. Wolfe before you had signed it, you would never have gotten into that mess."

"Does that mean you'll help me?"

"You *are* like my brother. He took advantage of me too, when I would let him. I'd hate to see you die and not get paid for it. I'll look over the contracts for you, that much I'll do. Just don't tell the Dean I had anything to do with this. I'm supposed to be a steadying influence on you two rascals."

That got me out of bed. I spread the offers out on the table and the three of us started looking them over.

"No lions or tigers," said B'oosa.

"Or bears," said Pancho.

"Sharks and bulls are out, too," I added. "After all, it's my body."

"Here's one," said Pancho. "Wrestling alligators in a place called The Glades. Alligators are just big lizards with lots of teeth."

"Let me look at that," said B'oosa. He studied it for a minute. "No good," he said. "The money looks fine on the surface, but it's all tied up with how much holo time they can sell. If they don't sell much time, you don't get much money. Better to look for one big show than to try to pick up a lot of little ones."

We eliminated most of the offers.

"This one looks interesting," B'oosa said. "No animals. It's a formal challenge from a gladiatorial team in Lusaka. If you come up with a team with a total weight of 400 kilograms, they'll take you on with a team of equal weight for a prize of P60,000. The prize is bonded, and independent of the sponsoring corporation's profit or loss. Sounds fair, but you'd need a team."

I looked at Pancho. "You interested?"

"Not me, man. 400 kilograms of Earthies is a real mob. They'd crawl all over us, likely bite us to death."

"Nonsense," said B'oosa. "Two good men back-to-back with quarterstaffs can hold off any mob indefinitely, as long as their opponents don't use long-range weapons. Gladiators are only allowed to use clubs, vibroclubs, quarterstaffs, and bolos. Only the bolo can be thrown effectively, and it's easy to counter with a quarterstaff. Just get them to set a time limit and you shouldn't have any trouble. It's certainly easier than sharks or bears. More dignified, too, I might add."

I had my doubts, remembering the time B'oosa flattened me with the quarterstaff. "It wouldn't work."

"Why not?"

"I'm not nearly good enough with the quarterstaff."

"You're not *that* bad, Carl. All you need is practice and some instruction. From what I've seen of the Earthies, they're not too good with the quarterstaff, even the best of them."

"But I only have a few days and . . . *hey!* Would you teach me?"

"Me? Why should I have anything to do with this? I don't usually spend my time teaching hard-headed kids how to go out and get themselves hurt. Besides, there are some museums I haven't seen yet."

"But you're good," I said. "The best in the University. Better than anyone on this planet, I bet. You could teach me a lot."

"Well," he said. "I suppose even someone like you could learn the rudiments if he tried hard enough. It would be a challenge of sorts. If I could teach *you*, I could teach anybody. Of course it would take years before you could become even halfway decent by Maasai'pyan standards, but it shouldn't take that much for you to hold your own against the Earthies."

"It might work," said Pancho. "I could handle the bolo."

"You?" I asked.

"Sure. On Selva we are practically born with bolos in our hands. I'm good with one. Before I joined *Starschool* I was village champion."

Champion? It began to look possible. Only . . . "We'd need to find another quarterstaffer." I looked at Pancho and grinned. He caught it right away.

"He'd have to be good," said Pancho. We both looked at B'oosa.

"Forget it," he said. "I'm not interested. I'm too old and too smart for that foolishness."

"Wouldn't work, anyway," said Pancho. "Mr. B'oosa isn't tall enough. It would take a lot of man to protect you. We'd better find someone larger."

"Nonsense," said B'oosa. "Size means nothing with the quarterstaff. I've already shown you that."

"Besides," said Pancho, grinning. "He would have to be someone strong and fast. Someone with courage."

"Are you saying that I—"

"That's right," I interrupted, looking at Pancho and ignoring B'oosa. "He should have brains as well. Someone you could trust in a fight."

"Look—"

"Someone who could fight as well as other people talk," said Pancho. "Where could we find someone like that?"

"I could place a wannad," I said. " 'Wanted: One strong courageous gladiator to help a couple of foolish schoolboys pay off a debt. Experience with quarterstaff a necessity. Maasai'pyans need not apply.' Someone would answer it. A bum, probably, a derelict who didn't know one end of a vibroclub from the other. We'd most likely both get killed trying to protect him."

"Enough," said B'oosa. "Enough."

"You'll do it?" I asked him.

"It seems I have no choice," he said good-naturedly. "If I don't, you boys are bound to get into trouble. Besides, winning this one should put an end, once and for all, to all this undignified sporting with animals."

Together, the three of us weighed in at 320 kilograms, B'oosa also being a giant by Earth standards, even though he weighed a paltry 95 kilos. That left us 80 kilos to round off the team. I had an idea where I could find 80 kilos of mean gladiator.

*   *   *

I found him in the Plaza de Gladiatores, but he looked like he'd been the one who fought the bear, not me.

"Shize, Springer," said the Heller. "I didn't think I'd be seeing you again."

"It wasn't your fault, Markos," I said. "And thanks for the warning about the bear."

He rubbed the side of his face. It was swollen and patched roughly with plasti-flesh. "There were other people who didn't care for that little conversation we had."

"They almost killed him," said Angelo, who didn't look too good himself. "It was very close."

"They ain't gonna kill me till they can't get one more dightin' pesa out of me. Gonna dightin' bleed me dry if they can," said the Heller. "But they're gonna have one hell'va fight on their hands. Old Markos don't give up easy." He took a long pull on the beer I'd bought him.

"I'm sorry I brought you trouble," I said.

"Shize, man," said Markos. "I bring my own trouble. Bad news is my middle name. But they had no call messin' up on my little friend here. It was none of his affair. How's he gonna find one of them *señoritas* if he keeps gettin' bashed up like that? He'll end up as ugly as me. Broke as me, too."

"I made it my business, amigo," said Angelo. "Your trouble is mine."

Markos shook his head, looked up at me. "But what

brings you here? Can't be you're looking for another bear.''

''No. I'm looking for a gladiator.''

''This is the right place. Whole dightin' town's full of 'em. What you got in mind?''

''I need a fourth for a team we're fielding against a bunch of Earthies from Lusaka. Has to be good with a vibroclub and weigh eighty kilos or less. Purse is P60,000. It's bonded. If we win, it's P15,000 all the way around.''

''I'm seventy-eight kilos and can do things with a vibe' that you ain't thought of. That kinda money I could get off planet and away from Wolfe. Start over. I'm your man.''

''I was hoping you'd say that.''

XII

BY THE TIME Markos and I got back, B'oosa had all the details ironed out. We were going to be facing a team of nine Earthies: four with quarterstaffs, two each with clubs and bolos, and one vibroclub. Each team was allowed only one vibroclub, it was some sort of a rule.

We would win if we had at least one man left after ten minutes. The referees would send a team member off the field if they judged him severely enough disabled. This meant unconscious, or worse. The match was to be held in one week.

It was a long week. We worked out constantly. Somehow we had to integrate the fighting styles from four completely different planets. Somehow it seemed to work.

What we ended up with was mostly a defensive strategy. Since they had so many more people, it was obvious that if we got down to one, the fight would end in seconds. So we worked out a conservative strategy, a waiting game. B'oosa and I would stay back-to-back while Pancho and the Heller worked from our sides. We figured we could hold off almost anything that way. It took a lot to convince the Heller of that. He was more inclined toward the "let's wade in and bash heads" school of thought. He also felt the quarterstaff was effete, a weapon for sissies. B'oosa took him down a notch or two the same way he'd handled me. There wasn't any problem after that.

Lusaka was hot and dusty. Tens of thousands of spectators surrounded the small, hard-baked clay ring. It was obvious who they were rooting for. The match had been billed as ''The Earth Against the Off-World Monsters'' or something like that. Anyway, we were the bad guys. I was tired of being the bad guy.

We were introduced in the center of the ring to a rousing chorus of boos and jeers. The Earthies got all the applause. They were small, but there were nine of them. Nine had never seemed like such a large number before. We shook hands, took our opening stances. Ten minutes, that's all. Ten minutes.

It started.

We moved cautiously to the center of the ring, B'oosa and I back-to-back, Pancho and Markos at our sides.

''Here,'' said B'oosa and we froze. The Earthies circled us warily, with a dart here or there, a small feint. Nothing serious.

Pancho started his move. The bolo is a heavy leather covered ball on the end of an elastic tether, tied around the wrist. Properly thrown, it will wrap itself around a person's ankle and bring him down. Then the idea was for Pancho to drag him close enough for Markos to reach him with the vibroclub, without leaving the protection of the quarterstaffs. One touch with a vibroclub is enough to produce a temporarily disabling paralysis. A blow to the head with one is always serious, sometimes permanently disabling, sometimes fatal.

The Earthies seemed bewildered and confused. Usually matches like this are a free-for-all, with individual battles taking place right from the start. I don't think they knew what to do with us.

Pancho scored first. He caught a staffer by the leg with his bolo and started pulling him in. We covered for him, inching sideways toward the fallen man. Markos hit him and he went out. The referee called time out and they removed the Earthie. Eight to four, now. Time started up again.

Same strategy. This time Pancho hooked a guy with a club. One of the staffers tried to cover for him, but B'oosa and I easily held him off. The man with the club stiffened as Markos hit him.

"Like fish in a barrel," said the Heller. I wondered about that. The only fish I knew on Earth were sharks.

Time started again. They had regrouped, copied our defense: two staffers covering a bolo and the vibroclub. But that left three men to rotate and they pressed us from the left as the rest of the crew came in a block from the right. Things got pretty busy. I caught a guy with a club in the stomach. He went down, but not out. Deflected a bolo, parried with a staff. I could feel B'oosa moving rapidly behind my back. Something from out of nowhere hit my left shin hard. I went off balance, staggered. A staff swung down at me and I barely knocked it aside in time.

"Take that, you dightin' dighter," said Marcos, and another of their staffers fell. The Heller was grinning, though the side of his head was all bloody and it looked like he'd lost a couple of teeth.

It was six of them to the four of us, and it looked like we had the edge.

This time they charged the Heller. At least it looked that way at first. Didn't notice the bolo man until he had worked his way around to the other side and caught Pancho by the leg.

"Carl," he shouted. He was being dragged out of the formation.

We shifted to try to give him some protection, but the others were all over us. B'oosa sent their other bolo player to his knees with a quick jab to the chin. A gentle tap to the side of his head dropped him to the clay. The referee should have called time then. He didn't.

Their club man had gotten to Pancho, was really working him over. Where was that referee? All Pancho could do was protect his face. The club man could see that we wouldn't be able to get over to him and he was taking his time, obviously enjoying himself. I heard something crack— ribs, maybe, or a wrist. Pancho was in real pain and would have fallen if the Earthie had let go of him. As it was, the club man held him up, beating him, until a staffer worked his way over. The staffer caught Pancho in the belly and lifted him off his feet. On the return swing, he caught him across the back of the neck. Pancho went down hard and didn't move.

Then the referee called time.

I was really mad. Pancho had obviously been disabled before the staffer got there. I started to protest, but B'oosa and the Heller stopped me.

"Remember the arm wrestlin'?" asked Markos.

I nodded.

"Like that. There ain't no real rules. Just got to *do* it."

Five more minutes. They had us, five to three. This time they threw everything at me. Guess they figured I was the weakest link. I parried the bolo twice, their staffers kept me pretty busy. B'oosa had trained me well, though. I was holding my own. But I never saw the Earthie with the vibroclub.

"Springer! Watch that dighter!" Suddenly I felt an elbow push me aside. It was the Heller, throwing himself between me and the Earthie. Then I got the bolo all tangled around my staff and the other staffer came in quick and in the confusion, somehow we got separated. B'oosa and I were still back-to-back, but the Heller was all out by himself, hunched over, facing the Earthie, vibroclub against vibroclub.

In a one-on-one vibroclub fight between two good opponents there doesn't seem to be much action, but there is. Everything is position. They circle each other, make small darting movements to try to draw the other off balance, to make him commit to a losing course of action. It's usually a lot of this and then a quick slice through the opponent's defenses. The Earthie was good, but Markos was better. He made a complicated movement and tapped the Earthie in passing, dropping him. The referee should have called time then, but didn't.

One of their staffers and a club man had Markos surrounded. The staffer flipped the vibroclub from his hand. We tried to move over to help him, but the bolo had me by the leg. I was trying to get untangled and their other staffer was beating me on the shoulders.

Without a weapon, the Heller didn't have a chance. They could have finished it quickly and easily, but they didn't. The clubber waded in and beat the Heller unconscious. Held him up for the staffer who caught him hard on the neck, twice, three times, four. The crowd loved it.

"He's out," I yelled. "He's out."

Something cracked in the Heller's neck and his head spun around in a crazy direction. They let loose of him and he fell to the ground. They kept beating him.

We worked our way over to him. I got in a lucky shot and dropped the bolo man when he came too close to me. Then B'oosa stepped on the discarded vibroclub. I could feel the jolt through his back.

Then the referee called time.

Things were pretty hectic. They took Markos off the field, along with the two Earthies. I started to argue with the referees, but I didn't get anywhere. I was mad. They ruled that B'oosa should stay in, since a Maasai'pyan on his knees was almost as tall as an Earthie.

"Carl," said B'oosa, in considerable pain, trying not to show it. "*That's* the only referee we can count on." He pointed to the large clock at the end of the field. Two minutes ten seconds to go. It started moving again.

They came at us, two staffers and a club. On his knees, B'oosa couldn't handle his staff. I sort of hovered over him, protecting him the best I could. Maybe the sting of the vibroclub would wear off and he could get back into action.

I tried to use my body as a shield, holding them off as well as I could with the staff. There were just too many of them. One of the staffers came in hard and caught me across the ribs. Something cracked and it wasn't his staff.

I could barely feel the pain, but I knew something had broken. The staffer, though, was in trouble; he'd come in too close when he hit me. B'oosa may not have been able to use his staff, but he wasn't helpless. He grabbed the staffer's leg, pulled him off balance. I gave him a nice tap on the side of the head and he went down. All of a sudden my side really started to hurt. Wish I'd hit him harder.

A quick time out while they hauled the Earthie off. My side was on fire, a couple of ribs busted, at least. B'oosa tried to stand, couldn't. They wouldn't let him use a discarded club or bolo. He could only use the staff or his hands. They seemed pretty quick to enforce the rules that were against us. There was a little over a minute left. I was dead tired, my body was covered with welts.

They came in for the kill. The staffer kept me busy from the front while the guy with the club attacked me from the back. It was all I could do to keep the staffer away and the fellow with the club was tearing into me. He got a good shot at the back of my leg and my muscles went all into knots. I had to lean on B'oosa to stay upright.

That was when I had the staff knocked out of my hands. Then the guy with the club jumped on my back and started beating my shoulders and head. The staffer came in to finish me off.

But I wasn't ready to be finished off yet. I reached over my shoulder and grabbed the Earthie's arm, flipped him over my head at the onrushing staffer. They got all tangled up, went down in a heap. B'oosa handed me his staff and I started toward them to break some heads.

Then the gun sounded.

I hurt so bad, I thought I'd been shot. It took a second for me to realize what that meant. The match was over. I was still on my feet. We'd won.

I had to help B'oosa off the field. It was almost as dangerous as the fight. There were a lot of unhappy people in the stands and they seemed to be throwing everything that wasn't nailed down in our direction. Some of them were trying to get on the field and the local police didn't seem too concerned about keeping them back.

In the office, however, everyone was all smiles. The match had been a huge success, with holo coverage live on Earth and syndicated to three other planets. I tried to find Pancho and the Heller, but they had been taken to a local hospital and immediately lifted to a regional intensive care center. It was that serious.

Neither one of them was expected to live.

It was a shock, stunned me. Up to now it had all been some sort of a game. People got hurt, but nobody *died*. And all for what? For me and my foolish pride. All for nothing.

I didn't even notice when they gave us the money. The check just sort of appeared in my hand. I looked at it. Numbers printed on a piece of paper don't equate with a friend's life. Everything went sour in my mouth and my stomach churned. I didn't want to have anything to do with the money, handed it to B'oosa.

"I've got to find them," I said.

B'oosa nodded. "Soon enough," he said. "There's nothing we can do now. First we have to fix you up."

I looked down at my body. It seemed to belong to someone else. I was covered with blood and bruises. I looked like a wild man.

I felt like a fool.

XIII

IT WAS OUR last night on Earth. B'oosa and I sat in a booth at the Plaza de Gladiatores. Pancho was already aboard the *Starschool*. In the infirmary, in a body cast from chin to toe. At least he was alive. The Heller hadn't been so lucky.

"Not a bad place for local color," said B'oosa, sipping on a beer. "I can understand why you preferred this to the museums."

I just nodded, my beer untouched in front of me. I didn't feel much like talking. There was something I had to do before we left, someone I had to find. This was the logical place.

B'oosa was trying to cheer me up. Sure, it hadn't been a fair fight; but it hadn't been the worst he'd seen, not by a long shot. We had each entered into it of our own free will, the Heller included. We'd known the risk. All in all, he thought it had been an educational experience.

"Educational?" I asked. One friend dead, another seriously injured. "What's the going price on education these days?"

"Whatever one is willing to pay," he said, staring off into the darkness of the cantina. "Some risk more than others. Life is never easy. On Maasai'pya that knowledge comes early. My brother was younger than you when he died."

"Died? I didn't . . ."

"It was a matter of some importance to him. I felt it was trivial, actually. But to the young, everything is important. It's possible I could have stopped it; he respected me. But I learned long ago that you can fight no one's battles but your own. If it hadn't been that, it would have been something else. He was headstrong and foolish. Yet he had the right to live his own life. And die it, too."

"I'm sorry," I said.

"Don't be. Death is part of life."

"Carl!" A voice came from the doorway of the cantina. It was Angelo. Little Angelo.

"Sit down," I said, pushing back a chair for him. I started to introduce B'oosa.

"I have seen this man," said Angelo, shaking B'oosa's hand. "He was with the quarterstaff at the fight. A brave man." He paused for a second. "I watched it on the holo."

"Your friend, Markos . . ." I started.

"He was a good man. An honest man, in a hard sort of way. He had many troubles, but he handled them to the best that he could."

"I want you to have this," I said, passing over a packet.

"What is this?" he asked.

"It's your friend's share of the purse. Markos earned it. I want you to have it."

He looked at the package carefully. "There is much that I could do with this money."

"Can I offer you some advice?" I asked.

"Si, amigo. To you I will always be glad to listen."

"Forget about being a gladiator. There is no glory there, only deception. This planet is full of men like Mr. Wolfe, ready to take advantage of you. The fights are vicious and wasteful, a circus that only exists to feed the violent impulses of an overcrowded planet. Once it may have been noble, but now it is anything but that. There is no heroism here, only desperation. It's not like this everywhere. Look around. Find something different."

"I think you speak the truth. As many fights as Markos had, he was always talking of going to Perrin to start over. Things were better there, he said. He was one who should know. I thank you. And in the name of my friend, I twice thank you."

"I only wish it could be more," I said. "Enough to buy you passage to Perrin."

"I think this should cover it," said B'oosa, dropping another packet on the table.

"What?" I said.

"This is my share and Pancho's share. He spoke to me of your little friend here. We felt it was the proper thing to do, under the circumstances."

"My friends from the stars," said Angelo. "You are truly rare men. I cannot thank you enough."

"It's only money," said B'oosa. "And money should serve some useful purpose. I'm glad it found one." He looked at his digital. "Carl, we had better be going to the spaceport. I'd hate to get stuck on this planet."

"May luck follow you always," said Angelo, embracing us as we rose to leave.

I didn't know what to say so I just hugged him, thought of Markos the Heller and wanted to get off this planet as soon as possible.

As we walked outside into the night air, I turned to B'oosa. "One thing bothers me," I said.

"Only one? What is it?"

"If you believe that a person can't fight anyone's battles but their own, why are you helping Angelo? Why did you help me?"

"I may be logical," said B'oosa, smiling. "But I don't have to be consistent."

I laughed and we headed down the street. Next stop on the tour would be the planet Hell, but after Earth it would look like Heaven to me.

HELL

Curriculum Notes—Hell

Hell is the fourth planet out from the star Delta Pavonis. Settlement was begun in A.C. 35, originally by Jewish immigrants from Selva. More than 90 percent of the immigrants perished in the first two years, the surviving fraction maintaining a precarious existence in the desert regions, which, though barely habitable, at least are free from most of the terrifying fauna that dominate the rest of the planet's land and sea areas.

In A.C. 62 these immigrants sold their charter to the corporation Mercenarios Universal, S.A., a firm of freelance soldiers who wanted to use the desert as a training ground. Over the centuries, the corporation extended its domain to include various subtropical and arctic areas. The scope of the corporation also expanded, to accommodate training military leaders of other planets, and finally to renting out desolate areas of Hell itself, for countries that want to wage war without risking one another's real estate . . . .

. . . students with religious or philosophical misgivings about this part of the Tour will be allowed—indeed, encouraged—to stay in orbit aboard *Starschool* while the others take the short course.

The Dean of this second Tour wishes that it be a matter of record that he opposed adding Hell to the curriculum.

I

MY KNEES FINALLY buckled and I fell to the sand, hard. I was dizzy, thirsty. My skin felt like dried parchment. I would have given everything I owned for a glass of water.

They had told us how tough Hell would be and I hadn't believed them. I did now.

I tried to wipe the sand out of my mouth and rolled over on my back. That was a mistake. The sun nearly blinded me. The pain in my side wouldn't go away. I couldn't seem to get much air and what I got was hot and dry.

A face blotted out the sun for a moment; a weathered, wrinkled face improved by puckered scars. It loomed over me, drew closer. The face was about ten centimeters from my nose and its breath settled on me like a poisonous fog.

"Shize, Springer," he shouted. "Can't you do no better than that? You lying there like an old lady. Get your butt off the sand and move those legs. Now! Move 'em."

I wanted to say that I'd had enough, that I was finished, that I felt like I was dying. It wouldn't have helped. That voice wouldn't stop until I moved. I hated the voice and the knuckle-dragging cretin that belonged to it; we all did. Bruno Santino, our drill instructor, who tried to push everyone to the breaking point, then beyond. I think he rode me harder than the others. Probably because I was the only one larger than he was.

The only way I could get him to shut up was to move. I pulled myself to my knees. It hurt, everywhere.

"That's it, Springer. We'll make a soldier out of you yet." He turned abruptly to harass another student. I never wanted to be a soldier. I was just a university student. He seemed to forget that.

Somehow, I managed to get to my feet. In the distance I could see the glinting black solar panels on the barrack roofs. The buildings were mostly underground, only the tops poked above the sand and scrub brush. Some of the students had already reached the barracks. They hadn't had as far to go as I did. Some brilliant mind had scaled the maneuvers this morning so that the largest had the longest trek. I could make a case for it being the other way around.

I put one foot out. It held. I tried another and slowly lurched across the desert.

Of course nobody had promised us that Hell would be easy. It had been the most unpleasant world in the Confederación, until Springworld was colonized. Now I figure it's a toss-up, though Hell might just have an edge. Sometimes when I'm all tired and beat, I almost feel like I was back home harvesting the volmer.

Hell has only one important industry: training people for violence by tempering them to violence. Just about everything that moves on this rotten planet can kill you, including the Hellers. Maybe especially the Hellers. Planets that are serious about war send their future military leaders here to learn their trade. They either learn it or they die. That's the hard course.

There's another course for important people like princes. Under controlled conditions they learn how to kill without being killed. If they fail they don't die, they just flunk out. They might lose face, and maybe a limb or two, but they live. Come out pretty tough, too. This is called the *easy* course.

Naturally, there's a third course for people like us— students and visitors who just want to get a taste of what goes on during the training process on Hell. This is called the soft course. They rolled us out of bed at 0300 this morning, and we've been going full tilt for sixteen hours. Somebody named Bruno keeps yelling in my face that he wants to make me a soldier. I'd yank his arm off if I had any strength left. *Soft* course!

When I finally got to the barracks, I headed straight for my bunk. It felt like it was made out of bricks and was at least a meter too short. For the first time, I didn't complain. I stretched out on top of the sheets and was asleep before my head hit the pillow. I could have slept ten years; it felt like ten minutes.

"Wake up, Carl," said a familiar voice, far away. "Only a half hour till chow." I opened one eye. My mouth felt like a carrion bird had been nesting in it. The sand between my teeth made interesting sounds.

Gradually the person on the adjoining bunk came into focus. Short, black-haired with a drooping mustache. Pancho.

"Gonna skip chow," I moaned. "Sleep. That's what I need. Lots of sleep."

"You need food, amigo," said Pancho, reaching over and shaking my arm. "Your body needs fuel."

What my body needed was a picket sign: On Strike. Every muscle was howling in protest of the last week of punishment.

"Let me think about it," I said, closing my open eye.

A harsh voice cut through the barracks. "Ah, the baby from Springworld, the giant baby, he needs his beauty sleep."

Damn Bruno. Even knowing we were *supposed* to hate him didn't help any. Somehow I managed to sit up, get both eyes open this time.

"I was just going to shower up and get something to eat," I said. There was no rule against sleeping during meals, but it was considered a sign of slacking off and slackers got pretty rough treatment. I didn't need any more of that.

Sitting on the edge of my bed, my eyes came about even with Bruno's. He was pretty tall for a Heller, but I still had an easy three-quarters of a meter on him as well as being some eighty kilos heavier. All other things being equal, though, I wouldn't want to tangle with him in earnest. Hellers were built tough. I swallowed all the things I really wanted to say about the species of his parents. Instead, I turned to Pancho.

"About that shower, amigo. You ready?"

Pancho grabbed two towels, tossed me one. "Let's go," he said.

The showers had two settings: cold and colder. The recycled water had a foul, musty smell. Were their recyclers inefficient or was it that way on purpose? They did a lot of obnoxious things on Hell to "build character."

The mess hall was noisy and crowded in spite of the fact that we were late. Balancing my tray, I looked over the room and saw a couple of empty seats. I plowed my way toward them and Pancho followed along in my wake. We sat down at a table with B'oosa, Alegria, and Miko Riley, who had joined the tour on Earth. I didn't like him much.

"Did you boys enjoy our little invigorating hike this morning?" B'oosa asked as I set down my tray.

"You've got to be kidding," I said. "Up at 0300 hours and I pulled late watch last night. Calisthenics till sun-up. Doubletime over the sand for thirty kilometers. Seemed more like a death march to me."

B'oosa laughed, an easy laugh, smooth as glass. "The desert reminds me of home," he said. "It was good to get out and stretch my legs. Even a ship as large as *Starschool* feels cramped after a while."

"I thought I was in pretty good shape until they started running us around," I said. "If this is their soft course, I'd hate to see their hard one."

"It's pretty mean, from what I hear," said Pancho between gulps of unidentifiable pasty food.

"They build tough soldiers on this planet," said Alegria. "It's their only export item."

I nodded. Hellers were known all over the galaxy as first-class scrappers. The only people nearly as rough as

Hellers were those who had gone through their training course. The hard one.

"We've got a long evening ahead of us," said Miko. "Full-dress exercises."

Oh, no. I hadn't checked the duty board after I'd gotten back. What else had I missed? I hated working out with a field pack. But I couldn't let them see it. Not Miko, anyway.

"Easier than the daytime running," I said, though I didn't feel very confident about it.

"I wouldn't count on it," said B'oosa, rising. "See you there." He placed his tray on a conveyor belt that led out of the hall. I imagined there was a monster at the other end of the belt, gobbling up any leftover food. It would have to have a titanium alloy stomach.

I looked glumly at my own tray. Three piles of amorphous gray slop filled it from rim to rim. It was supposed to be nutritious, guaranteed to keep a body full of energy. It tasted even worse than it looked.

Pancho was shoveling it away. I wondered what they normally ate on Selva that could have possibly prepared him for this, but I didn't want to think about it too much.

"At least it'll be cooler in the evening," said Alegria.

Pancho nodded. "But those field packs are heavy," he said.

"Feel like they weigh a thousand kilos," said Miko. "Like carrying a bear around on your back."

"It's only 37.5 kilos," I said, and then wished I'd kept my mouth shut.

"Not much for you," said Miko. "The rest of us have to get along with normal bodies."

We could have been kidding, but we weren't. Miko and I were not the best of friends. He saw me as a rival, and I saw him as an interloper.

Alegria had gotten on *Starschool* at Selva, the stop before mine. We got to be pretty close friends and, in spite of her being so short, I guess it was always in the back of my mind that someday we might be more than friends. Well, Miko got on at Earth, and Alegria liked him instantly—she liked everything about that damned antique of a planet.

I guess I was a little obvious in my dislike for him, and that got Alegria to taking sides. Then the impudent little dwarf challenged me in the gym. He started it; I couldn't back down. I just did what I had to do. It only took a dab of plastiflesh to patch him up. Alegria was mad. Pancho, too. Me, too—only Miko didn't seem to mind. He'd done what he wanted to do.

Alegria stood up from the table, picking up her plate. "I'm finished," she said, walking away. Miko followed her, even though he still had food on his plate.

"What'd I do?" I asked Pancho.

He just shook his head and we finished eating in silence.

We were late to the briefing session and had to stand at the rear, at attention. A Heller officer stood at the front and surveyed us with a look of weary contempt.

"Hell is no place for soft people," he began. "You students are softer than most. We don't have much time with you to change that, but we're going to try. You're on this tour to learn and we're here to teach. To teach you a few things about life and how to keep it. It won't be easy. What you've done so far has been child's play compared to what will follow. Our objective here is simple: we want to push each and every one of you up to your own individual breaking point. Then we're going to push you a little harder. You'll hate us for it. Maybe later, at some important time in your life, you'll thank us for it. Pay attention. In the next two weeks you just might learn something."

He looked around the room, relaxed a little, leaned against the top of the desk.

"I suppose you students don't like it out here in the desert. You should. It may not be comfortable, but it's safe. Not many dangerous animals in the desert. Oh, there are a few, but not too many. The really mean ones are large and we can see them coming."

They'd warned us about some of those creatures, but we

hadn't seen any. Just hearing about the sandlizards was enough, though. Hoped I'd never meet one.

"We put tour groups and people like you in these desert compounds. That way we don't lose too many. Most regular recruits spend their first few days in Panoply. You'll be jumping there tonight, in full field dress. It's a little more dangerous than here, but I think you'll be able to handle it. We jump at 1800 hours. I'll now turn you over to Sergeant Santino, who will dismiss you. That's all."

He turned and left the hall abruptly. Bruno came forward.

"All right, children, I guess your butts have had enough exercise for now, so let's get the rest of you in shape. Gonna be a long night. As you leave here I want you to do twenty laps around the complex. The last ten people to finish will do twenty more. Move!"

At least I was standing in back. I got a head start.

■

VERTIGO. The desert suddenly dropped out from beneath my feet. I gripped the webbing tightly and closed my eyes. B'oosa laughed. It was 1800 hours, to the second.

They had loaded us into three of those huge floaters for the jump. I had a good view, too good. My two and a half meters wouldn't fit into one of the regular seats, so they put me up front where there was some room for my legs to dangle. B'oosa sat beside me, Bruno was next to him. It was a long way down. The barracks looked like a scattering of small black mirrors. Soon they were gone.

We slipped over a mountain range and headed out over the water. Panoply was an island quite a distance from shore. That was one of the things that made it "safe." The other was that periodically a team of Hellers swept from one end of the island to the other. It was supposed to be just about as safe as any non-desert place in Hell could be. The thought didn't cheer me.

The trip took a little longer than it should have. We had to skirt around the southern edge of Purgatory because there was a war going on. An interplanetary war.

I guess I should explain.

The Confederación forbids actual interplanetary wars. By that I mean that we don't have ships fighting it out in space or bombing planets. It was tried once, by a planet

111

called October. October doesn't exist anymore; the Confederación moved in and sterilized the planet, wiped it clean. That pretty much stopped anybody from trying it again. Of course, I could never see much use for it, anyway. There's just not much cash flow between planets, not enough to fight a war over.

Occasionally there's a big gripe between two planets and they fight it out on Purgatory. Purgatory is a fair-sized continent that the Hellers lease out to factions who don't want to dirty their own planets up. Each side puts up a bond and they slug it out according to the rules. The rules are simple: nothing stronger than class three, low-yield nukes. Everything else goes. Part of the bond goes to clean up the mess on Purgatory when it's over, but the Hellers pocket most of it.

The Confederación doesn't care what people do on their own planets, so there are always a lot of candidates for Hell's unique training program.

No Springers, of course. On Springworld we have our hands full just fighting the planet. Who has time for anything else? Besides, we don't try to impose one rigid system on everybody. If something isn't working, we just try something else until we find one that does. It seems like a waste of energy and resources trying to "prove" that one system is right and another is wrong. It either works or it doesn't. Seems simple to me.

(There have never been any wars on Hell between Hellers. They may know something the others don't.)

We dropped down close to the water and skimmed along about a meter above the whitecaps until the shore of Panoply rushed up. The island was surrounded by a narrow, sandy beach cut off immediately by a wall of impenetrable jungle. Turning into a small cove, we came down on a landing pad near a cluster of buildings set in a clearing.

We got off the floaters and split up into our training units—TU's, they call them. Love their abbreviations. There were five in ours, the maximum number: B'oosa, Pancho, Alegria, Miko, and me. All across the field people gathered in small clusters. A Heller came up to our group. We sat on the grass. My ears still rang from the wind that had torn at us in the open floater.

"Name's Vito Fargnoli," said the Heller. "Most people call me Skeeter, so you might as well." As he talked he drew a knife from his belt, flipped it from hand to hand. "I don't know what you've been told about this place, but it ain't no holiday here. Safer than most places 'round here, but that ain't saying much. You're going to take a tamed version of the survival test we run all raw recruits through. You'll have it easier than them, but not too much. We swept the island a couple of weeks ago, but it's a big island. Could have missed a sucker or two."

Suckers were round animals about the size of the palm of my hand. They liked to drop out of trees. Their bodies were soft, but their skeletons were a lot of sharp spines. When they hit, their spines stuck and the animal created an instant mouth where the spine had pierced its victim. Enough of them got you at once and they could bleed you dry. They tended to come in bunches, too.

"Isn't it the big ones we have to watch out for?" asked Miko.

The Heller spit on the grass. "Not necessarily," he said. "Biggest thing on the island is a beast we call the masher. Six meters tall and all teeth. Three rows of teeth and if you get close enough to count 'em they'll be the last thing you'll ever see. You'll never have to get that close. They got no natural enemies here; they just clump around and make a lot of noise. You can hear them a couple klicks away. Just head the other way. A vibroclub'll bring one down in a second. Stunner's better, though, don't need to get as close.

"Mostly you should watch for the small things, the night bats, the land eels. If you stay on the path, you shouldn't have much trouble."

"Path?" I asked. "What path?"

"*Students*," he said. "What do you know? Nothing. It's all very simple. We take you out to a place and drop you. You follow the paths back to here. The paths are kept clean, cleaner even than the rest of the island. If you stay on them you should have no trouble. You watch your step, you follow the path, you come back here. I would think even a student would understand that.''

He pulled a small box, about ten centimeters square, out of his field pack and set it in front of him. ''This is a transmitter,'' he said. ''What it does is transmit a call for help and give us your location. All you have to do is press this little button on the side. The red light shows you're transmitting, the green light shows we receive you and are on our way to pick you up. One of you carries this. Don't lose it.''

B'oosa reached out, picked it up.

''I suppose you've worked out in field packs before,'' said the Heller. We all nodded. It was an understatement. We'd drilled with the things on our backs every day. I almost felt naked on Hell without one.

''You have the standard week's ration of dehydrated food, but I don't expect you'll use much of it. Shouldn't be out much more than a day. We'll issue your group two vibroclubs and a stunner. Please try not to injure each other with them.''

I tried to hide a smile. I knew my way around a vibroclub pretty well, as did B'oosa and Pancho. I didn't see any trouble there. If worst came to worst, B'oosa could make a staff from a branch. There's nothing he can't stop with a staff. I bet he could even handle a masher.

The Heller gave his knife a casual backhand flip. It landed about five centimeters from my left foot.

''You,'' he said, looking at me. ''Where you from?''

''Springworld,'' I said.

''Heard of that place. Supposed to be a pretty rough planet. That true?''

I nodded, pulled the knife out of the ground.

''Well, you got to be more than tough out there.'' He nodded his head toward the jungle. ''You got to be smart to stay alive.'' He looked at his digital. ''You won't get any smarter talking to me. Let's go.''

I handed him his knife back. I would have tossed it back to him, but I might have missed. It might have made him mad. Never make a Heller mad.

The small floater lifted off, skimming the treetops. As it disappeared, the jungle noises started. They weren't loud noises, just a background of crunching and scurrying sounds. Occasionally a growl or squawk. We were all standing very close together.

Four paths led away from the clearing. "Which way do we go?" I asked. "The floater went in so many circles I lost my bearings."

"We find water," said B'oosa.

"Why?" asked Pancho.

"A stream will lead us to the coast. From there we can find the camp."

It sounded as good as anything to me. We split into two groups and checked the paths out. Pancho and Alegria found one with a stream running beside it. We followed it.

At first it wasn't so bad. The path was pretty clear and wide enough for two people to walk side by side. That didn't last very long. Soon the jungle closed in overhead and then it was pressing in from the sides. The blocking off of the sky made it quite a bit darker. The air was heavy with the smell of rotting vegetation.

"Are you sure this is the right way?" I asked B'oosa. He was behind me as we walked slowly, single file, down the dark path.

"Not really, but it's close," he said. "The sun was setting in roughly the right direction. I'll get a better fix when the stars come out."

"You studied the star chart for this planet?" I asked.

"Sure," he said. "Didn't you?" He laughed and I knew he didn't need an answer.

"*Down!*" yelled Pancho. He was guarding the rear of our line.

As I hit the ground, I rolled onto my back. Somehow I had a vibroclub in my hand. By then it was all over.

About a meter above my head I saw the red and yellow

flash of the tail end of a slasher. I broke out in a cold sweat. That had been close.

A slasher is something like a cross between a snake and a bat; long narrow body and leathery wings. Its whole body is covered with razor-sharp plates, that bristle forward when it attacks. If it brushes your shoulder you lose an arm.

Shaking, I got to my feet. B'oosa was looking off into the brush where the slasher had disappeared. I swear he was smiling.

"Guess they missed that one," said Miko.

"Maybe, maybe not," B'oosa said.

Alegria got to her feet. "What do you mean?" she asked.

"They clear off a lot of animals when they check the island, but not all of them. Some they miss, but some they deactivate."

"Deactivate?"

"The scales on that slasher were filed down. If it had hit you it would have bruised you, nothing more. Unless it scared you to death. There are a lot of declawed and defanged animals around here."

"How do you know that?" I asked.

"I've been doing more research about this planet than studying star charts. Not just in books, either. Last night while you were on guard duty I was out having a couple of beers with the instructors. Bruno gave me that interesting piece of information. They don't like to kill off students, even if their insurance covers it. Which it does."

Bruno. "Did your buddy also tell you which paths to follow?"

B'oosa just smiled. "We'd better get moving. It'll be getting dark soon and we don't want to have to set up camp by starlight."

We picked ourselves up, feeling scared and foolish, and headed down what was left of the path. Occasionally we had to hack away some vines or underbrush to make headway. Vegetation grew fast in the humid jungle. We saw another slasher, but it wasn't near us. I couldn't tell whether its scales had been blunted or not.

Just as I thought the trail was going to give out, it took a hard left turn and opened into a small clearing. It looked like a good place to set up camp. We couldn't see where the trail left the clearing, but it was getting dark and we figured we'd find it in the morning.

Alegria and Pancho popped up the tent while Miko started getting dinner ready. B'oosa, Pancho and I checked out the perimeter of the clearing and gathered wood for a fire.

The perimeter seemed clear, for the time being. We piled the wood and broke a couple of fire sticks to start a campfire. The rations we had for dinner were serviceable, if tasteless. The fire was more for our peace of mind than anything else; it might or might not keep animals away. We sat around it and the flickering light played shadows across our faces. Some sort of a frog started croaking and soon it sounded like there were thousands going all at once. At least it drowned out some of the more unpleasant noises.

B'oosa reached into his field pack beside him and drew out a small musical instrument. I assume it was from Maasai'pya; I'd never seen one like it before. He blew through it and the sound that came out was soft and reedy. He played for a long time and I leaned back and listened. It was a side of B'oosa I'd never imagined.

The fire died down and I rolled another log onto it. Pancho and Miko bedded down. It was getting late.

"I'd better go relieve Alegria," I said. We'd drawn straws for the watches. I had the second one.

B'oosa nodded, stirring coals with a long stick. "Be turning in myself, shortly," he said.

I walked to the edge of the clearing where Alegria was sitting on a log.

"Quiet?" I asked her.

"Not quiet," she said, "but uneventful. I don't think this place is ever quiet."

"I guess you could get used to it after a while," I said.

"You can get used to anything after a while," she said. "But that doesn't mean you have to like it."

"Does it bother you?"

"The jungle? No."

"Do I?"

"Do you what?" she asked.

"Do I bother you?"

"Why do you ask that?" She turned to me, half her face outlined by the fire, the other in darkness.

"You seemed to . . ." I groped for words. "I mean, since Miko came on the tour . . ."

"Let's not start that again, Carl. You're my friend and he's my friend. Leave it at that."

"But I thought—"

"That's your trouble. You think too much. For a big guy, you sure get messed up by little things." She handed me the stunner. "I'm going to turn in. Holler if you see any beasties."

"But Alegria . . ."

"But, *what*, Carl? What?" She looked tired.

"Nothing," I said. "See you in the morning."

She walked back to the camp without saying anything else. I felt foolish, stupid. I don't know why I always seem to say the wrong things around her. I'm usually okay with anyone else, but around her my brain gets all fuzzy and my foot heads right for my mouth. Sometimes I feel like such a dightin' fool.

I saw B'oosa and Alegria stoke the fire and turn in. Feeling restless, I shouldered the stunner and walked around the perimeter of the clearing. That didn't help much, so I turned around and walked back the other way. As far as I could see, there wasn't much moving around our camp. There were a lot of grunts and rustlings from the jungle but most were just frog noises. Everything else seemed far away. Once I saw some night bats fly overhead, but they're not much of a problem unless they come close. I sat back on the rock.

Funny thing, I started thinking about Springworld. I

don't guess I'd given it much thought since I got on *Starschool*.

I was the first in my family to have the opportunity to have such a fine education.

I was the first in eight generations of Boks to be able to escape a life of harvests, a life ruled by the whims of a hostile planet, the whims of heartless traders who have you at their mercy.

I was the hope of my family. Their dreams were pinned on me.

And sometimes I felt like it was all a waste; I didn't know anything at all, never would.

Sitting on the log, I could just barely make out a few stars through the tops of the trees. I felt a long way from home.

My leg had fallen asleep. I moved it around until the circulation came back. Listening carefully to the night sounds, I walked around the clearing again. Maybe Alegria was right. Maybe I do think too much. Not well, but too much. I kept walking. Soon Miko joined me; he had the next shift.

I gave him the stunner and told him where I'd left the lantern. So far we hadn't had to use it.

I put a couple more logs on the fire, then I went into the tent and crawled into my bag. Alegria was in the bag next to mine, a thousand light years away. I fell asleep quickly and wandered into troubled dreams.

I woke when someone stepped on my shoulder. It was B'oosa, looking out the tent flap. I started to sit up. He turned and put a finger to his lips.

"What is it?" I whispered.

"Trouble," he said. "Big trouble."

I got out of my sleeping bag and crawled over to him. Looking out, I could see five or six shapes at the edge of the clearing. Miko was stretched out beside the log, asleep or dead or unconscious.

"What are they?" I asked. "I can't make them out."

"Killer snails," he said flatly.

That *was* big trouble. They called them snails because

they had a shell on their back. That was where the resemblance stopped. They weren't slow; they moved on about a thousand little legs. Quickly. Spaced around their shells were several thick tentacles, which secreted an acid-based poison. Even if the poison didn't kill you outright, the acid would tear away at your skin.

"Are they, uh, deactivated?" I asked.

"I doubt it. Take a deep breath."

It was unmistakable, the sharp tang of hydrochloric acid. One of the creatures moved toward Miko. It was going slowly, its tentacles waving ceaselessly in the air.

"What should we do?" I asked.

"Wake the others."

"We're awake," said Alegria from behind me.

"We've got to get the stunner," said B'oosa. "That's the only way we can handle them. Miko's okay so long as he doesn't move. He may only be asleep. Who's got the fire sticks?" he asked.

"I do." It was Pancho. "About a dozen of them."

"We might be able to create a diversion using them. If you toss them in the fire it might confuse things enough that we could reach the stunner."

"All of them?" asked Pancho. "That would—"

"I know what it'll do," said B'oosa. "A lot of noise, a lot of light and a lot of fire. It can only help us."

"Who goes for the stunner?" I asked.

"We all do. I'll follow Pancho out of the tent. When he tosses the fire sticks I'm on my way. You all follow. Carl, you take one vibroclub, Alegria has the other. Don't use them unless you have to. If you're close enough to hit it with a vibroclub, it's close enough to hit you with a tentacle. Don't try anything fancy. Once we get to the stunner we can handle them with no trouble. Try and keep Pancho between you. He's the only one without a weapon."

"You," said Pancho. "Where is your weapon?"

B'oosa reached down beside him and lifted a good-sized staff. "I cut it last night."

"What about the one by Miko?" asked Alegria.

"We'll just have to handle it ourselves," said B'oosa.

"I'm counting on the fire distracting it. If we tried to yell to Miko, he'd move reflexively and it'd be on him in a second."

"I've got the fire sticks," said Pancho. I'd already grabbed one of the vibroclubs; Alegria had the other.

"You get up front," said B'oosa. "Go when you're ready, we'll follow you out."

Pancho sprang out of the tent, running low, and we followed. I was just untangled from the flaps when I saw the fire sticks arc toward the fire. I grabbed the ground; the concussion lifted me and rolled me over.

I picked up the vibroclub and staggered to my feet. The creatures seemed confused, from the explosion and the sudden variety of meals; they shuffled back and forth as if in indecision. Alegria and B'oosa were on their hands and knees, between the fire and one of the killer snails. I moved toward that one.

Vibroclub probably wouldn't do anything to the shell. I shouted at the beast and it spun around, surprisingly fast. It charged, jaws grinding, tentacles waving. When it was a few meters away I tossed the humming vibroclub under-hand, right in front of it. It scurried over the weapon and gave out a terrible gurgling howl, then flipped forward, landing on its back, centipede legs writhing.

I cautiously retrieved the 'club and looked around. Miko was on his feet now, but there was a killer snail between him and the stunner. B'oosa was holding one at bay with his staff, protecting Alegria as well as himself.

I stood there one second too long, deciding—the upside-down creature's tentacles were flailing around and one of them brushed my hand. It was like being slapped with a burning torch. I flinched away and dropped the club.

Pancho ran over and scooped up the vibroclub, then charged the snail that was blocking our way to the stunner. He started to circle it warily, but had come in too close; a tentacle whipped out and wrapped around his left leg. I ran to help, but he took care of it himself, banging the monster on the face when it pulled him in for the kill. It flipped with the same somersault reaction mine had; Pancho rolled away, holding his leg and moaning.

I went for the stunner and fired off six or seven quick shots and suddenly everything was quiet. Except for the crackling of the fire and Pancho, cursing in a strange, soft monotone.

Alegria and I bent over Pancho. The acid had eaten through his pants leg and was starting on his flesh. B'oosa pushed me aside and pulled a first aid kit from his pack. He ripped Pancho's pants leg open up to the knee and applied a salve. He seemed to know what he was doing. I noticed B'oosa was the only one wearing his pack. I automatically looked toward the tent where I'd left mine. There wasn't anything left of the tent but some smoldering plastic and blackened poles.

B'oosa applied some salve to my hand, too. The salve was cold and took away the sting, but left a deep, throbbing pain. I could imagine what Pancho was feeling.

Miko sat down next to me. "What happened?" he asked.

"That's what I was going to ask you," I said sharply.

"I must have . . ." he said. "I mean, I never saw them."

"What you mean is you fell asleep," I said.

"I guess so."

"That could have killed us. All of us." I was thinking more of Pancho than myself. Suddenly, I was filled with anger and frustration. "That was stupid, plain—"

"Carl," said Alegria. "That's not going to get us anywhere."

"She's right," said B'oosa. "We'd better call for help."

Reaching into his pack, he pulled out the small transmitter. He thumbed the switch, but the red light didn't go on. Neither did the green one. He flicked it back and forth a few times. Nothing.

"Looks like we're on our own," he said.

"I don't suppose Bruno said anything about this," I said.

He just shook his head. "How do you feel, Pancho?"

"It hurts, amigo, but I can make it."

"We'll leave at dawn," said B'oosa. "It shouldn't take too long."

We gathered up what equipment we could salvage. It wasn't much. B'oosa and Miko were the only ones who had their field packs. Everything in the tent was lost.

The rest of the night we just sat around. Nobody slept. Every time my hand would start hurting I'd think of Pancho and try to ignore it. He must have been in real pain. I avoided Miko, though B'oosa and Alegria both had long talks with him. It may not have been rational, but I blamed him for all of this. When it started to get light we cut some poles and made a sling between them with vines to carry Pancho. He couldn't possibly walk.

Miko and B'oosa found the path leading out of the clearing. The fire had died down and the clearing was a charred mess. The snails weren't dead, but they wouldn't be moving for a long time; I hoped something would come along and eat them. We pooled what food we had, shared a little for breakfast, and started out.

Pancho's leg was infected. It hurt when he bounced around and had ugly red streaks around it. He'd need expert medical attention soon. My hand throbbed and was starting to swell and get puffy.

We settled into a routine. I carried the head of the stretcher and Miko carried the foot end. I had to walk bent over most of the time and even then my end was quite a bit higher than the other. B'oosa took the lead, chopping the path clear and keeping an eye out. Alegria followed, wearing Miko's pack and keeping an eye on our rear. She saw two slashers; one came too close and she shot it with the stunner. Its plates were razor sharp.

I plodded along behind B'oosa. Pancho wasn't heavy, but we covered a lot of ground and my arms were beginning to tire. Occasionally, B'oosa would rub some more salve on my hand and on Pancho's leg. It helped a little. Just before we stopped for lunch, Pancho got delirious and then passed out. We ate lunch without tasting, without talking. Miko sat on a rock, his eyes dull. I couldn't think any farther ahead than one foot after another. B'oosa fiddled with the transmitter. Nothing seemed to be working. We finished eating and walked on.

I was ready to lie down and give up. My body was throbbing a thousand protests; my hand felt like it was sitting on a bed of coals. We ran out of salve. Pancho was running a high fever. I had a cramp in my left leg and was staggering; I didn't think we were ever going to get back to the camp. We might even be going the wrong way. Maybe B'oosa was mistaken. I began to feel feverish myself. Things started to get blurry.

Twenty more steps and I figured I'd quit. I counted out twenty steps and decided I'd do twenty more. Then twenty more. I went down the path convinced that each step was my last. I think I fell a couple of times. I think I remember B'oosa helping me up. Only then it wasn't B'oosa, it was somebody else. Somebody familiar. Scooter? Skeeter! Vito Fargnoli, the Heller who had dropped us off. Bruno was there too. I tried to say something to him and all the hate welled up and everything went blank. It was just like sliding down a tunnel. A black tunnel.

When I came to I was stretched out on a bunk. The first thing I noticed was that it was too short. Then I noticed the small bandage on my hand. I sat up and Pancho grinned at me from the next bed.

"Buenos dias, amigo," said Pancho. "Did you enjoy your sleep?"

"Sleep?" I asked, shaking my head, trying to clear it.

"You've slept the day around," said Pancho. "How do you feel?"

"Okay, I guess. But you . . ."

"I'm okay, amigo. Look." He pulled back his sheet and showed me his leg. You could hardly see where the plastiflesh joined with the real flesh. I peeked under my bandage. My hand looked just as good.

"They must have some pretty good doctors around here," I said.

"The best," said Pancho. "They import them from Earth."

"Of course."

"They brought you some broth," said Pancho. "Give it a try."

I looked at the bowl on the stand by my bed and remembered Pancho shoveling away the gray, pasty food the other day. But I was hungry and sipped it. It wasn't half bad. I was surprised, first decent food I'd had on Hell. I drank it all.

"Watch this," said Pancho, slipping out of bed.

"Wait," I said. "Don't . . ."

"It's all right, Carl. No problem at all. Mostly it was just the poison in my system. One shot and I was good as new. See?"

I saw and was impressed. I'd figured at best he'd be laid up for a week or so. Last time I'd looked at him I'd thought he was almost dead. The wonders of modern medicine. I moved my fingers and they worked fine. More wonders.

"What am I doing still in bed?" I asked.

"Beats the bananas out of me, amigo. Sleeping, I guess. You always were one for lots of sack time. Let's get dressed and find the others."

It sounded good to me. We dressed and went wandering. Found B'oosa in the canteen, alone. He didn't know where Alegria and Miko were. I don't know why it bothered me, but it did. B'oosa looked preoccupied. We sat down anyway.

"What's the good word?" asked Pancho.

"Not much," said B'oosa, pushing his coffee cup away from him. "Not many good words at all."

"What's wrong?" I asked. I'd never seen B'oosa quite so upset.

"They were there all the time," he said softly.

"Who? Where?"

"The Hellers," said B'oosa, shaking his head. "We were never out of their sight. Skeeter and Bruno were there all the time. They only stepped in at the last minute."

"You mean they let all that happen?" I couldn't believe it.

"Afraid so," said B'oosa. "All part of the 'soft' survival training course."

"Survival? They could have killed us."

"I doubt it," said B'oosa. "They would have done something if it had gotten too serious."

"Are you sure?" I asked.

B'oosa looked thoughtful. "No, I'm not sure, but I'd like to believe it."

"And the transmitter?"

"It was never supposed to work. But the next one will, they assured me."

"Next one? What next one?"

B'oosa nodded toward the door. "Here they come. Let them tell you."

Skeeter and Bruno were walking toward the table. I felt like knocking a few heads together.

"Hello, students," said Bruno. "Ready for some cold weather?"

"What cold weather?" asked Pancho.

"We jump at 0800," said Bruno, dropping an envelope on the table. "Here's the schedule. Pick up your gear this evening. Tomorrow we'll be on the high plateau. See you then." He turned and left. Skeeter stayed for a second.

"You okay, Pancho?" he asked.

Pancho shrugged. "I guess I'll live."

Skeeter looked nervous, blushed a little. "Hey, I'm sorry about what happened. If I'd had my way—"

"Skeeter. Get a move on," shouted Bruno from the door.

"Sorry, Pancho. Really I am," he said and left.

B'oosa had opened the envelope. "Same procedure," he said. "Only arctic conditions this time. Too bad about that, don't like being cold. Heat I can take, but cold . . ."

"Who's going?" I asked.

"Same crew," said B'oosa.

"No way," I said. "I refuse to go out with Miko again. Not when my life may depend on him staying awake."

"Calm down, Carl," said Pancho. "He feels real bad about it. I think he wants to make it up to you—to us."

"I don't care," I said. "I won't do it."

"Yes you will," said B'oosa quietly. He slid the assignments across the table. There were signed by the Dean.

I could get out of it if I really wanted to. If I wanted to flunk, to look like a coward, to look like a fool. Trapped again. If the Dean hadn't signed it, I might have had a chance. He doesn't sign many documents like this, so he must have wanted this crew together for some reason. Offhand, I couldn't think of a single good one.

I wondered how cold it would be.

III

It LOOKED SIMPLE, which by itself made me suspicious. They set us down on the peak of a small mountain. The place we were headed for was on the far side of the valley below us. We could even see the tops of the base's antennas in the distance. All we had to do was get off the mountain and cross the delta. Couldn't have been more than thirty klicks. A piece of cake.

At first we split up and looked for an easy way down the mountain. There weren't any. I found about a dozen places I could have gone down alone, but not with everybody else tied to me. On Springworld I'd climbed mountains like this since I was five years old. Of the others, only B'oosa had any experience on mountains. The rest were all flat-landers, as we call them at home.

B'oosa found a route he thought we might be able to manage together. It started out as a more-or-less sheer face that led down and across to a vertical fissure. Formations directly above the fissure would have made rappelling difficult; we'd have to transverse, go down sideways to it. After the fissure it didn't look like it would be too hard.

"What do you think?" asked B'oosa.

I took a long look at the sheer face. The surface of the cliff was uneven and ought to provide fairly good foot and hand holds. It was cold, though, probably be some ice. I looked at the sky. It was a slate grey from horizon to horizon, could be a storm coming in. Ordinarily I wouldn't even consider starting a descent under these conditions.

"Guess it'll do," I said. "At least it's not snowing."

"Not yet," said B'oosa.

We got everyone together and explained what we had to do. B'oosa would go first and I'd take up the other end. Nobody moved until they were told to by B'oosa or myself. We double checked our equipment and headed for the edge.

B'oosa went over. I watched him descend. He was pretty good, no doubt about it. Only one arm or leg would move at a time. He checked each hold carefully before committing his weight to it. As he went down he'd drive pitons into the rock face, sliding the rope through their clips. He went sideways as much as down, guided by the nature of the cliff rather than our wishes. Soon he stopped, hollered up to the rest of us to follow. I had a good, secure position, the rope played down from me to B'oosa without kinks or sharp bends.

Pancho was the first to follow. He went slowly, checking each hold several times. Each time he reached one of the pitons, he'd pull some slack from the far side of the rope and slip it through the clip on the right side of his belt. He'd hang there for a second before he unclipped the trailing section of rope from his left side and moved on past the piton. It was slow progress, but he was doing a good job. No such thing as being too careful on the side of a mountain.

Alegria was the next over. She started when Pancho was about halfway to B'oosa. She came easily, gracefully. I'd never seen anyone take to the ropes so naturally. If I hadn't known better, I'd have thought she'd been doing it all her life. Her moves were careful, but smooth. She went along the rock as if she was part of it. I couldn't detect a single trace of nervousness. She moved like a cat and I figured she was a good person to have in the middle.

Miko went over after Alegria. He wasn't surefooted, but at least he didn't do anything stupid. A couple of times he stopped and didn't seem to be able to find the next hold. I could see them from where I was. I started after him and helped him along.

I immediately slipped into the old rhythms and patterns. Funny how you never seem to lose certain skills once you learn them, even if you don't practice them. I felt right at home. Even having Miko in front of me didn't bother me too much.

Most people would think that going first in a line like this would be the most dangerous position. It isn't true. The person taking up the rear runs the greatest risk. I know, I've done it both ways. Many times.

It got a little harder. Once B'oosa trapped himself in a dead end, found himself with no place to get a forward hold. He could have driven in a piton and tried to swing out and find one, but the others wouldn't have been able to follow. We had to back up and follow a different tack. It worked a little better, but that had cost us some valuable time and the wind was picking up. B'oosa signaled us and we started forward again.

By the time we caught up with B'oosa, the wind was coming full force. There was nothing to do but grit our teeth and keep on going. When we got to the fissure at least we'd be sheltered from the wind. I guessed it would take two more stretches. B'oosa took the slack rope and moved on.

It was starting to rain. Just a little at first, but the wind made it seem colder than it was. It made the rocks slippery, too, and the going was slower. I wanted to get to the fissure before things started icing up and I guess that was where I made my mistake, going too fast. If I hadn't been in such a hurry it never would have happened.

Miko had gone ahead while I fooled with a troublesome kink in the rope. Everyone was out of sight around a ledge and I was in a hurry to catch up. I only had a two-point hold and too much slack when I reached around the ledge. It was a stupid thing to do.

I had a good hold with my left foot and my left hand was fairly secure, but my right side was blocked by the ledge. I was sure there would be a hold on the other side, so I swung my body around. As I passed a certain point in my swing I felt my balance shift and realized I was in trouble. Too much slack. Too far from the nearest piton. If there wasn't anything to grab on the other side of the ledge, I was going to fall. It was as simple as that; all physics and the motion of falling bodies. There wasn't anything to grab. My fingers slid over wet, smooth rocks. I fell over backwards. Everything seemed to happen in slow motion.

It wasn't the first time I'd fallen, so I knew what to expect. I'd only go down until the rope stretched to the next piton, then I'd stop and swing. I tried to let my body relax. There was a sharp double-yank on the rope. All bets were off, that was probably a piton pulling loose. No telling what would happen now.

The rocks slapped and tore at my face and hands as I fell. I tried to grab anything that slipped by. If I couldn't hold it, at least it would slow me down. It didn't look as though I was going to be able to get a good grip on anything; the rocks were wet with rain and my fingers were wet with blood. Somewhere I heard someone yell. It could have been me.

My right foot hit a small outcropping and I threw my body hard against it. Pain ripped through my side as the rock tore along my body. It slowed me down. I scrambled for toeholds, footholds, mouth holds, anything. The outcropping caught me in the chin, I hugged the side of the cliff. Somehow I stopped. I waited for the others to come falling past me, dragging me along with them. Nothing. All I could hear was my own labored breathing.

I have no idea why I didn't keep falling. As far as I could tell I didn't have a single hold. Arms spread wide, I pressed myself as close to the cliff as possible. It was ridiculous to have gotten myself in such an awkward position. I couldn't move a muscle without losing what little grip I had.

It seemed like I hung there for hours, but it couldn't have been more than a few minutes. I could feel the rope moving and occasionally muted voices would drift down to me, but I could never quite make out the words. Dirt and small pebbles fell past me as they worked their way down to me. My left leg, in an awkward position, started to twitch. My nose itched, like it always does when I can't scratch it. I felt more dumb than scared. I'd made a bad mistake. More than that, I'd involved other people in it. If I'd done it at home, I would have paid for my mistake alone; here I'd almost dragged four other people along with me.

"Trying to find the quick way down, Carl?" B'oosa's voice startled me.

"I missed my grip," I said. "I slipped."

"We all slip once in a while," said B'oosa. I could hear him driving in a piton, but I didn't dare move my head to see him.

"Almost there," he said. "Just a second . . . Ah, that's got it. I've got the rope secured about two meters above your head and a meter to your left. If you let go and swing to your left, you should find a good grip."

I had no choice but to trust him. I *knew* he'd done a good job—I don't think he's capable of doing a bad one—but as I swung out, I'll have to admit I wondered if he'd underestimated my weight. He. hadn't. I found the grip easily.

"Thanks," I said, breathing hard. "I didn't think that piton would pull loose."

"It didn't pull loose, Carl," B'oosa said slowly.

"What do you mean?"

"It broke. Snapped right in two."

"That's impossible. I know I'm heavy, but those pitons are built to take it."

"That one didn't," he said in a tone of voice that made me shiver. "And I'm not too sure about the others."

I didn't like the implications.

"I'm going back to the other end," he said. "Unless you'd rather I took up the rear."

I knew what he was saying. In his usual roundabout, polite way, he was asking me if I'd lost my nerve.

"No, I'm okay," I said. We made the fissure in ten minutes and then we rested.

The fissure was actually a vertical crack that ran the rest of the way down the face of the mountain. It would be fairly easy to work our way down; clear sailing after that. Almost a hike to the valley.

The top of the fissure was narrow and I could hardly squeeze into it. The others fit comfortably. It had an uneven surface and it was easy to prop your feet against one side of the crack and your shoulders against the other. We rested that way for several minutes before moving down. The storm was gaining in intensity, but we were fairly well sheltered in the fissure.

B'oosa led the way down and I took up the rear position. It went fairly easily. I'd anchor the line and B'oosa would guide the others down as far as the rope would allow, then I'd come down to them and we'd start all over again. It worked real well, except for the time that Pancho slipped, but even that wasn't serious. We decided to camp at the bottom of the fissure, since it was level enough for our tent. It was starting to get dark and the storm showed no signs of letting up.

I drew first watch. There really wasn't too much to watch for. I couldn't imagine any animal being out in weather like this, but if there were any, they'd probably be large, mean and cold. The rain turned to sleet and when Miko came to relieve me, I headed straight for the sack. I listened to the wind howling for about ten seconds before I fell asleep.

B'oosa woke me up and gave me a hot cup of tea. The wind was still roaring outside the tent. If anything, it was louder than the night before. I had about a thousand scrapes and cuts from my little spill the day before and I could feel every one of them.

I stepped outside the tent and the cold sank into me, bone-deep. Everything was covered with a thin layer of ice.

Although we'd come a long way down the day before, we were still fairly high up. Visibility was rotten; I couldn't even see the valley floor. It was still sleeting. Pancho came out and stood beside me.

"What do you think, amigo?"

"Look at all that ice," I said. "I think it's going to take us all day to get off this mountain."

It took two.

They were two hard days. It wasn't that the descent was steep; it was just that the weather never gave up for a second. It was hard to keep your footing on even relatively level ground. We spent a lot of time slipping and sliding around. I could see why they had given us five days to reach the station.

Late in the second day, B'oosa took a bad spill on an icy rock. I thought he might have sprained his ankle, though he never said anything. I don't think that guy would complain even if it had been a compound fracture.

The sleet eventually turned to snow. It wasn't really much of an improvement, but we were grateful for even small favors. We camped at the foot of the mountain, with the delta area spread out before us. It was flat, treeless and cold. A very bleak place.

The delta was a sloppy network of thousands of little creeks and rivers, branching off from a major river that flowed into the northern sea. The smaller ones were probably frozen; it was the others that would be trouble.

It was a big area. We were glad to have the transmitter, and hoped it worked this time. Were they watching us? It would be hard for them to find places to hide.

We broke camp early; the snow stopped just before dawn. The sky brightened to a uniform dull slate, no trace of blue. The wind was strong and gusty, the driven snow constant cold specks of pain on your face.

Walking was difficult. There was about ten centimeters of new snow on top of a hard crust, the melted top of the old snow, which was about twice as deep. All of us except Alegria were heavy enough to break the crust: step, crunch, drag; step, crunch, drag. We kept getting caught in the vegetation, too, which was usually low enough to be hidden by the snow. A mat of interconnected brambles.

The ice was about two meters lower than the shore, with steep banks on both sides. We tested the ice carefully before putting our full weight on it. I went first. Figured if it would hold me it would hold anybody. It wasn't a very wide branch and we got across without any difficulty. If the rest were as easy, we'd make it in fine shape, so long as the weather held.

The rest weren't as easy and the weather didn't hold. It started sleeting again, wet and cold. The next branch we came to was slushy on top with several large holes in the ice.

B'oosa shook his head. "This looks bad."

"You don't think the ice will hold?" I asked.

"It's not that." He scrambled down the bank and we followed, to rest for a minute out of the wind. "These holes are part of the winter ecology of this area. A lot of animals come to them for water; some come to fish."

"Big animals?" Alegria said.

"That's just it. Large predators hang around the holes to feed off the animals that come to drink. Some of them are large enough not to be afraid of five humans." He told us about the snowbeast, the worst one. The size of a small floater, it had six powerful legs, the front pair of which could be used as hands, centaur-style, when it wasn't running or swimming. It had large claws and teeth—in a mouth wide enough to decapitate a person in one snap— and was covered with silky white fur. Its eyes were saucer-sized and also white. In a snowstorm you could walk within ten meters of one and never see it, never know what killed you. Vibroclubs would be useless, except on the eyes or mouth.

We didn't see any snowbeasts that day, or any other kind of animal larger than a seabird, even though we crossed four rivers with the water holes (giving the holes wide berth, admittedly). It sleeted constantly, until we stopped for the night and put up the tent. Naturally.

It was hard to tell how far we'd gone. The maps they'd given us were crude, on purpose, and one small stream looked just like any other. The visibility was too poor to see the mountains, and back-triangulate. When we got to the main river, we'd know we had covered about a third of the distance. What that meant in terms of time would depend on the weather and the terrain.

The sky was perfectly clear the next morning, and we made pretty good time. We got to the main river after a couple of hours of slogging.

It was a lot wider than it had looked from the mountain. Ice granules floating in a scum of slush rattled along the bank, but the middle was clear except for large chunks of ice drifting lazily along. We would have to paddle about two hundred meters.

Miko took the raft from his pack and pulled the tab that inflated it. It was big enough for three normal people; we'd have to make three crossings.

The first two went without incident, though it was scary to be left on one bank while the stunner was on the other. I kept my knife out and didn't inflate my safety vest until the last minute, to stay maneuverable. Pancho, Alegria and Miko went over first, then Pancho came back for B'oosa. He was going to come back for me next, but he'd gotten a cramp on the second crossing, so I drew Miko. B'oosa was too big and Alegria too small. That didn't please me too much, but I was glad to finally pop my vest and step aboard the raft.

"Current's not bad until we get to the middle," Miko said. "We have to put some back in it then."

The damned thing didn't steer at all; we paddled straight and drifted in a curving diagonal toward the opposite shore. We also used the paddles to push ourselves off the ice floes, some of which were big enough to stand on.

Miko had more boating experience than I did, but I was in front, for being stronger. We were heading toward what looked like a whirlpool. I pointed at it with my paddle. "Does that mean there's a rock underneath, or something? Should we—"

"Wasn't there before," he said quickly. "It's no rock."

Suddenly the water heaved and a huge mound of white fur surfaced. It swiveled around slowly and fixed one large white eye on us. It was no more than ten meters away. The stunner warbled from the opposite shore; the snowbeast turned to look at it and sank leisurely.

"That was too close," Miko said.

I was paddling like a madman. "Idiot! What it was was *too far away!* You can't drop an animal that big from—" Suddenly we were out of the water, tipping crazily, and I had a glimpse of the thing's massive back before I plunged into the black icy water.

A strong man might survive five or six minutes in that water. It only felt cold for an instant; then I was just numb and stinging. I bobbed up coughing, knife in hand, for what it was worth. I tried to find the vibroclub, but it was on the outside of my pack, stuck under the life jacket.

I couldn't see the snowbeast anywhere. Miko was swimming furiously toward a large ice floe. I was closer to the raft, so I set out for it.

I don't know how long it took. Trying to stroke and breathe regularly and not think about the mankiller swimming below, ready to kill me with one bite. Somehow I got to the raft, no paddles, and heaved myself half aboard. Started kicking my feet, moving slowly toward shore.

After a few minutes I heard shouting. I looked up and saw the other three hollering and pointing. B'oosa dropped to a marksman's crouch and fired a long burst from the stunner.

They were pointing at Miko, who had made it to the ice floe. He was lying on top of it, evidently unconscious. The snowbeast was just downstream, only its head showing as it swam closer.

Two paws broke out of the water and grabbed for Miko, but he had pulled himself far enough from the edge for the claws not to reach him. The beast howled and started scrabbling aboard. It didn't pay any attention to the stunner, which B'oosa was firing steadily.

It finally got all of its bulk up on the floe. I knew I should be kicking, make it to shore before I became dessert. But I was fascinated by the horror, frozen in more ways than one.

It stood over him, half again my own height even with four feet on the ground. But instead of grabbing Miko and tearing at him, it stood there with its arms limp, shaking its head. The stunner was having some effect. B'oosa never let up firing.

The creature's four knees buckled and it fell, its terrible head less than a meter from Miko.

"Get him!" B'oosa shouted. "In the raft! We'll get a line out." It looked like a long way. I wondered how long the snowbeast would stay unconscious.

I started kicking my way downstream. You couldn't leave anyone to that sort of thing, not even Miko. But I couldn't even feel my legs anymore, and it was getting hard to breathe.

By the time I reached the floe I was in a sort of trance from the pain and exertion. I did manage to get up on the ice, but standing there was very strange, as if I were floating two meters off the ground, and didn't exist from the waist down. I may have stood there for a long time, enjoying being out of the water. Someone was shouting from the shore. The beast lay there with its eyes open, one nostril flap moving slowly. We looked at each other for a while. Then I came more-or-less to my senses, pain waking up my legs, healthy fear seeping into my brain. I dragged Miko to the edge and managed to manhandle him into the raft without drowning him. When I slipped into the water it was like a bath of fire, then numb again. We were about seventy meters from shore. In the serene knowledge that we would never make it, I started kicking.

They were yelling for me to get into the raft. That didn't make any sense, but it did look like a warmer place to be. It took a long time, everything did, and I had to be careful not to dump Miko overboard.

The exertion was almost too much. I felt a new, squeezing pain in the center of my chest. Heart attack? I lay down, using Miko as a pillow. I blacked out, then woke up, then blacked out again.

"Can you reach it?" Miko was whispering. I was annoyed that he woke me up.

"Reach what?"

"The rope. They floated a rope, they say." I could hear shouting, but my ears were ringing too loudly for me to understand. I levered myself up far enough to peer over the edge of the raft. There was a rope, all right, one end tethered to an inflated life jacket, and we were slowly moving toward it. They had thrown it out to where it would hang up on an ice floe; we moved slightly faster than the ice because of the wind.

But the tight pain was still in my chest and my arms felt paralyzed. I waited until the raft touched the rope, then heaved one arm overboard. Sitting up, I dragged the arm back into the raft, and the rope came with it. My hands wouldn't close, to hold the rope, but I managed to twist it around my arm and lean back. Miko tried to help, but all he could do was twitch.

They pulled, and the rope started to slip. I rolled over on it and the world went away, different this time, white sparks instead of blackness.

I managed to make one eye work. There was a light, amorphous and shot through with rainbows. A few good blinks and it sharpened somewhat: a blur that was recognizably B'oosa, sitting under the tent lamp, reading. Another blur, next to me, was Miko wrapped up in a sleeping bag. So was I; it took a certain amount of effort to free my hands, to rub sight back into my eyes.

"Feeling better, Carl?" B'oosa said, without looking up.

"Better than what?" My body was a collection of dull aches and sharp pains. Must be alive. "How long have I been out?"

"Almost two full days."

"Two *days!*"

"You were suffering from exposure. Badly, as was Miko. It was better that you get some rest. The med kit has marvelous little pink pills for that."

"Where are we?"

"We're still by the river."

"And that noise outside?"

"A storm, a bad one."

I counted sleeping bodies. "Where's Pancho?"

"Outside, keeping watch."

We'd been gone five days, it occurred to me. "They ought to be looking for us by now, right?"

B'oosa shrugged. "Perhaps."

"Did you call them on the transmitter?"

"I tried," he said, holding up the small box, "but I got no results."

"Not again."

"I thought that was strange, too. So I opened the transmitter to see if it could be repaired. This is what I found." He opened the front of the box. Inside the shell it was empty: no wiring, no crystals. "This is not just a broken transmitter, this is a dummy transmitter. It was never intended to work."

"It sounds almost like they were trying to kill us," I said.

"I've given that some thought," said B'oosa. "Unlikely, but possible."

Just then Pancho burst into the tent. "B'oosa, I've—oh, hi, Carl—I mean you told me to—"

B'oosa got up, left the tent in a hurry. Alegria followed him out. I went too, after I'd found my clothes.

Outside, I could hardly stand up, the wind was so strong. B'oosa and Alegria were bent over the tent supports. They had been braced and double-braced. Even from where I was, I could see that they weren't going to hold for long.

"We'll have to strike the tent," B'oosa shouted. Alegria nodded.

"I'll help," I said, stumbling forward.

"Get back in your sleeping bag," said B'oosa. "You're too weak."

I started to protest when my legs gave out and I sprawled sideways into the snow. He was right, I *was* too weak. I crawled back into the tent.

They collapsed the tent on top of the three of us. With a

low profile, the tent might stay. They lashed it down pretty well. Eventually Pancho crawled in with us.

"Where's B'oosa?" I asked.

"He's outside, amigo," said Pancho. "Keeping an eye on the tent, and watching out for the snowbeast. He told me he would come in if it got too bad, but frankly, I am worried."

"Why's that?" I asked.

"Those two days you were out were very hard on our riend. I do not think he is well and he tries to do too much. He pulled you and Miko from the water, you know."

I didn't know. I would have expected it and it was like him not to say anything about it.

"Very bad out there," Pancho said. "I saw the storm come in. It started in the mountains, and like a solid wall it came, a solid wall of ice. Then the wind came up the delta from the sea. They met in the valley and it has been getting worse every hour. When I came in, I honestly could not see my hand in front of my face."

We had such storms on Springworld, during mid-winter. Nobody went out in them, of course. There were stories of people who stepped outside and got lost a few meters from their homes, and started going in circles, to be found at spring thaw, kilometers away. "How long does B'oosa stand guard?"

"One hour, two hours. He'll come get me or Alegria when he's ready."

"Or me," I said. "I couldn't stand a full hour, but—"

"Only if you sleep, amigo." He turned off the light and I could hear him burrowing deeply into his bag. Good idea.

"*Wake up!* Everybody wake up!" It was Alegria, and there was the sound of terror in her voice.

"What is it?" Pancho sounded fully awake.

"B'oosa! He's disappeared!" We struggled out of the tent to be greeted by a pale blue sky, no wind, the sun almost warm. No B'oosa, no footprints. No stunner.

Miko staggered and grabbed my arm. I held him up by the shoulders. Being smaller, the exposure had hit him even harder than me. "Shize," he said weakly. "What are we going to do now?"

"We have to look for him," Alegria said. No one would suggest otherwise, of course, but the same thought must have possessed all of us: B'oosa pacing to keep warm, getting turned around, the steep river bank not ten meters away.

Pancho trudged to the bank and peered over. "No sign."

"What we need is a floater," I said. "If he's . . . passed out even half a klick from here, we could search for days and not find him." Especially if his body is buried in a drift.

"We'll quarter the area," Pancho said. "And search for six hours. Then we break camp and set out across the delta."

"With the sun out," I said, "he would start heading in the same direction. If it doesn't start snowing again, we should run into his tracks." I didn't believe it and they didn't believe it, but they all nodded.

We only had three vibroclubs. I gave mine to Alegria, then took B'oosa's staff and lashed my knife to the end of it. Go for the eyes, sure. Pancho assigned directions and we all walked off, searching.

After an hour or so of toeing drifts, I heard somebody yelling—yelling loud, for me to hear him over the ringing in my ears. It was Pancho, back near the campsite, waving and pointing.

I looked for a long minute and finally saw the silver speck of a floater, drifting down over the mountains, heading straight for us. I started to run and fell on my face. Got up and hurried carefully.

I got there the same time as the floater. This wasn't the simple open platform they used to ferry us around; it was a streamlined airfoil with a bubble top. The top slid back and Bruno stepped out. A man I'd never seen followed him. He wasn't dressed for the weather: mottled green

combat fatigues with a jacket. He rubbed his hands together and blew into them.

Bruno studied us. "Where's the big black one?"

"He was on guard last night. We lost him."

"Lost him." Bruno turned to the other man. "Sorry.
He was the best one."

The man shrugged. "Quantity, not quality."

They both laughed and Bruno unsnapped the holster on
his belt. He leisurely drew out a squat black pistol I
recognized to be a "neurotangler."

"You're all dead," he said flatly, and clicked off the
safety catch.

My home-made spear wasn't balanced for throwing, and
I was never that good at underhand, but I flung it at him as
hard as I could. At the same instant the 'tangler buzzed
and I felt a million tiny pins prick the front of my body,
and what strength I had left started to drain away.

The spear struck Bruno squarely in the chest, then fell
away. Body armor. Rubbing the spot where it had hit,
Bruno dropped everyone else with a negligent wave of the
'tangler.

"He's a fighter," the other man said approvingly. "Good
reflexes."

I fell slowly back into the snow. Was this blue sky the
last thing I'd ever see? "Bears are good fighters, too," I
heard Bruno say. "But they're dumb. Let's dump this
shize into the river."

I heard them dragging the tent; heard it splash.

"Doesn't seem fair," the other one said. "You get
insurance for all five. I just—"

"Tough. We made a deal. Help me with the big one."

They grabbed my feet and dragged me. My front was
totally numb, but the shocking cold of the snow shoveling
up the back of my tunic helped keep me awake.

They didn't drop me in the river. Instead, they muscled
me upright and tipped me into the floater. I heard my nose
crack on the floor, but didn't feel anything. I saw snow;
the floor was transparent plastic.

One by one, they piled the others on top of me. Then they slid the top shut and we took off.

I watched the river drop away and traced my erratic path back to where I'd been searching when the floater came. I wasn't looking for anything, and almost missed it—more footprints! About a hundred meters farther than I'd gone. So B'oosa had survived the storm.

But my hopes evaporated as quickly as they'd risen. It must have still been dark when the snow stopped. The steps went straight to another river, and stopped.

IV

"COME ON, TROOPS. Rise and shize." Something hit me hard on the foot and I woke up from a confusing dream.

We were in a white windowless room, with two rows of beds, mostly empty. The man who'd hit my foot with a stick was the one who had been with Bruno in the floater. He had on a different uniform now, with the cluster of circles on the arm that identified him as a Heller sergeant. Not my favorite branch of the human race.

Besides the four of us, there were two strangers groggily getting out of their beds. We all wore white hospital gowns. Somebody had undressed me—somebody had undressed *Alegria* while she was unconscious. If it was this sergeant I'd break his arm. I'd break his arm off, and beat him with it.

"*Stand* at attention. In front of the bed, stupid." He had a 'tangler on his hip.

"This training has gone too far," Pancho said. "I'm going to—"

"I'll tell you what you're going to do." The sergeant jabbed the air with his stick, a few centimeters from Pancho's face. Pancho didn't flinch. "Very soon now."

I was still groggy from whatever they'd given us to keep us asleep. My nose hurt, but not as if it were broken. Had they had time to fix it? I took a deep breath and held it, trying to force the fog away.

He stepped to the room's one door and opened it part way. "By your leave, Commander."

The man who walked in looked too young to have white hair. He was deeply tanned and tall, built like a young athlete. He wore a closely-tailored uniform I couldn't identify, with gleaming gold insignia of rank. He stood for a moment, arms folded on his chest, and looked at us with a totally neutral expression. When he spoke, his voice was deep and quiet.

"I am Captain Forrestor of Her Majesty's Marine Corps. I will be your commander for one year. Less, if we win in less time."

"Whose Majesty?" Pancho said. The sergeant stepped toward him and raised his baton to strike.

"No, Sergeant." He looked at Pancho. "You haven't been briefed yet?"

"I don't know what you're talking about."

"*Sir!*" the sergeant hissed.

"I don't know what you're talking about sir," Pancho said in a monotone.

"For the next year, all of you will be employed by Her Majesty Queen Phylle II. Of Sanctuary, on the planet Spicelle. We are here to resolve a dispute between Her Majesty and the reigning monarch of Feder. Also on Spicelle. We will meet Feder's armies in the northeast quadrant of Purgatory, for a clean Class 2/D war, beginning two days from now."

"Sir, there's some mistake," I said. "We aren't soldiers."

"You can say that again," the sergeant muttered.

"You are now," the captain said. "I have your papers."

"This can't be legal," Alegria said. "I'm a citizen of Selva, a student. We were kidnapped."

He smiled slightly. "You won't find many lawyers on Hell. Not this Hell, at any rate." He took an envelope from an inside pocket and removed several sheets of paper from it. "You would be Private Alegria de Saldaña, *for-*

merly of the planet Selva. Now a slave conscript, leased to Her Majesty by Manpower, Incorporated.''

"*No!* We're students, we were on a training—"

"I'll explain, sir," the sergeant said. "When you crossed that river you were on Northland soil. Slavery is legal in Northland, isn't that barbaric? You were legitimately captured by Manpower, Incorporated, and leased through me to Her Majesty."

"We won't fight," I said. "Sir."

"Not all of you will have to fight. It takes more than combat troops to win a war . . . Private Saldaña, for instance, is being assigned to an aid station, because she's had paramedical training. You would be . . ." He looked through the papers. "Carl Bok. You will fight, of course."

"No, sir. We don't have war on Springworld. I'm a farmer and a pacifist."

"Here it says that you hired yourself out for gladiatorial combat on Earth. That's an odd trade for a pacifist."

"It's not murder."

"I've heard differently. At any rate, you will fight when ordered to do so, or face certain death. Either by military tribunal or a real-time field decision."

"What are we fighting for?" Miko said. "I've never even *heard* of Sanctuary, or your Majesty."

"That's immaterial. Do you know what a Class 2/D war is?" Nobody answered. He turned to the sergeant. "I thought you said they were trained."

"Physically trained, sir."

"Ah. Well, for your information, a Class 2/D war is a very good kind of war for you untrained soldiers. We chose this type because our own Marine Corps is not large, and we had to buy most of our footsoldiers here. Frankly, Sanctuary is not an extremely wealthy land, and we could not afford a large number of trained Heller mercenaries. So most of your comrades-in-arms will also be leased conscripts.

"A Class 2/D conflict uses no nuclear weapons, nor lasers, nor any other weapon invented after the year 1900, on Earth, with the sole exception of cybernetic aids to these primitive devices. A reasonably intelligent person can master all of the allowed weapons in a day or two.

"We have further agreed, with Feder, that no artillery be allowed, nor aerial observers, nor fragmentation weapons other than simple hand grenades."

"What's a hand grenade?" Miko asked.

The captain sighed. "This is Sergeant Meyer, my Field First Sergeant. He will be training you for the next two days. With God's help he will not only teach you what a hand grenade is, but teach you how not to kill yourself with it.

"Just keep this uppermost in your mind: what has happened to you may seem grossly unfair. But individual justice was never war's domain. If you fight well and carefully you may survive to win your freedom. If you balk, or in any way impede the progress of our endeavor, you will most . . . certainly . . . die." He turned to Meyer. "Sergeant, you will deliver these six to the staging area at 0900 Saturday, fully trained and cooperative."

"Yessir." They saluted, raised fists, and the captain marched out. The sergeant turned to us with a malevolent smile.

"Let me explain that in more detail. There are three ways the army can kill you for disobedience. One is a trial, a court martial. If the presiding officer finds you guilty, and he usually does, you'll take a deever; hang by the neck until dead."

"Choke to death?" one of the strangers said.

"It only hurts for a few minutes," the sergeant said. "If you disobey under combat conditions, of course, any officer or non-commissioned officer, such as me, can kill you on the spot.

"The third method is the most useful. The meat squad, TDU, Tactical Diversionary Unit. In essence, we strip you of arms and use you as bait, to draw the enemy's fire. Often we can patch you up and use you again."

I didn't know what I was going to do. I could probably kill somebody who was trying to kill me. But kill in cold blood for somebody else's politics? I wouldn't even kill for my *own* politics!

But the alternative was dancing at the end of a rope. Was I willing to die for my pacifism? I was probably going to die anyhow. I wished B'oosa were here.

They took Alegria off to the aid station and put us with a group of about fifty men who were doing weapons training. None of us was very enthusiastic, but as the officer had said, the weapons were simple. We used rifles, knives, and hand grenades. The hand grenades were bombs that you threw toward the enemy; when they exploded they shattered into thousands of tiny fragments, so you had to throw them far enough not to get caught in the blast yourself. Or get behind something.

The rifle shot metal bullets, powered by explosive powder, and was deadly simple to use. Looking through the telescopic sight, a bright dot showed you where the bullet would land. It incorporated a rangefinder that also evaluated the speed and direction of the wind between you and your target. So the dot drifted around as the wind shifted, or as you moved from target to target.

We were training in some neutral part of Purgatory, in what amounted to a large prison compound. It was about two kilometers by three, inside a shock-fence, with armed guards on elevated platforms every half-klick or so. When we weren't practicing with the weapons, we were running, doing push-ups, toughening-up in general.

That was curious. Since they'd taken our watches, we didn't know what the date was, and didn't know how long we'd been unconscious. But while we were under they had done something to restore our strength: at our Northland camp I wouldn't have been able to do one push-up, let alone fifty at a time.

We didn't have much time for conversation, but I was able to find out a few things. Most of our fellow-conscripts were military students, sent here from other worlds, who were sent out on Northland maneuvers in small groups, as punishment. One man was a hunter and another was a casual vacationer, who had been talked into signing up for a Northland tour.

It was inconceivable that Hell authorities didn't know about this recruitment-by-kidnapping. And it was obvious that none of us would ever live to tell about it.

Our only hope was to try to make an escape from the battlefield, and try to find our way back to the capital, Hellas. There was only one land bridge connecting Hellas with Purgatory, so no matter where we were, if we could find the coast and follow it, we would eventually get there. Our chances of escaping were probably as slim as our chances of surviving the long trek, but there didn't seem to be any other way out.

Once in Hellas, we could get help from some Confederación official. If the military didn't find us first.

That first night another alternative presented itself. It was grotesque, but it had one advantage: it might keep the army from killing us as soon as the war was over.

We trained for eighteen or twenty hours and then staggered back to the barracks, for cold gruel and hard beds, both welcome. While we were eating and exchanging desperate whispers, Sergeant Meyer walked in.

He sat down on an empty bunk, and set a clipboard beside him. "You didn't look so bad out there today. With practice, you might become decent soldiers."

He tapped the papers on the clipboard. "I'm going to give you a chance to find out for yourselves, if you want to. These are recruitment forms. Sign them and you'll be bona fide private mercenaries, with rank and pay and opportunity for advancement."

"For how long would this be?" Pancho asked.

"Ten years." He put his hands on his knees and looked straight at Pancho. "You wouldn't be fighting all of that time, of course. Sometimes months go by without a war."

"And in between times?"

"You would stay in a barracks. Like this one."

"A prisoner."

He shrugged, stood. "Think about it, talk it over. There are advantages."

He dropped the clipboard on the bed where Pancho and I were sitting. "If the idea appeals to you, sign one of these forms. Write above your signature 'Signed without coercion, 17 Diazo 49.' "

"The seventeenth? We've only been here two days?" That matched with day-after-tomorrow being Saturday, but we were sure we'd been under for a week or even two.

"That's right; the regeneration clinic is very efficient. As you'll find out if you're wounded. They don't like to see soldiers wasting time in bed."

"You don't call this coercion?" Miko said.

"No. No one has to sign."

"We just might live longer if we do," I said.

"I'll be back in ten minutes. Talk it over." He walked away, then stopped at the door. "I was picked up the same way you were, eight years ago. It's not such a bad life. It's a life."

Nobody said anything for a minute. Then one of the military students came over and signed a form. Pancho took the clipboard from him and also signed.

"They can only kill us once, amigo," he whispered. "This way, we can wait for the best opportunity."

I wasn't sure that that increased our odds very much, but I signed. So did Miko. Eventually all the barracks did.

Meyer came back and picked up the clipboard; riffled through the forms. He nodded but didn't smile. "Usually turns out this way . . . sweet dreams, angels. Heavy day tomorrow."

The first day we had practiced with blank ammunition and dummy grenades; the second day was for real. I suppose what happened was inevitable; at any rate, Meyer was prepared for it.

The rifles were modern copies of a primitive design: instead of firing whenever you pulled the trigger, you had to cock a sliding bolt between each round. They seemed slow and awkward, and each cassette of ammunition only had ten rounds.

Meyer led us out to the firing range and his corporal

handed each of us a cassette. We knew how to operate them from endless drill the day before.

One conscript, who had not said a word in two days, slipped the cassette into place, pointed his rifle at Meyer, and fired. Meyer was wearing body armor, of course; the bullet knocked him back a step but he immediately drew his neurotangler and dropped the man. He quickly scanned the rest of us, then returned the pistol to its holster.

He stood over the fallen man. "Well, well. Corporal?" The other Heller noncom had his own pistol drawn and was looking excited about it. It was a laser, not a 'tangler. "What should we do about this poor cob?"

"Kill him here. Less paperwork than a court martial."

Meyer nodded thoughtfully. "We should make an example of him. He's obviously too stupid to be an infantryman."

"Burn 'im?" He clicked the safety off.

"No. Might as well get some use out of him. We'll use him as meat." The corporal stooped and handcuffed the paralyzed man. Meyer raised his voice. "Tomorrow or Sunday you'll see this man die, our first TDU. With luck, he may save your life, by showing us where enemy fire is coming from." He put his hand on the butt of his pistol. "Any other volunteers?"

None of the rest of us was that desperate, or that resigned. We took our places on the range.

Our targets were man-shaped dummies that popped up at random from trenches fifty to two hundred meters downrange. You had one second or less to aim and fire. It was more difficult with real bullets than it had been with blanks. The noise was louder and the rifle butt kicked back against your shoulder in recoil. It was hard not to flinch in anticipation of the impact, which would throw your point of aim off by as much as several meters.

After five or six hours' practice I was pretty good at it, but some people, including Miko, never did get the feel of it. Meyer remarked sarcastically that they were sure to improve when the targets started shooting back.

Then we lined up behind a transparent wall of scarred-up plastic. Ominously, an ambulance floater settled behind us. We put on the heavy steel helmets we'd be wearing in combat.

This was the grenade range. When you got to the front of the line, Meyer would hand you a grenade. You stepped to the other side of the wall, pulled out the safety pin, and threw the grenade at a concrete target thirty meters away. And hit the dirt.

The fragments were deadly out to ten or fifteen meters from where the grenade exploded; some people could barely throw it that far. The plastic wall often rattled with stray chunks. One man put a couple of deep dents in his helmet and managed to shear off the last joint of his little finger. Meyer said that earned him a one-day vacation and a position in the leading trench, "where he could get lots of practice."

We practiced using the knives as spears, clamped over the end of the rifle barrel. This was supposed to be useful if you ran out of ammunition. I don't suppose it would be of much use if your enemy still had a bullet or two.

When night fell we had our "graduation exercise": being shot at. We had to crawl down a zigzag trench while somebody fired over our heads with a gatling, a gun that shot a continuous stream of bullets. The trench was full of mud and scarcely a meter deep. The other people were small enough to go on all fours; I had to belly down. It was pretty scary, especially since Meyer was crawling along behind us, throwing grenades. None of them rolled into the trench, though, and we finished the exercise with the same number of people we'd started with.

They gave us a good meal—meat, vegetables, and wine—and let us go to bed early. That would have been fine if I could've slept. I stared at the ceiling until well after midnight, wondering what it was going to be like, wondering whether I would live to see another sundown, wondering what would happen if I actually did have to kill someone. Pancho and Miko and I had talked it over. It would be easy enough simply to miss, shooting at people with the rifle. But what would happen if we had to fight in close quarters? Miko swore he would die before he would kill someone for Her Majesty. I agreed with him. But it was just talk. I was pretty sure I would kill to save my own life; I certainly wouldn't have hesitated during the games, on Earth.

When I finally slept I dreamed about home, but it wasn't a pleasant dream. I had to face a harvest with no more weapons than I was taking to the war. I kept getting attacked by droolers and one-eyes.

I don't think any war makes sense, but this one seemed even more stupid than the ones I'd read about. What was involved was two hills, named 814 and 905, with a small valley between them. Sanctuary was to position 500 soldiers on hill 814; Feder would do the same on 905. They were to fight until one group had possession of both hills.

The valley was about two kilometers wide, filled with a network of deep trenches. Evidently that's where most of the fighting would be done. Neither the rifles nor the gatlings were effective at a two-kilometer range; you could get a bullet that far, but you couldn't aim. So the obvious strategy was to divide your group, leaving part of it to defend the hill, with the other moving from trench to trench toward the enemy's hill. The second bunch had a more dangerous job, it seemed to me, but also would have better opportunity to escape.

About a third of the force were specially-trained men such as snipers, who had heavy rifles of great accuracy, demolition engineers, medical workers, and so forth. The other two-thirds of us were fodder.

They woke us up before dawn and herded us aboard floaters. We didn't go directly to the hill, but to a "staging area" about ten klicks from it. That was as close as floaters were allowed to go, to prevent aerial observation. We walked the rest of the way, pushing carts full of supplies.

We were about a tenth of Sanctuary's total army. The others had been on the hill for several days, setting things up. The war was to start at noon. We hauled the carts up the hill at about 1130, exhausted.

Sergeant Meyer was fresh as a flower after our little hike, not having pushed a cart. "Stow your gear in that bunker," he said, pointing at a hole in the ground, "and fill a few sandbags." Sandbags? He walked briskly away without elaborating.

When Pancho and I hauled our cart around to the bunker, we found two men filling plastic bags with mud. Wet sand, I supposed.

"Here comes the green meat," one of them said. "You got a shovel in that shize?"

I found one. "You two fill; we'll stack." They talked as they built a wall over the hole, two sandbags thick. They were Tanner and Darty, veterans of more than a year of fighting, who had been given the privilege of helping us build our bunker. They already had a large pile of sandbags, and they stacked with speedy efficiency.

The hole was sort of a cave, facing down the hillside. They explained that the sandbag wall would protect us against any amount of rifle or gatling fire, in theory, since a bullet could only penetrate a couple of centimeters. But there had to be ports to shoot through, and a lucky sniper or a rifleman who got too close could get a bullet through the port. If you were shooting out of it at the time, you would most likely get a head wound. Darty showed us a bald crease along the side of his head, and giggled.

The shooting ports were wooden rectangular boxes two sandbags long, open-ended, with enough room to stick a rifle in and move it around a little. The end that pointed outward was covered with a flap of see-through gauze, the same color as the mud. That way, theoretically, no sniper could tell where the port was unless he was looking right at it when you fired in his direction.

More dangerous than bullets was the possibility of somebody getting close enough to toss a grenade or firebomb over the wall. There was a "grenade well," a deep hole, in the middle of the bunker floor. If a grenade came over the top, you could kick it into the well, which should channel all the fragments straight up. If it was a firebomb the only thing to do was try to get out of the bunker as quickly as possible.

The best strategy was not to let anyone get close enough to throw at you.

"But listen," Tanner said, "don't shoot to kill unless you have to."

"Tanner. . . ." Darty drawled.

"Shut up, hard case. Shoot for legs, arms, hips, shoulders. Those guys are the same as us, most of them, they just want to live through it. We get real bloodthirsty and they're going to come back the same way. You can't say it isn't true, Darty. I've seen it."

Darty just scowled at him.

"Unless you see Heller insignia. Crazy dighters all wanna die anyhow." A whistle shrilled from above them. "Ammo call. Let's go."

We clambered, slipping and falling, up to the top of the hill. Captain Forrestor and Sergeant Meyer were there, and about a dozen other Heller noncoms. Alegria came out of a bunker beside them, dressed in white, along with nine other white-clad medics, two of them women. She waved at me and Pancho and gave a weak smile.

It got pretty crowded up there, five hundred people slipping around. They herded us into our ten companies, each area marked with a stack of boxes and a company flag. All three of us were Brave Company, though Miko was assigned a different bunker.

When the whistle blew again it was 1200, time for the war to start. They gave us each two hundred rounds of rifle ammunition and five grenades and broke us down into squads of ten. Pancho and I were in D squad, led by an Earthie corporal named O'Connor.

"We've got it lucky today," O'Connor said. "We're one of the defense squads, stay on the hill. Most of the fighting be down in the valley for a while. You all have bunkers assigned?" We murmured yes.

"Good. We'll spend the next few hours one-on-one-off.

Sleep for an hour, keep watch for an hour. How many of you green meat?''

Five of us raised our hands. He sighed. ''I always get 'em. Listen. You haven't had much training and I know you aren't ready for this. When it gets hot, you're going to forget everything. One thing you don't dare forget: always shoot to kill. Always shoot to kill. You aren't getting out of this alive unless we can weaken their forces enough to take that hill. You wound some cob, he'll be back shooting at you next week. Always . . .''

From across the valley drifted the faint tap-tap-tap of a gatling being fired.

''Shize. They're bein' cute already. Get into your bunkers, up against the sandbags. I'll be by later.''

I looked at Pancho and opened my mouth to say something. Then there was a whipping sound and a flat splash: a bullet made a crater in the mud about three meters away.

I guess I could slide faster than him. I was in the bunker a good three seconds before he fell on top of me.

He wiped mud off his arms. ''Thought those things couldn't go this far.''

''Guess they just can't aim them. Just trying to throw a scare into us.'' Succeeding, too; we could hear people shouting and scuffling. My heart was beating fast and Pancho didn't look too tan.

Our own gatling started to return fire. I stuck my rifle through the shooting port and cranked the telescopic sight up to its highest power (the aiming dot fell to the bottom of the field of view and blinked red). Hill 905 was covered with scurrying ants.

Experimentally, I aimed the rifle down the hill, toward the trenches at the base of it. The dot turned yellow and drifted back up to center.

''Don't you think we're going to have enough of that later, amigo?'' Pancho said. ''And your rifle isn't even loaded.'' As if on cue, a rifle barked in a nearby bunker.

''Save it,'' someone shouted. ''Can't get halfway there.''

''Who rests first?'' Pancho said.

''You go ahead. I couldn't.''

"Me neither. Odds or evens?"

"Evens," I said. He produced two fingers to my three.

"Pleasant dreams," he said, and slipped a cassette into his rifle. Suddenly there was an even greater commotion, as a crowd of men came bustling and sliding down the path by our bunker—armed, helmeted, carrying the small combat packs that held extra ammunition, grenades, and a little food—flying to the temporary safety of the trenches below. The assault squads, over two hundred men.

One man pitched forward and slid ten or fifteen meters until he stopped, unmoving. Another skidded to a halt beside him, looked him over, then shouted "Medic! Concussion!"—and continued down the hill with redoubled speed.

Two male medics rushed down and checked the man quickly, then grabbed him under the arms and carried him up over our bunker, and started lowering him inside. "Here, give us a hand."

We wrestled him down to the floor, gently as possible. One of the medics hopped down and selected a syrette from a case on his belt, and gave him a shot in the arm.

The man groaned and shook his head. The medic unstrapped his helmet and set it next to him. "Where am . . . what th' shize . . ."

"Bullet bounced off your helmet, knocked you out," the medic said. "Come up to the medic bunker when you can walk." He started to lift himself out. "Or when it stops raining." He followed the other medic uphill, fast.

The man picked up his helmet and ran his fingers over the large dent in the top. Then he gingerly touched the egg-sized swelling that was growing on his crown, and stared at his fingers. "Close one." He swallowed, turned pale.

"You were lucky, amigo."

"I—I've never been hit before."

"How long have you been fighting?" I asked.

"First couple of minutes, that's bad luck. What?"

"I said, 'How many wars have you been in, and not get wounded?' "

"Three shows," he said, touching his head again, wincing. "Four months since I signed up."

"Signed up? You don't look like a Heller."

He looked at his fingers again. "At least it's not bleeding—no, I'm from Earth. Too dightin' big for Earth. Made some money in the games and came here to open a liquor store. Got into debt." He shook his head slowly. "Shoulda stayed on Earth, if I knew it'd come to this. Coulda made a fortune. Who cares if people stare."

"We were in the games," I said. "Pancho here was bolo; I was on the quarterstaff."

"Well, damn me." He smiled for the first time, and stuck out his hand. "Jake Newmann, vibroclub."

"I'm Carl—" With a shower of dirt and mud, O'Connor, the little Earthie corporal, slid into the bunker. "What the hell is this," he said. "Three men in one dightin' bunker and no one on guard?"

"Medical emergency, sir," I said.

"Don't-call-me-sir-I-work-for-a-living," he said automatically. "You're the one that got hit goin' down the hill?"

"Yeah, corporal, one of those gatling rounds. Bounced off my pot, knocked me out."

"So early," he said, shaking his head. "Bad luck." Were all soldiers this superstitious?

He turned to me and Pancho. "You cobs don't really have to look out for another hour or so. The Blues aren't gonna come running across the valley." We were the Reds; both sides wore identical mud-colored uniforms, but we had armbands to keep us from being killed by our own men in close quarters.

"I just don't want you to be slack then. See, they can send snipers around the flanks of our main assault bunch—bet yer bum we're doin' the same—and they could be here in an hour or so.

"Most likely, first thing we know of a sniper is when he kills his first man. He's not gonna risk givin' away his position until he's sure of a kill. Everybody's lookin', then maybe we can see the muzzle flash or some smoke."

"S—corporal," I said, "won't we be able to see him,

himself, when he shoots? I mean, there aren't any bunkers down there, are there?''

"No bunkers. But they've got PCU's, portable camouflage units. Sort of like your shooting ports. If you don't see him putting it up, and they're hard to catch, then you won't be able to tell it from the rest of the trench. Not unless you have all the ground memorized, down to the last pebble. That takes a couple of weeks. By then they're only shootin' at night.'' I was glad the rules of the game didn't allow night-glasses, like we used guarding the harvest at home. Snipers would be too powerful then.

"You cobs green meat?'' Jake Newmann asked.

"They sure are,'' O'Connor said. "Why don't you stay with 'em until your squad gets back—unless you wanta go catch up with 'em.''

"Sure thing, corporal, alone in nomanland.''

"I'll clear it with Sergeant Dubi; headed up that way. Shouldn't be any problem.''

"No place else to go,'' Jake said. "Besides, we're blood brothers. We were all gladiators, on Earth.''

The corporal looked at us strangely. "This must seem pretty tame for you, then.'' Pancho and I kept our mouths shut. "Just wait,'' he said softly, and pulled himself up out of the bunker.

"I got a feeling he don't like gladiators much,'' Jake said. "Why'd you come here? Get disbarred or something?''

We explained to him about *Starschool* and the kidnapping. He wasn't surprised, of course.

"You're sure the ship's left by now?'' he said.

Pancho shrugged. "We were reported killed in training, in a remote area. I have the idea that Bruno has done this often enough to know how to cover his tracks.''

"And the ship was scheduled to leave yesterday,'' I added.

"Still, these *Starschool* candies must be pretty sav,'' Jake said. "Hell, even *I'd* see a skim job there. You might just see that whole damn ship set down in nomanland tomorrow.''

"Never lands," I said. Still, the Dean was nothing if he wasn't thorough.

"It may be that you are right, though. Perhaps we have been trained too much out of optimism, out of hoping."

"Sure. Just stay alive. They'll come for you—look at it *their* way. *Starschool*'s way. They're gonna go home and tell your folks that you got wiped on some damn training exercise? They an't. They just an't."

I was fighting against hope. "We signed releases with *Starschool*. They aren't responsible for . . . Oh my God."

"What?" Jake said.

"We signed up. We signed up as mercenaries, and had to say that we'd signed it without coercion."

Jake laughed out loud. "That piece of paper an't worth bumfodder. Not with witnesses around, like your Dean. *You an't Hellers!* You're offworlders—if you contest a contract it goes to the Confederación fer adju'cation. They won't let it."

"How is it that you know so much about these things?" Pancho asked.

"Look at me!" He spread his arms wide. "I'm a merchant, not a soldier." He laughed, softly but a little crazy. "I had a liquor store on Earth, before I had to go to the games. Believe me, I know. I could have been a registered alien, but taking citizenship here gave me a ten percent tax advantage. Shize, I wish I could . . . go back. Better broke and deported than broke and drafted." He laughed again. "But believe me, I know the law. I saw this coming, I saw it for a year or more."

"There's nothing you can do?" I said.

"Live for ten years." Suddenly grim. "Seems less likely than it did yesterday."

"This whole dightin' planet doesn't make any sense," I said. "Why don't they just . . . well, on Springworld they'd send in a government manager, monitor your standard of living—"

"Oh, my liquor store's got a government manager. And no debts. You can't sue the government here—who would dare to? When I get out, theoretically, I get back my store and my debts. Plus interest. Which ten years at private-and-corporal pay will exactly pay. Which is why I got drafted.''

''I thought you said you'd signed up,'' I said.

''Sure. Like you boys did. I had the choice of enlisting or going to debtors' prison. Nobody gets out of debtors' prison, except they come out in a box.''

''But wouldn't you have . . .'' Pancho realized what he was saying, but continued: '' . . . lived a natural life span?''

''Yeah. Where were you when I needed your advice?'' He stood up, leaned on the sandbag wall for support.

''Why don't all the unwilling ones simply refuse to fight?'' asked Pancho. ''Just sit down or something?''

Jake laughed. ''It'd be a toss-up to see who'd kill you first. There are a lot of Hellers out there that'd love to do the job. Some draftees, too. They start out hating it and end up loving it. Seen it happen lots of times.''

I shuddered, remembering the arena. There were dark sides to every man.

''I'd better go get my rifle,'' said Jake. It was still in the mud where he'd fallen. ''Before it gets dangerous out there.''

''Stay here and rest, amigo. I'll get it.''

''Pancho—'' The gatling was still tapping away.

''Before it gets dangerous,'' he said, lifting himself out of the bunker. He was fast about it.

''Thanks.'' Jake took the rifle and started cleaning it carefully with a rag.

''Like I say, you boys may only have to last a day or two, before they come get you. Just keep your heads down and don't do anything stupid.'' He waved at the shooting ports. ''Put all your cassettes on the wooden shelf there; all facing the same way. You're gonna have to reload in the dark. Put a couple grenades up there, too. Use 'em when you don't want to give away the position of the bunker at night. Try not to throw 'em in the direction of the bunker below.

"Keep your sights clean; keep your gun clean. Might save your life."

"Do you shoot to kill?" I asked him.

"I just shoot. Let the bullet decide." He looked thoughtful. "If a certain Blue sergeant comes up the hill, though, I'm going to aim very careful."

"Do you think they will be coming up the hill tonight?" Pancho asked.

"Probably not. My second show they did; took every dightin' man off their hill and tried a mass attack. Didn't work.

"Usually they'll just get a few snipers down there. Each one of them has two or three PCU's; that way they can keep shooting at us from different angles. Nighttime, they might try to move some sappers in, sneak up and drop grenades in some bunkers. Likewise, after it gets dark, we'll send a squad of commandos down after the snipers. That's nasty work. Have to be real quiet about it. Sometimes the commandos goin' down meet the sappers comin' up. That's a bloody mess."

"Think they'll make us be commandos?" I asked.

"No. Those're usually Hellers, or other real mercs. Like I say, they have to be quiet. That's knife work." I shuddered.

He rubbed his face with both hands, hard. "Wonder if I oughta go see the medics."

"He said—"

"Yeah. But I sure hate doctors." He put his helmet on his head and flinched. "Guess I better. They might send me down the hill for a couple days."

He pulled himself up out of the bunker and there was a sound like a hard slap. "Oh," he said softly, and slid back down.

I caught him before he hit the ground and eased him down on his back. I heard Pancho gasp.

His skin was grey with shock and a dark red stain was spreading on the front of his shirt. He was staring at it. He said one word: "Didn't." Then he gurgled terribly and his neck went loose, his head dropped back to the ground, his eyes were dead.

"*Dios*," Pancho said. "*Mierda*."

My hands were shaking so I could hardly manage the slider on his shirt. When it opened I tasted acid vomit, stood up, and choked it back. I was not going to stick my head over the parapet just to empty my jumpy stomach.

The center of his chest was a hole big enough to put my fist in. Mostly red and white and yellow. Splinters of bone. It looked like the bullet had smashed right through his heart.

"Medic," Pancho yelled, then yelled again, louder.

"What is it?" a voice drifted down.

"We—we have a dead man."

"Are you sure he's dead?"

Pancho looked at him for an instant and jerked his head away. "He's dead all right."

"Just a minute."

We waited. I took the rag out of his pocket and covered his face with it. That made it a little easier. They say that when medical students do autopsies the first thing they do is remove the face.

"Hey you." The voice wasn't any closer. "Leave him be. We'll come get him after dark."

That was jolly. "Should . . . should we put him outside?"

"I don't think so," Pancho said. "Why don't we both stand guard for a while?"

"Good idea." I stepped over the body and sat down to look through the gunport.

"What a terrible thing," Pancho whispered. "He—"

Someone jumped into the bunker behind us. I grabbed my rifle and spun around.

"Don't shoot, bumhole." It was O'Connor. He toed the body. "Same guy." He peeked under the rag. "I'll be damned. I will be damned."

I thought that was likely but didn't say anything. "What happened?"

"He was going up to see the medics. Maybe it was a sniper."

"Naw. That's a fifty-caliber wound." He turned the body part way over; there was a circle of blood on the back of its shirt.

"See, there's the entrance wound," he said with detachment. "Higher than the exit wound. Sniper, it'd be lower." He let the body drop. "Better *hope* they don't have a sniper with a fifty."

"Just one of those random gatling rounds," I said.

He stood up and wiped his hands on his shirt. "Sometimes a cob just runs outa luck. Twice! Would you—"

Two medics scrambled down to the edge of the bunker. "You guys wanta hand up that meatball? Goddamn lieutenant says we need the parts."

"Don't need no goddamn *parts*," the other one said.

"Listen, I'm a corporal," O'Connor said.

"You're a dightin' fleet commander, I don't care, just give us that dightin' meatball so we can get back to the dightin' bunker!"

I grabbed one arm and O'Connor grabbed the other. A dead body is heavier than a live one. The medics took it without thanking us and dragged him away, the toes making parallel furrows in the mud.

O'Connor kicked mud over the pool of blood and sat down with his back against the sandbags. He lit up a weed and offered us the box. I refused but Pancho took one.

For a minute we sat and stared at where the body had been. The gatling chattered softly and every now and then there was a wet sound when a bullet hit nearby.

"They must have a ton of ammo," O'Connor said.

"Why aren't we shooting back?" I asked.

"Well, probably because somebody thinks that *they* want us to. To use up ammo. That would mean an assault tonight, big one, human wave attack. So we're saving ammo. But I'm just guessing."

He took a deep drag. "That would be nice."

"A *human wave* attack?" Pancho said.

"Get it over with, one way or another. Rather fight in the trenches, though. Mobility."

Down in the valley there was a sudden pair of shots, then several grenade blasts.

"First contact," O'Connor said, an edge of excitement in his voice. There was a short volley of rifle fire.

He stood up and ground his weed out on our floor. "Better go to the command post." He started up, then turned around. "Say, either of you cobs good with a knife?"

"No," I lied.

"Never used one," Pancho said.

He nodded and hauled himself out; walked away without hurrying.

"That man is more dangerous to us than any Blue," Pancho said.

I was thinking. "Wait. Suppose he did send us out on a commando raid. That would give us all night to slip away—and when we didn't come back they'd probably think we were killed."

"The only flaw in your logic is that we probably *would* be killed." He looked through the gunport. "I wonder if they made it halfway."

I used my telescopic sight, scanning. There was a spurt of white smoke and mud, followed by the sharp report of a grenade. I focused on it; the aiming dot was close to the bottom but wasn't blinking red.

Suddenly a couple of dozen soldiers jumped out of a trench and started running in our direction. They had blue armbands; their rifles had bayonets.

"Open fire!" someone shouted, and the bunkers around us immediately started firing. I aimed high and squeezed the trigger—the rifle was loud inside the bunker—then cocked another round in and shot again.

"*Lead* th' motherdighters! Bullet takes a second to get there." We didn't seem to be having much effect. Then one of the soldiers fell to his knees, dropped his rifle and started crawling back.

Out of a trench some twenty meters in front of them,

Red soldiers popped up and started firing and throwing grenades. Several of the Blues fell immediately, but the rest started shooting back as they ran. Someone shot off a signal gun, and a bright green star glowed over their position. Calling reinforcements, I guessed, but both sides would see it.

About half of the Blue soldiers made it to the trench, jumping in with their bayonets.

"Hold fire!"

Without looking up from his gunsight, Pancho said, "I'm just as glad that we are here and they are there."

"Wish it would stay that way. You shoot anybody?"

"No, I aimed high."

"Me, too." I winced as a grenade went off in the trench. That seemed self-defeating, at close quarters.

A louder shot, almost as loud as the ones from other bunkers, stood out from the noise of the battle, and someone on the top of the hill screamed. A sniper. "Now we're in for it," I said.

"Did you see anything?"

"No." The person he had hit was shouting for a medic. I wondered whether I would have gone to help him, if I were dressed in white instead of mud. They weren't supposed to shoot at medics.

I had a sick vision of Alegria having to run out and tend the man, exposed, her life depending on the sniper's respect for the rules of the game. There weren't any women fighters, though, so maybe the female medics only worked under cover.

There was another shot that seemed to come from a different direction, but apparently no one was hit. A couple of seconds later, the bunker above us started firing furiously; they must have seen the shot. They threw a grenade but it fell short, narrowly missing the bunker below.

"Do you see it?" Pancho asked. I could see mud splashing where the bullets hit, but that was all.

Then there was another shot, and this time we could

hear the bullet whirr over our heads. The bunker above stopped firing. Sensible. Why ask for trouble?

"There!" Pancho said.

I thought I'd seen a little flicker of motion, too. "Just left of that white rock?"

"That's it."

After a moment I said, "Are you going to shoot?"

"It's not my war . . . is it yours, amigo?"

"No." But staring at that spot, I started thinking about Morality as Arithmetic, or vice versa. What if he lived to kill ten more soldiers, for my not pulling the trigger? I would be responsible for all ten, in one sense.

But if he saw the flash or smoke and I missed, and he aimed back . . . I felt more like a coward than a moralist.

"Do you think what Jake said made sense?" Pancho asked.

"About the Dean running in and saving us? I wouldn't put any real money on it."

"I fear I wouldn't either. Should we volunteer for this commando thing?"

I thought for a minute. "Not yet. They might get suspicious. *I* would, anyhow."

"Wait and see what happens, I suppose. That battle appears to be over." There was no more shooting there. Seven dead or wounded men lay between the two trenches. A white-clad medic (with a blue armband) walked from body to body. How many more were in the trench?

There was no more sniper fire. We assumed they were waiting for dark, or for somebody to show himself. I had to pee in the worst way, but decided that stepping outside would *be* the worst way.

Pancho stood guard while I tried to sleep. I almost wished O'Connor was here. Did that battle mean, because it involved so few men, that we wouldn't have the human wave attack? Or could there have been three or four hundred more men stalking through the trenches. It gave me cold sweat to realize that that would make sense: sending a dozen men up to divert the enemy's attention, while the main body moved in for slaughter. No, there would've been more shots. Unless they'd rushed with bayonets. But we had two hundred men out there, somewhere. How many were in the battle? Nothing like two hundred. And the trenches were a complicated maze; that's how the snipers managed to work their way in undetected. If two men could sneak through, could five hundred? It didn't seem likely. It didn't seem impossible, either.

I woke suddenly to the sound of gunfire. "It's down in the first trench," Pancho said. "Not the slit trench, the first real trench." The slit trench was a shallow straight one, as opposed to the deep zigzags that scored the valley.

I looked through the gunport and could see wisps of smoke rising from the trench. Was this the first rank of the human wave? It wasn't quite dark yet.

"See any people?"

"No," he said, "not yet."

The firing stopped abruptly. Then dozens of soldiers came pouring out of the trench—with red armbands, to our relief. "Maybe they caught the snipers," I said.

"At least they're coming back. It will make the night easier."

I stretched, then felt a sharp pain. "Lots of targets now. Think I'll go water the grass."

"Me next," he said.

The sanitation facilities were one large can, about two hundred liters, across the path. The returning soldiers scrambled by as I stood there relieving myself, some of them with entertaining comments. Some were bandaged and bleeding; some had to be carried. They had got two snipers.

I traded places with Pancho and watched it grow dark. When I could barely see through the sight, I heard someone approach the bunker and slide in. "O'Connor?"

"Right. You both awake?"

"Yes," Pancho said.

"Here." He handed me a heavy bundle; same to Pancho. "Pistol and trench knife.

"Gladiators have to be brave, right?" We didn't say anything. "Well, this is a job for brave men."

"What sort of job?"

"You two are going after snipers tonight. Crawl through the first few rows of trenches and kill them silently."

"I thought the assault squads cleaned them out."

"They'll be back. They love the night."

"Corporal," Pancho said, "these pistols aren't silent, are they?"

"No. You don't want to use them except in an emergency. Take a few hand grenades; they're better.

"Here's what we're going to do." I liked that "we."

"At 2225 we'll fire a double star shell. Two bright flares. As soon as they burn out, get out of the bunker and down the path. You have five minutes of darkness."

"Unless the enemy shoots a flare."

"True. In which case you freeze, as you were trained. It's really quite hard to see a man if he doesn't move. In addition, you'll find a camouflage kit on the pistol belt. Rub the cream all over your face and hands and the back of your neck." He rattled something. "These pills both improve night vision and darken the whites of your eyes. Take one now." We did.

"How do we know when it's 2225?" I asked.

"You don't have watches? I'll throw a pebble into your bunker. If you hear a whistle instead—" He put a whistle to his lips and blew softly. "—that means it's called off."

"Why would they call it off?" Pancho asked.

"Need you more here; signs of a mass attack. Did your training cover how to kill a man with a knife?"

"They showed us." We didn't practice on each other.

"For this sort of thing the best way is to come up from behind, put your free hand over his mouth and nose, and then either go for the throat or the kidneys. Throat is an easier target but the kidneys'll stop him faster. You, with your big hands, you might just choke the dighter until he's unconscious, then finish him quietly.

"Noise is the main thing. It's likely you've got another sniper nearby. Maybe some sappers, too. Best to have one person stand watch while the other goes for the kill."

"But surely he will be hard to surprise," Pancho said. "Surely he is expecting something like this."

"Maybe not. We're sending out a TDU, one of your group who fired at the Field First Sergeant. He will be outfitted for commando work. But one of his boots squeaks, ever so slightly. After they kill him, they will be less watchful." Carefully shielding the flame, he lit a weed. "Also, it's best to attack while there's firing going on. Every now and then the gatling up on the top of the hill will spray the trenches with random fire. That's a good time to strike.

"There's another gatling covering the break in the barbed wire. He will hold his fire when you go through." He smoked for a few seconds. "Coming back. It's safest to wait until dawn. Wait in the slit trench. Hold up an armband and wave it. The gatling will let you through."

"But what about snipers?"

"There won't be any left, not if you do your job. But the gatling will lay down a field of fire, just in case."

"Is everybody down there a Blue?" I asked.

"Yes. We have some units in nomanland, but they're all over by the other hill. If you hear or see a group of men, it's probably a Blue sapper squad. Throw a couple of grenades at them, from hiding. If they're Reds, they're disobeying orders." Severe punishment, I thought. "Any other questions?"

"Just this," Pancho said. "Why us? This sounds like the sort of job you would give to experienced soldiers."

"I only have five mercies in my squad. I want to save them." He turned as if to go, then said: "Well, that's not the whole story. I shouldn't tell you this. You must have done something to get the Field First pissed. He asked me to put you on a dangerous assignment. Do well and you might get on his good side."

I wasn't sure being on his good side would be much of an improvement.

"Your friend, the other one, has a similar assignment."

That would be Miko. "He didn't say why?" I asked.

"I've told you too much. But no, he didn't. Good luck." He left.

We listened to him tiptoe away. "Not very promising," Pancho said.

"Sounds like they want to get rid of the evidence," I said. "Wonder what they have lined up for Alegria and Miko."

"Should we desert them?"

I hadn't thought of it that way. "We must. There's no chance for any of us unless we can get word to the Confederación."

"I suppose." I heard him settle in. "Wake me when you're tired."

I went back to the gunport and watched the scenery grow slightly more clear, as the pill took effect. But I was dazzled whenever a star shell burst. There wasn't too much action. The gatling down by the wire fired a few rounds once, and a sniper returned fire, but his bullet just ricocheted off the gun's metal shield. One flare caught a Blue in the open, and though several people fired at him, he managed to roll to the safety of a trench. His rifle looked larger than ours, with a heavy 'scope and a bipod near the muzzle: a sniper. So we would have at least one to contend with, or avoid.

O'Connor had given me an idea. If necessary, I *could* choke a sniper into unconsciousness, and still stop short of killing him. Though it would be better simply to sneak around them.

Pancho woke up on his own, and in whispers we outlined a preliminary plan.

Nomanland was a rectangle about two kilometers long by one wide. The longest close trench was the third one out, which would take us to within twenty meters of the perimeter of nomanland. We would go straight to the third trench and follow it all the way to our right; then get out and run for it. As far as we could tell, there wasn't even a strand of barbed wire there, though there might be alarms. They said that putting one foot outside of the perimeter was desertion; automatic death penalty. Maybe that was enough to keep most people inside, where the death penalty was at least delayed.

I don't think I slept for more than five minutes at a time, with flares and gunfire and terrible dreams waking me up. I was mortally afraid, and so was Pancho: in the light of one flare I saw him staring down at nomanland, his jaw muscles bunched with tension, rivulets of sweat beading on the dark camouflage paste.

Finally the double star shone, and a pebble rattled off the top of our parapet. We strapped on our pistols and knives and, as soon as the flares winked out, scrambled out of the bunker and made our way down the path as quickly and quietly as possible. Going through the barbed wire, I almost had a heart attack when the gatling opened up. But he wasn't shooting at us; it was support fire, evidently, to keep the enemy's heads down.

Pancho and I had both done a lot of hunting, so moving quietly was second nature. I felt terribly exposed, though, as we crept over the ten meters of open ground between the slit trench and the first of the main trenches. There were no flares, luckily, and we lowered ourselves into the trench without incident. We had to go to the left about a hundred meters, to get to the cross-trench.

We came to within about three meters of a sniper before we saw him. He was in a sort of alcove cut in the side of the trench, and he seemed totally absorbed in his business, luckily for us.

We couldn't risk sneaking behind him, though. I made a patting motion to signal Pancho to stay put, and in a couple of quick steps I was on the man. I clamped both hands around his throat and leaned into him, jamming him up against the wall so his thrashing wouldn't make too much noise. The only sound he made was a faint squeak, like a kitten. Eventually he stopped struggling, and went limp. I gave him a few more seconds and lowered him to the ground. I slipped the bolt out of his rifle and put it in my pocket, then motioned to Pancho.

There was another sniper just before the cross-trench. We started to handle him the same way, but when I grabbed his neck it was cold and slimy. He fell back against me and just as that moment a star shell went off and I stared at the jagged hole in his head. I let go of him instinctively and he fell with a heavy noise. We waited for an army to pounce on us but nothing happened.

We slipped into the cross-trench and moved as fast as we could. If our own gatling opened up we'd have no place to hide; they were right in line. There was a dead man in the middle of the trench, with a red armband. Maybe the TDU who had been sent out as a decoy. We didn't stop to investigate.

We hesitated at the intersection, where the cross-trench met the second trench, and that was a lucky thing. We heard footsteps. Several men were coming from our left.

They couldn't see us yet, because of the sawtooth pattern of the trenches (this gave you some protection from grenade blasts and prevented one squad, or one man with a gatling, from being able to hold an entire trench under fire).

We crossed quickly and flattened ourselves against the walls. Pancho had a grenade in his hand; I took one out, too. So much for the moral equation. But we didn't have to use them. They came within a few meters but never even looked our way. They turned down the cross-trench and moved quickly away from us. Six-man sapper squad.

Then a flare popped and the gatling opened up. Pancho and I jumped back into the crossroads and took shelter. The sapper squad was caught in the passageway. There were a couple of horrible screams and one man called out for a medic. The gatling kept firing until he stopped.

I wondered about Miko being out in all this, too. He couldn't be much better off than we were. He might even be alone. I didn't wonder very long, though. He'd have to take care of himself.

When the last flare died down we continued up the cross-trench. I fought the impulse to sprint. We'd seen how noise carried.

Third trench, right turn, half-a-klick to freedom. It was less likely that we'd run into snipers here, but we used the same caution: Pancho leading, he'd sneak forward a few meters and stop; then I, the larger target, would follow, watching him for hand signals.

We got to the end of the trench without any trouble. Evidently both armies were staying close to home tonight, good luck. We had a whispered conference and decided to stay in the trench until the next flare; when that died away we'd make a run for it.

It seemed to take forever, but finally a flare popped and we tensed for the run. In the lurid dancing light we could see a warning sign above the trench:

WARNING!

YOU ARE NEARING THE PERIMETER. TURN BACK NOW. PENALTY FOR LEAVING NOMANLAND IS DEATH.

The flare went out and we scrambled up and started running. After a few steps I felt a sharp pain in my chest. I barely had time to wonder about it when it got suddenly more and more intense, and brought me to my knees. Pancho stumbled to the ground beside me.

"My chest," he croaked. *"Dios!"*

"Me, too. Have to go back."

"Back?" He didn't have it figured out.

"Come on." As we crawled back the way we had come, the pain diminished, finally disappearing as we tumbled back into the trench.

"I think I understand," he whispered, panting. "They put something in our bodies."

"Yeah. And there's some kind of signal generated by the perimeter, sets it off."

"I'm sure it would have killed us if we'd gotten much closer." He shook his head. "What now?"

"Like Jake said. Stay alive for a couple of days. Then a couple of days more, I guess. Right now we have to stay alive till dawn."

"This is a safe place, here."

"I don't know. The longer we stay here, the more Blues

we'll have to pass to get back. Assuming they've sent more than two snipers and six sappers.''

''And if they haven't, we're safe anywhere,'' he said, somehow with a mix of hope and sarcasm in his voice.

I stood up. ''We'll go back half as fast, twice as quiet.''

''And try not to kill?''

''I guess—damn!''

''What is it?''

''I didn't take the bolt out of that dead sniper's rifle. When the one I choked wakes up, he'll just switch weapons.''

''If he stays. If I were him, I'd start easing back toward my own hill.''

We retraced our path in total silence, and didn't meet anyone. There were only five sappers' bodies in the corridor, but we found the sixth on the floor of the first trench. The dead sniper still had a bolt in his rifle; I removed it. The one I'd choked had disappeared.

I started to go over the wall but Pancho grabbed my leg. ''No, amigo,'' he whispered. ''We're safer from our own fire down here than in the slit trench.''

He was right. We settled into a niche there and all hell broke loose.

There were several muffled grenade blasts, all within a few seconds. Then sporadic rifle fire and the deeper, faster banging of pistols. People were screaming, shouting orders, calling for medics. Flares popped. There were people running all over the hill.

''Sappers,'' Pancho whispered.

Four men were running down the path, shooting back at our people with pistols. They ran through the barbed wire opening unscathed; they must have gotten the gatling bunker. They jumped the slit trench and ran toward us. Rifle bullets spit all around them.

They would hit the first trench a few meters from where we were. There was no way they could miss us.

''God forgive me,'' I muttered, and pulled the pin from a grenade, and hurled it at them.

My aim was good but my timing was bad. The grenade

hit one of them full in the chest. It bounced in front of him and, without breaking stride, he kicked it right back at us. It bounced once and fell in the trench between me and Pancho. It was close enough that you could hear the fuse sputtering.

I could have been a hero and thrown my body over it, to save Pancho. Or I could have been smart and jumped away, flattening with my feet pointed toward it (which is what Pancho did). Instead I was stupid, and picked it up.

My memory of it is in excruciating slow motion. As soon as I picked it up I knew I'd done the wrong thing. Then as I swung to throw it back at the advancing sappers, I knew I'd done the second wrong thing; I should have just tossed it down the trench a few meters, and the zigzag would have protected us.

It must have detonated about a meter away from my hand. It didn't hurt, just a big sting and a blinding flash, and I fell back on to the floor of the trench, right on top of Pancho.

I heard the sappers jump into the trench and then I heard someone cock a pistol, and someone else say Don't waste it he's dead. Then I heard the gatling start up and slowly fade away.

"Carl! Wake up! *Dios!*" I woke up to a sudden universe of pain: my chest and face felt like they had been chewed off and nailed back on. My right arm felt like it was being deep-fried.

Only one eye worked. I used it to look at my arm and almost fainted again. Thumb and forefinger were gone; middle finger was broken off and swung loose, held by a scrap of flesh. The whole arm looked like a skinned animal that had been flayed alive. Spurting blood.

Pancho was working on a tourniquet. Blood stopped spurting as I watched. "I have to go get help," he said. "Hold on to this knife." He guided my left hand to the trench knife he had used as a pivot for the tourniquet. "Don't try to sit up. You've got one eye out of its socket, I don't know what to do about that."

My mouth was so dry I couldn't talk. I tried to tell him to go on, I was dead, don't risk himself and a medic. But he was gone. I fell asleep again. Did Pancho give me a shot?

The next thing I saw was Alegria's face. She smiled. "You're going to be all right, Carl." I was in the aid station on the top of the hill. "You'll be able to use the hand in a week or so." My vision was blurred; I touched the bad eye and it was sore, but there.

"They put the eye back in. You looked pretty creepy when they brought you up." Her voice was shaking. I wondered if she'd cried.

"How's Pancho?"

"Hardly a scratch. And you can thank him for finding your thumb and finger, while you were waiting for the medics. You were lucky it . . . it all came off in one piece. That made the bone graft easy."

" 'Hardly a scratch'? He was hit, then."

"He was hurt a little when that grenade you were playing with went off. Just some scalp cuts, though; he didn't even notice them."

My senses were starting to come back. "Are we alone?" I whispered.

"Yes, we are."

"Look, they'll be sending me back to the main hospital, won't they."

"I suppose. . . ."

"I can escape! Find my way back to the Confederación."

"It's not that easy. Miko tried last night and they—"

I heard a door open.

"Can he stand up?" said a voice I couldn't place.

"I don't know, sir," Alegria said. "I don't think he should."

"Have him try." I rolled over on one elbow and levered myself up, then sat up on the bed. Oddly, only my eye hurt.

The voice belonged to Captain Forrestor. He was standing there with a pistol in his hand, loosely at his side.

Behind him were Pancho and Miko, their hands tied behind their backs, and Sergeant Meyer, behind them with a rifle.

I lowered my feet to the ground and stood up, groggy. Alegria held on to my good arm. "What's going on?" I said. "Sir?"

"You know what's going on. I'm sorry the surgeon wasted so much time on you last night. You'll die today.

"You and Private Bolivar did willfully try to desert last night. The sensors implanted in your chests identified you. If someone had awakened me I would have had you shot, and saved some trouble." He looked at Meyer sharply.

"In addition, there is the matter of Private Riley's attempt at desertion last night. That he got farther than either of you is only a tribute to his ability to withstand the pain of the sensors." Captain Forrestor half turned, gave Miko a cold glance. "Private Riley managed to reach the perimeter and deactivate a portion of the warning network. If he had kept going there is no doubt he could have escaped. Foolish as it may seem, he chose to return. If he had simply taken the woman he would have had no trouble. It was only when he attempted to rescue you that he was apprehended. Stupid loyalty. Pity they didn't kill him."

I looked at Miko. He averted his eyes and it was only then that I noticed the thin line of plastiflesh that covered half his face. His nose had been rebuilt.

"Therefore, I have good and substantial reason to believe that a conspiracy to escape exists among the four of you. I have but one reasonable course of action. You are all condemned to die." He raised his pistol. "Sergeant?"

Meyer leaned his rifle against the wall and picked up a thick roll of surgical tape. He bound Alegria's hands behind her back and bound mine in front, the good one against the one in a plastic cast. Then he taped everyone's mouths shut.

"Take them down to the wire and dispose of them with the gatling. Make a little speech first. We'll get *some* use out of them."

Meyer pushed us, not too roughly, out the door, and

followed us down the path to the bottom of the hill. Miko was beside me.

I felt stupid for all the things I had thought about him. There were things I had to tell him, important things. I'd never get the chance. I caught his eye and, somehow, I felt he understood.

"It's no consolation," said Meyer softly, "but I don't like doing this."

Pancho had worked a corner of the tape loose on his shoulder. "But you *are* doing it," he said, mumbling.

"To save my skin. I didn't wake that bumhole up last night because I figured any bumhole who can sleep through a sapper attack must really need his sleep.

"You might as well have the whole story. He got a request—not an order, a request—to send you four back to base camp. It seems some Confederación official made an inquiry about our recruiting procedures. About the four of you, specifically. There will be a hearing. He would rather you weren't alive to testify, which is why you had such interesting jobs yesterday. Your trying to escape only made it easier for him."

"We were kidnapped—so were you! Can't you see that setting us free could mean *your* freedom?"

"No. It would mean a bullet in the brain. Besides, we were *legally* kidnapped. I think he could solve the whole thing in court, in Confederación court. But he's an impulsive bumhole, and the Confederación scares him shizeless—what the hell is that?"

We were about halfway down the hill. There was a low warbling sound, full of nervous subsonics.

I had never seen a Confederación police cruiser before. A shiny black inverted bowl half the size of the hill we stood on. It settled down over the first three rows of trenches, gently as a dust mote. The top-mounted gigawatt laser swiveled to point toward us.

"WE DO SUBPOENA FIVE INDIVIDUALS: CAPTAIN HARVEY FORRESTOR, SPICELLE; ALEGRIA SALDANA, SELVA; FRANCISCO BOLIVAR, SELVA; CARL

BOK, SPRINGWORLD; AND MIKO RILEY, PERRIN.
COME FORWARD.'' It had the voice of a minor god.

"Shoot the dighters!'' Forrestor was on top of the hill,
waving his pistol. He fired; the bullet sang over our heads.

Meyer slammed a round home and pointed his rifle at
the officer. "Drop it, Captain! They'll fry us all!''

He kept the pistol pointed at us for a second and then let
it drop from his fingers. "Ramirez! Tulo! Sandiwell! Someone *do* something!''

All of the camp was staring from behind their bunkers.
Nobody raised a weapon. "Guess I better go with you,''
Meyer said. "Come along, sir.''

Keeping his eyes and rifle on Forrestor, he said, "Mor-
rison. Would you set these people free?''

After announcing that the war was temporarily suspended, the police vessel took us aboard, and in a few minutes
we were back at the spaceport in the capital city. Guards
armed with 'tanglers escorted us to a floater, and we were
taken to a tall building in the center of the city. Down a
lift to a corridor; down the corridor to an office. In the
office was a huge desk, bare except for four pieces of
paper—our enlistment forms—and three people: a Heller
with an ornate uniform that featured five stars, Dean
M'Bisa—and B'oosa!

The Dean flinched when he saw me. B'oosa said: "Still
have all your arms and legs, Carl. I'm surprised.''

The general said, "Who are you?''

"Sergeant Meyer, sir. I had to escort the—''

"I only asked who you were. You may leave.'' He
turned to us. "Sit down. You remain standing, Captain.''

He waited for us to sit. "Captain Forrestor, do you
realize you are guilty of a profound violation of the law?''
He just stared. "In connection with the recruitment of
these four individuals?''

"Sir, I bought them from—''

"Silence! I don't know how they got into your camp,
and I don't care.'' With a well-manicured forefinger he

pushed the documents two centimeters toward Forrestor. "This is what I'm talking about."

"They signed without coercion, sir."

"Well and good." He leaned forward and his voice dropped almost to a whisper. "But they are minors, Forrestor. Minors. They can't sign such an agreement without their parents' permission."

He turned to the two black men. "In this case, Dr. M'bisa, who is acting *in loco parentis*.

"It may not please you to know that we have already hanged one man in conjunction with this . . . terrible scheme. The sergeant who supplied these four to you. He kidnapped them, reported them killed in training, and collected a part of the insurance as well as an enlistment fee from you.

"You will have a chance to defend your own role in this affair, at a general court martial this afternoon. You are dismissed."

"But . . . General . . . everybody—"

"You aren't helping your case, Captain. Dis*missed*." The guards escorted him out the door.

When they were gone, the General said, "His confusion might be understandable. On his world, people reach their majority at eighteen. On Hell, it's twenty-five."

"Of course," M'bisa said.

"So it isn't a Confederación matter at all, though we are of course grateful for the help of Confederación officials in resolving it. The rest may be taken care of within the structure of the Universal Code of Military Justice." You could hear the capitals.

"Unless we should choose to press the matter," M'bisa said.

"Let me be frank." He indicated us with a sweep of his hand. "It happens that the same document is used for enlistment in the mercenary forces and enlistment in our military school system. Minors may sign the latter."

"But it's difficult to get out of, I assume," B'oosa said.

He nodded slowly. "Even if this is desired by the parents. The natural parents."

Dean M'bisa stood up, his posture and face showing his age. "I think we understand each other, General. Good day."

"Good day, citizens."

B'oosa had seen the whole thing, from behind a snowbank. He stamped out a message in the snow, in Pan-swahili. Not too many Hellers understand the language, but most Confederación employees do. A weather satellite picked it up, and he was rescued by the same vessel that rescued us.

I spent a day in a Hell hospital, where Earthie doctors worked on my hand and face. Then we went back to *Starschool* and left Hell behind. Dr. M'bisa announced that the planet had been dropped from the school's itinerary.

What did I learn there?

It's hard to sort out. I was already pretty well-educated in fear and pain and exhaustion. The animals were no stranger or more ferocious than the ones at home. Except the human animals.

I guess what finally comes out of it is something cold and dry, like The Perseverence of Institutions, or The Imperfectibility of Man.

Those Hellers were not less human than I was.

What keeps me up at night is the thought that they might be more human.

CONSTRUCT

Disclaimer

The preceding fourteen sections have outlined the various Tour stops, along with a tentative schedule. However, *Starschool* cannot guarantee that all of these stops will be made.

The political situation of some Confederación worlds is not stable from year to year. If prudence dictates, one or more stops may be skipped, according to the Dean's discretion.

There is also the possibility that new stops may be added, if in the Dean's opinion they offer unusual potential for learning. . . .

I

HELL DREW US together. After all we'd been through, we became a tight-knit little crew. It happens that way. Sometimes you have to get knocked around before you can see what was in front of you all the time. We had five different backgrounds from five different planets. We learned a lot from each other. I even came to an uneasy understanding with Miko, though there was still a little friction, on account of Alegria.

Even Dean M'Bisa seemed to show a little fondness toward us. Or maybe it was just that he was keeping an extra sharp eye on us to make sure we didn't get into any more trouble.

He needn't have bothered. Trouble was the last thing we wanted. As a matter of fact, we took great pains to avoid it. We were model students on Odalys, the planet-fall after Hell. Except for that small incident on the algae raft, we didn't cause any real difficulties at all. Well, hardly any.

Lately, we'd been too busy to get into trouble. Macroeconomics can get pretty complicated when you're dealing with planetary systems and we had a battery of exams looming on the near horizon. I'd been bashing my head against economic theories so hard I even dreamed about them. What a waste of perfectly good dreams. I hadn't been to the gym in over two weeks. As a matter of fact, I hadn't been anyplace except classes and study hall for a long time. Until today.

The Dean had called all the students to the auditorium. That in itself was unusual, since he made most of his announcements over the ship's intercom. I'd never even seen all the students aboard *Starschool* in one place before, not aboard ship. As I entered the auditorium, it was impressive. And noisy. Seemed like everyone was talking at once.

I scanned the crowd, looking for familiar faces. It was easy to pick out B'oosa; he stands out almost as much as I do. He was sitting with the rest of our friends. There seemed to be an empty seat, so I pushed my way through the milling students.

"Saved you a place, Carl," said Alegria, patting the chair beside her.

"Didn't think you were going to make it, amigo," said Pancho as I sat down.

"Even I know what compulsory attendance means," I said. "I'm busy enough without working off demerits."

B'oosa laughed. He could afford it, since he was holding up the high end of the curve in Macro. I was doing my best to keep the middle from collapsing. It was a struggle all the way.

"Any idea what the Dean's going to spring on us?" I asked.

B'oosa shook his head. "Whatever it is, it must be important."

"Nothing's more important than that Macro exam next week," I said.

"If you didn't put everything off until the last month, you wouldn't have so much trouble," Alegria said.

She had me there. What could I say? I always put things off until the last minute. A place as big as *Starschool* has a lot of diversions. I was as human as anyone else. More than some others, I guess.

The Dean entered and everyone took seats, quieted down. He walked purposefully to the lectern, adjusted his throat mike. Personally, I didn't think he really needed the amplification, having been on the receiving end of more than a few loud conversations with him. He looked deadly serious.

"Students, I'll keep this short and to the point," he said. "There's been an unexpected change in plans. We are no longer headed for Dimian. That stop on the tour has been cancelled due to a message we recently received. Our course has been changed. We estimate arrival at Construct in six days."

He paused to let that sink in. Construct!

"I don't need to tell you the importance of this. All classes are cancelled until further notice. You will begin planet-fall training immediately. Check your data-boards at your study terminals for all available information on Construct. I assure you it won't be a long listing." At that, he turned and left. The room was absolutely quiet as we sat in stunned silence.

Construct. An enigma wrapped in layers and layers of mystery. Proof that man was not alone in the universe.

"I guess that you can forget about that Macro exam," whispered B'oosa.

"That's the farthest thing from my mind right now," I said. That was *almost* true.

Construct. Mankind's touch-point with alien races, alien cultures. The Confederación kept a tight lid on whatever went on there. It was shrouded in mystery to such a degree it seemed almost a mythical place. But we were headed there! Us.

Construct.

■■

THE DEAN WASN'T kidding when he said the listing on Construct would be short. The truth was that we just didn't know much about it. Not even its real name.

It was an artificial planet, built maybe fifty thousand years ago. Maybe half a million. It circled a tiny red dwarf star that had no other planets. The view was stupendous, with the Orion Nebula sweeping over half the sky, but I guess nobody ever looked at it. They all lived inside.

Construct was really sort of a cross between a spaceship and a planet. Or maybe a senate and a zoo. It was a hollow sphere inside another hollow sphere inside etc., nineteen of them, the biggest six hundred kilometers in diameter, the smallest about a tenth that size.

It was built this way so as to provide economical artificial gravity by rotation. The different levels gave you higher gravity as you moved outwards, from about a one-third gee to about three gees. So everyone could be comfortable.

"Everyone" was 277 different species of intelligent life, from 246 different planets. Each had an area of Construct that duplicated the conditions of its home planet. Springworld wasn't duplicated there, but Earth was.

There were waterworlds and baked arid places where water was poison. High-gee frigid zones where they swam around in liquid ammonia. A half-gee shell was almost vacuum, just a wisp of chlorine for the barely mobile rocks who wove sculptures there.

Some of the ones who lived on Construct were more-or-less humanoid. Most of them were something else. We were warned that some weren't too easy to look at.

Like the Linguists, those who long ago built the planet. They were almost human; at least they had one head, two arms, two legs. But they were taller than me and impossibly skinny. Their white skin was covered with pulsing red veins. Their arms and legs had extra elbows and knees. Their eyes rolled instead of blinking; their mouths were toothless wide rubbery slits. They would be our guides.

This seemed to be what the Linguists *did*: introduce various species to one another and watch what happens. It was probably why they built Construct, though we couldn't be sure. It was hard to get a straight answer out of them.

Humans were invited to set up shop on Construct about ninety years ago. We had a couple of thousand xeno-biologists, xeno-anthropologists, xeno-you-name-its living there, studying and being studied by the other creatures' xeno-people. Except for scientists hand-picked by the Confederación, almost no humans ever got to Construct. The invitation to *Starschool* was a first. It was kind of unsettling.

We'd be working on Construct, but it would be an odd kind of work. Just walk around in small groups, with a Linguist, and talk—or try to talk—with the various aliens. The Linguists were slightly telepathic; they would pick up our nonverbal reactions, as well as translating back and forth.

Pancho and I went up to the observation deck to watch the docking. It was an eerie sight. At first, Construct was a dim slender red crescent hugging a circle of black. It expanded into a half-circle, blood-red, that grew larger second by second, to become a vast curved horizon. A black dot suddenly appeared, blossomed, became the mouth of a dark tunnel, and swallowed us.

After a minute of blackness we emerged into the central

sphere; a weightless, airless volume of pale blue light, radiating evenly from every direction. There were hundreds of spaceships parked inside, mostly of alien design, some much larger than *Starschool*.

"I wish we had had more time to prepare for this," Pancho said.

"Not that much to study."

"That is not exactly what I mean."

"What, exactly?"

"They'll be watching us. Closely. They haven't had very many humans to observe before. I'm afraid we'll do something wrong. We don't know what they expect of us. What if we offend someone, step on some creature's taboo?"

"That's a chance we'll have to take. We'll just have to be careful and keep our eyes open."

"I still wish we had a better idea of what to do."

"I guess we'll just have to be ourselves. They're probably expecting that."

"That's what I'm afraid of," said Pancho.

We were hovering over a docking platform that looked like it could hold five *Starschools*. When they built this place they sure weren't thinking small. Everything was on a scale that made even me feel like a midget.

A bell sounded and we reluctantly left the observation deck to join up with the rest of our group. From here on in, we'd be on our own.

"Are you ready for this?" asked Miko when we arrived.

"As ready as I'll ever be," I said. Miko was really excited at this. B'oosa was taking it in stride, like he took everything in stride. He was unflappable. Alegria kept her feelings pretty much to herself. She seemed a little awed.

The lights flickered once and a faint background hum I had hardly been aware of stopped. We must have completed docking. We stood around nervously for a few minutes. I noticed we tended to talk in whispers. Eventually Dean M'Bisa came over to us.

"They're ready for you," he said simply.

We left the ship through a large umbilical, pulling ourselves along in the zero-gee by grabbing what I guessed were handholds. They could have been tentacleholds for all I knew; there were lots of different shapes and sizes. Sort of a universal walkway, I suppose.

The air inside was fresh and clean, provided by Construct. I imagined it must have been the way the air once was on Earth. Mankind's home planet hadn't had an atmosphere that good in a long, long time.

When we emerged, we saw our first aliens. Linguists. Even though we were as prepared as possible and they were humanoid, it was still quite a shock. Their similarities to humans only emphasized their differences. In both obvious and subtle ways they were totally unlike us. When they walked, they moved in impossible directions. They held their bodies in a position just a little off-center, a position human bone structure wouldn't allow. One detached himself from the crowd and came our way. Seeing him up close, I shuddered. Even as I shuddered, I remembered they were telepathic and wondered if I'd made our first mistake.

"You may call me Guide," he said in perfect Panswahili. Perfect, that is, except for emotion. His voice was as flat as a machine's.

"My real name is not possible to duplicate, given the physiological parameters of your species. Half of it is 'spoken' on a telepathic level. I will remain with you during your stay. You may ask me questions. I will respond. At this time I will take you to the Earth level." He turned abruptly and we followed.

His voice may have been expressionless, but his face wasn't. The trouble was that his expressions didn't match what he was saying and his face was inhumanly mobile; seeing him smile or frown made your own face hurt.

The Linguist led us to a line of small cars. Sleds, he called them. They seemed to be nothing more than oddly shaped seats on a platform surrounded by a flimsy-looking shell. Each sled hovered about ten centimeters above a thin metal rod set in the floor. As we got in a transparent roof swung over us. In a pouch on each seat there were silver necklaces; Guide explained their function.

"Construct does not have many rules, but one rule never broken is the one of free access. Any being may visit any area; there are air locks to separate different environments, but anyone may pass from one to another.

"Of course, some of the environments are dangerous, or even toxic to you. Use the key on the necklace before you pass through any door. It will tell you whether you can survive unprotected on the other side."

"But it won't stop you from going?" M'Bisa asked. "Even if the environment will kill you?"

Guide covered his face with both hands and made a whistling sound. "Good joke," he said. "Strap yourselves in now."

We waited a few seconds while the stationary docking platform lined up with one of the transport tubes that were slowly rotating with the rest of Construct in front of us. They ran from the center to the edge of the artificial planet. Specific ones would take us to the Earth level. When it came by, we accelerated down it smoothly. The docking port dwindled away behind us.

"We will pass through seven levels before we reach yours," said Guide. "You may adjust your seat to any angle by using the lever on your left. Some species find our mode of transportation disconcerting."

Moving through the semidarkness, I couldn't understand what he meant. The transport tube was huge and substantial, no problem there. Beyond was the exposed gridwork of the planet, massive beams in some places, spiderweb-thin wires in others. Tubes and ductwork wove in and out of the complex structure. Most of Construct was composed of open spaces like this, some for storage, some filled with the machinery necessary to operate the planet. The living sectors were actually located only in an area sliced through the sphere at the equator. Even that was huge by any standards.

Ahead I could see a dim circle of light where the tube pierced the wall. The circle grew larger, slowly at first, then more quickly. Suddenly it rushed over us and we were through it.

Instant vertigo.

The "wall" we had passed through was actually the ceiling of the first inhabited level. We were looking straight down at the rocky floor several kilometers below us. I couldn't shake the feeling I was falling. Without hesitation, I reached for the lever. The seat swung around so that its back was to the floor of the sled and I was facing out through the tube. It was quite an improvement. I noticed the others had done the same, all except Guide.

The level we were in was gigantic. It must have been a good twenty kilometers from the roof of the sky to the floor of the ground. On the far horizon I could just barely make out another tube like ours. The ground was covered with jagged rocks, no signs of buildings anywhere, or at least nothing I recognized as a building. We were still fairly high up, but I searched the ground looking for aliens. I nearly missed them when they came. They were in the air.

They hung like faint gossamer curtains in the air around us, expanding and contracting with a regular rhythm. Their edges seemed blurred and indistinct, and they moved with a graceful undulating motion. One drifted toward the tube below us, flattened itself against the transparent surface. It extended its edges around and completely circled the tube. In an instant we were past it. All I could see was a blur of pastels rushing by. I wondered if it was trying to say hello or trying to eat us. Could have been anything.

"What was that?" asked Miko.

"They are Whisps from the planet known as K'allsón," said Guide. "Some say they are great composers of music, though it is not to my taste. You would not be able to hear it, as they communicate on a frequency far beyond that which you are equipped to receive."

We were getting closer to the ground now. It seemed to be coming toward us faster. Overhead the Whisps had drifted away from the tube and were sailing across the sky like fragile pastel clouds. The ground rushed up and in an instant we had popped through to the next level.

At first there wasn't much to see, as we were in a heavy

cloud layer. But the clouds were orange and they bubbled and churned like some evil brew. Chances are it would be just as deadly, too. At least to us humans.

We broke through the clouds and a yellow crystalline world unfolded below us. As far as it was possible to see, the landscape was an uneven, jagged mass of sharply pointed crystals oriented in every conceivable direction. Some were incredibly massive, towering a kilometer or two into the air, branching off in impossible directions and angles. It looked like some complicated chemical solution left to dry. The bottom of their world resembled a petri dish covered with a sulphurous crystalline residue. I couldn't see any aliens, nor any buildings to house them.

"You won't be able to see the Clingers," said Guide. Was he reading my mind? "Their bodily structure is that of a thin, flexible film the same color as everything else on their planet. Their lives are spent in contemplation. They are excellent theoretical mathmaticians and dabble occasionally in other sorts of philosophy. They have produced no artifacts, yet their thought processes are quite interesting. Without a Linguist you would be unable to communicate with them. As it is, you cannot exist in this area without a life-support system. The atmosphere is highly caustic."

As the ground rushed up to us, I thought I caught a glimpse of another color. It went by too fast for me to get a good look, but it seemed to be grey. Then it was gone and we were enclosed in darkness.

"The inhabitants of this level have requested privacy from casual observers. To this end they have opaqued the tubes which pass through their domain. This is within their rights. They must still, however, provide open access to all who take the trouble to enter."

Next we passed through an area filled with reddish fog. The aliens living there looked like they had their insides on the outside. Nauseating.

The next sector seemed to be one big city, or at least that was what I guessed its function was. It spread out over ten kilometers, an interconnected maze of ramps and what seemed to be walkways. What I took to be buildings were large round structures joined by the ramps. From up high it looked like one of those models they use to teach molecular science. I didn't see what the aliens who lived there looked like. Probably just as well; I was getting overloaded with sensations totally different from anything I'd ever encountered. It would take a while to sort them all out.

In that respect, it was a relief to pass through another opaque area. It was followed by a waterworld that teemed with life of all sorts, most of it big, ugly, and full of teeth.

Then we entered Earth, an Earth that probably hadn't existed for several hundred years. The first thing that hit me as I gazed down from the top of the sky was how cool and peaceful everything looked. Green was the predominate color, from the forests to the fields. A river cascaded from the distant hills to a central valley below us. Where the tube hit the ground, there was a small city, modern and clean. What this sector cost in terms of energy was staggering to think about. Multiply this by all the other habitats in Construct and you have some idea of the massive expenses involved.

We came to a smooth, soundless halt at a loading platform. Somehow I felt a sense of relief, almost a feeling of being home, although this imitation Earth had no resemblance at all to Springworld. What was familiar was form and function. Everything was built to human scale and human needs. I could tell what almost everything was meant to do, unlike all those alien worlds where I could only guess.

We left the tube and gathered in a large room overlooking the loading dock. Other groups from *Starschool* were arriving now, each with their accompanying Linguist. From there we took a lift to the upper level of the building where the dorms were. The room they gave us looked comfortable, spacious in comparison to what we were used to on the ship, with an impressive view of the city and tube, with the fields and forests beyond. So much green.

"You are free to come and go as you please during your

stay here," said Guide. "There are no restrictions save those you choose to impose upon yourselves."

"How do we get around?" asked Miko, anxious as always.

"Everything on Construct is at your disposal. This is true for all the beings on this planet, regardless of their intentions."

I waited for him to explain, but he didn't. "Do we use the sleds?" I asked.

"You may," he said. "If you desire."

"Do you drive us around?"

"If you desire."

He wasn't giving us any direct answers. I thought of something else.

"Can we drive ourselves?" I asked.

"If you desire," he said. I felt like I was caught in a computer loop.

"How do we operate the sleds?" I asked. It seemed like a pretty direct question to me.

"Like everyone else," he said and left it at that. I was beginning to understand how the humans could have been here so many years and still not know much about the Linguists.

"It is preferable to form small groups in order to experience as much as possible," said Guide. "Your time here is limited and should be utilized to the fullest extent. Impressions can be shared, but time cannot be expanded."

We talked it over and decided it would be a good idea to split up. Pancho was going with me, B'oosa and Alegria would go together, and Guide would go with the Dean and Miko. Miko seemed to be impressed that the Dean had chosen to stick with us, but I was a little chagrined. It looked like he was keeping a close eye on us.

I felt a little old to be carrying around my own personal babysitter.

III

PANCHO AND I started out by checking out the Earth sector. Even though the city was fairly small, it looked like it could easily hold five or six times the number of people currently stationed there. Everyone wanted to talk with us, catch up on the latest gossip from Earth and the other planets. I hadn't seen much of Earth outside the stadium walls, but that didn't seem to matter much. I think they were glad just to see a few new faces.

We were sitting with Carlos, an engineer from Earth, on a veranda overlooking the river. He'd been on Construct two years. The view was fantastic.

"How do we get around to the other sectors?" I asked. We were pumping him for information as much as he was pumping us.

"Didn't they tell you kids anything?" He looked amused.

"Our Linguist wasn't what you would call full of facts," said Pancho.

"That explains it," said Carlos. "I should have guessed. Most of what I've picked up around here has come from other people. Hard to get anything at all out of one of those Linguists."

I nodded. That was an understatement for sure.

"You use the sleds," said Carlos, leaning back and putting his feet on the table between us. "Just insert your key in the slot at the front of the sled. This activates it and programs the right atmosphere. Single stick by the front seat controls it. Push it forward to go, pull it back to stop. Simple.''

''What's the key and where do we get one?'' asked Pancho.

Carlos just shook his head and tapped the slender metal rectangle dangling from his necklace. ''Key,'' he said. Pancho and I were both wearing one.

''They didn't tell us,'' I said.

''Wouldn't have expected them to,'' he said. ''I gather you're supposed to fish around and find out everything the hard way. That's the way it was with all of us.''

''We don't have much time,'' said Pancho.

''I can help you some, but not a whole lot. Construct has more questions than answers. Did your Linguist explain *anything* about the necklaces?''

''Not much,'' I said. ''Just about using it to check before entering a level.''

''That's only one of its uses; activating the sleds is another. The key is also a kind of communication device. It will connect you with your Linguist, if your Linguist happens to be nearby. Otherwise, it's kind of a simple computer. You can ask it questions and it'll answer as best it can. They're kind of dumb, though. I wouldn't—''

He was interrupted by the arrival of an alien—a short, multi-armed creature covered with loose folds of brown and white spotted skin. Carlos seemed glad to see him, and as the creature settled into a chair, he introduced us.

The alien's name was roughly One-Who-Looks-And-Finds. He was from the planet Savrot and occupied a sector in the one-g level adjacent to Earth's. He had been on Construct for fifty Earth years—a short time by Savrotian standards—and could speak passable Pan-swahili, though his voice was rough and hollow, like a dog barking.

''We know more about Look/Find's culture than anyone else's,'' said Carlos. ''Our atmospheres are pretty similar, which helps a lot.''

''We also do not look at each other as food items,'' said

Look/Find. "That too helps." He made a noise like a drawn-out growl. I took it to be an expression of humor since Carlos was laughing.

"What can we do for you, Look/Find?" asked Carlos. "I know you too well to think you came over just for the pleasure of my company."

"I am looking and I have found. We heard about the students and are curious. Can you lend us some?"

"Students aren't the kind of things we lend," said Carlos. "They can go with you if they want to."

The alien turned to us. "Will you go with me?" he asked. "We are interested in students."

I looked at Pancho. Seemed as good a place to start as any. "Sure," I said.

We went down to the loading dock and took the first sled in line. Look/Find showed us how to activate them. There really wasn't much to it. When the sled was ready, the top flipped open and we climbed in. Since Look/Find had used my key—in what appeared to be a matter of courtesy on his part—the atmosphere was Earth-normal.

"We take a transverse pathway," he said, starting the sled in motion. "They run underneath every level and connect with the vertical tubes."

Once we left the loading dock, there wasn't much to see, just a lot of metal struts and braces. Tubes, ducts, and wires ran in every direction. It was like being inside some giant, complicated machine. I had to really concentrate to realize that the ground of Earth was just above my head and someone else's sky was right below us. Soon the light became brighter and we entered another loading area. A vertical tube ran at right angles to our path. The docking area was different, much simpler than the one at the Earth sector. We left the sled and started for the entrance, an airlock arrangement not too different from those I was used to. We started to follow Look/Find through, but he stopped us.

"Even though this level is safe for you, it is good to obtain the habit of inserting your key before entering anyplace." He showed us the slot.

I inserted my key and when I removed it, it was flashing green. It spoke to me and I was so surprised I nearly dropped it.

"The physiological constraints of your species allow you to remain in this sector for an unlimited period of time without irreversible damage." It spoke a clearer Pan-swahili than Look/Find.

I grinned sheepishly at Pancho, who inserted his key after mine. He looked so superior and smug when it talked to him—like he'd expected it to do that all along—that I almost broke out laughing. We followed Look/Find through the airlock and into his sector.

I don't know what I'd expected to find in the Savrotian sector; a city maybe, a village. I'd tried to keep an open mind about that. But nothing prepared me for what we walked into.

It was a steaming jungle, hot and humid, with a thick atmosphere that smelled like yesterday's garbage. I started sweating immediately. There were no signs of civilization at all, just plants and trees. Lots of them, all strangely shaped. They completely surrounded the small clearing we were standing in, intertwined so tightly they seemed to be a solid wall.

"Welcome to Savrot," said Look/Find. "This is not quite like our home planet, but a very close approximation."

"It looks . . . uh . . . pleasant," said Pancho, not believing any such thing. I wondered if Savrotians could read human facial expressions.

"We find it accommodating," said Look/Find. "You will please to follow me." Making good use of his multiple arms he scampered into a tree and disappeared into the dense vegetation.

"How are you at climbing trees?" I asked Pancho.

"I think we're about to find out," he said, walking to the nearest tree. Its bark was smooth, not much to grab at. "Give me a boost, will you?" he said.

Standing on my shoulders he could just barely reach the lowest limb. With a great deal of commotion he pulled himself up. About that time Look/Find reappeared and dropped a vine down to me.

"Apologies are mine," he said as I climbed up. "I had forgotten you are not used to our ways." We awkwardly made our way balanced on interlocking tree limbs into the jungle. It was like being on another world.

"At home we are more comfortable in the trees," explained Look/Find. "You will please to make allowances."

I could see what he meant. The tree limbs formed a huge maze above the ground. It wasn't too difficult to get around, provided you had lots of hands to steady yourself. Look/Find moved easily, even gracefully, his arms in constant motion.

Below us the jungle floor was a twisted mass of dangerous-looking plants. Everything seemed to be covered with an assortment of brambles, thorns and barbs. Needle-sharp spines stuck up everywhere. No wonder they kept to the trees.

Something in the brambles caught my eye. It was grey, half-hidden in the undergrowth. I stopped, tried to get a better look in the dim light. As I watched, it moved.

"What's that?" I said. "It looks dangerous."

Look/Find stopped, hanging by three arms from a sturdy branch.

"There is nothing dangerous on our planet," he said. "What is it that you see?"

I pointed out the creature to him. It had moved into sight now. It had a hard, chitinous shell and several complicated, multijointed arms, some of them coming to points like claws. If it wasn't dangerous, I sure didn't want to meet anything that was. Several bulbs I took to be eyes peered out from armored projections in its carapace.

"We call them Hardshells," said Look/Find. "They live on another level. Your friend Carlos-From-Earth calls them Lobsters. Only the Linguists can pronounce what is assumed to be their actual name. It involves the clacking of mandibles and is most difficult to reproduce. Nothing is known of them."

"Nothing at all?" asked Pancho.

"Nothing. They do not communicate, at least not in a way that has been determined. They seem to be content to sit and watch. Every level has one or more of them. They do nothing. They say nothing. Nothing is known of them except that physically they are very weak. They are easily immobilized by falling limbs or trapped in the tangles of our plants. We free them when this occurs. How they exist in so many varied conditions on all the levels is unknown. They have never been seen to eat. This one has been on this level for ten of your years."

"They give me the creeps," said Pancho.

"What are creeps?" asked Look/Find. "That is not a word I know."

"Creeps. Shivers. They frighten me."

Look/Find gave that silly growl of his. Seemed to find something funny about that.

"You humans have many strange words and concepts. To be frightened you must have fear. To have fear in that way implies what you call 'conflict' or 'strife.' A terribly confusing concept. We have no understanding of that."

"I thought conflict was pretty basic," said Pancho.

"Perhaps it is to you humans, but not to all species. We have no 'enemies' on Savrot. We are vegetarians: all our food comes from the trees. We have never had what you would call 'opposition,' therefore we have had no 'strife.' I hope I have used those words in a correct fashion. Their definitions are not clear to me."

"I'm not sure they're clear to any of us," I said, thinking of the many times in my life that enemies had become friends and friends had become enemies. Not to mention all the times that strife and conflict had existed only in my head.

He looked at us for a moment. I tried to read his expression and failed. There was very little human about this creature in spite of his ability with our language.

"We proceed in an upward direction from here," he said, lifting himself up.

Actually, moving up was no harder than moving sideways. We were always surrounded by the branching tree limbs. All we needed were a couple extra arms. A tail wouldn't have hurt either. The ground dropped far below us. There seemed to be no end to the towering jungle.

I lost track of how far we climbed. My muscles ached and I could imagine what it felt like to Pancho with his shorter arms and legs. He didn't complain, though. He was probably as cúrious as I was, maybe more so. Getting used to the air was another matter entirely. It *still* smelled like rotting garbage.

"We're almost there," said Look/Find from five or six meters above us. As I looked up toward him I could see the bottom of a large platform. It seemed to be made out of tree limbs lashed together. Primitive, but substantial. It didn't take us long to get there.

I was surprised at how large the platform actually was. The end of it was lost in the branching tree limbs, but the part I could see as we reached it covered an area more than twice the size of *Starschool*'s gym.

Up close it was even more primitive than I had imagined. There was nothing metallic in sight; everything was made out of wood of one kind or another. Vines lashed together oddly shaped tables and chairs, formed flimsy partitions to set off rooms. There was no roof. Several Savrotians were waiting for us. Look/Find went over to them and spoke rapidly in what I assumed was their native language. He came back to us.

"These are Elders. Most of them are also Teachers. Although my job is finished—I have looked for you and I have found you—I will remain to translate. The Elders do not have much contact with humans and are not comfortable with your language." Several of the Savrotians started talking at once, an unintelligible clatter of sounds. Look/Find cocked his head, a remarkably human gesture. "They have many questions," said Look/Find. "I am sure that you have some. A balance will be sought for exchange of information."

I *did* have a lot of questions, and I'm sure Pancho had some, but we didn't get a chance at first.

"Since they are Teachers and you are Students, they

are naturally curious about you. They want to know when
you will Change.''

"Change?" asked Pancho.

"When will you stop being Students and Change into
something else? They hope it will be soon. They would
like to watch."

"I don't think we ever really quit being students," said
Pancho.

"I do not understand," said Look/Find. "The concept
of a perpetual Student is contradictory."

"I think what Pancho means is that we never stop
learning."

"But what does that have to do with being a Student?
Surely you must undergo the Change."

"I don't understand what you mean by change," I said.
"And I don't think you understand students."

"I understand Students," said Look/Find. "I was once
a Student, though of course I don't remember that time of
my life. I couldn't be a Seeker if I hadn't been a Student
first."

"Maybe we should talk to a student," said Pancho.

Look/Find did his growl laugh and translated for the
other aliens. Soon everyone was laughing except Pancho
and me. He shrugged his shoulders, as confused as I was.
It sounded like feeding time at the kennels.

"We will take you to our Students," said Look/Find,
leading us across the platform. "You may talk with them
if you desire." He laughed again.

We entered a large room partitioned off by vines. There
were no aliens in sight, only a bunch of large leather cases
suspended from the overhanging branches. One of the
cases moved. Then another. They seemed almost alive.

"There are our Students," said Look/Find.

"Students?"

"Yes. Those-Who-Are-Learning. Students. It is a stage
of our life just as it is a stage in your life. We must
be Students to learn. Then we Change and take our
work/name."

One of the other aliens walked to one of the suspended

cases. I guess they might have been cocoons. He growled and Look/Find translated.

"He will show you the Teaching and sing the songs of learning. Perhaps it will induce a Change. This Student is nearly ready."

The alien approached the cocoon and spread his folded skin. On the underside of the folds were thousands of small discs like suction cups. In the center of each disc was a tiny barb. He wrapped himself around the cocoon and attached himself to it. Then he started a rhythmic series of grunts and growls in a low, soft voice.

"He is singing to the Student, Teaching it what it will need to know as an adult. It will be a Builder/Forager, skilled in woodworking and gathering food. The Student sings back as it learns, but that can only be felt as vibrations through the growing-sac. The Teacher is also injecting the growing-sac with nutrients and a fluid that helps transmit knowledge."

The "song" grew louder and louder. It raised in pitch until it hurt my ears. Sounded more like an animal whining than any kind of language. The cocoon was writhing around now, twisting on the strand that suspended it from the branch.

"Fortune is yours," said Look/Find. "You are about to see a Change."

Suddenly the cocoon burst open, spilling a greenish fluid on the floor. A pale white mass slid to the ground. It took me a moment to realize it was a partially developed Savrotian.

"He has Changed, now he can grow," said Look/Find as two aliens carried off the small wet bundle.

One of the Teachers walked tóward me, spreading the folds on his skin. I got a good look at those suction cup things with the sharp points inside. Too good. They looked dangerous. I backed away.

"He would like to Teach you," said Look/Find. "It is considered to be a great honor. If possible, he would induce a Change in you so that we may observe." ·

It took some fast talking to get out of that one. Eventually I convinced them that their Students were just a whole lot different from our students. Once I got this across their Teachers lost interest in us. Look/Find apologized for their lack of interest, but not for the problem about the definition of student. I couldn't shake the feeling that he still didn't understand and was kind of disappointed he couldn't see us Change.

As he led us back down through the trees he explained a little about their home planet. They had no enemies and food was abundant and easy to get. The weather on Savrot was remarkably constant—always warm and calm. Consequently, they'd never developed much in the way of a technological society. Hadn't needed to. Everything on their planet was there for the taking. Competition in any form was unheard of. They didn't have the background to understand the concepts of war and strife.

Personally, I didn't think they had much of a handle on "student," either.

Making our way toward the exit, I caught a glimpse of the Lobster in the underbrush. Ten years in one place seemed like a long time to me, but I had no idea what their life spans were like. I could swear it was watching us.

When we arrived at the airlock, Look/Find showed us how to call for a sled using the key. We said our goodbyes, and when a sled came we got into it.

The first thing I did was take several breaths of the clean air. After the foul atmosphere in the Savrotian sector, it was pure pleasure just to breathe again.

"That was close, amigo mio," said Pancho as we strapped ourselves in. "I thought you were in line for an early graduation back there."

"It was just a misunderstanding," I said, feeling a little embarrassed by the whole thing.

"A misunderstanding like that can kill you," he said.

"Where do we go from here?" I asked, anxious to change the subject.

Pancho looked at his digital. We had a couple hours before we were due back at the dorm. "Let's just look around," he said.

"Suits me." I shifted the position of the lever beside me and we started moving.

The first two places we stopped didn't work out. The key casually informed us we would suffer immediate irreparable physical damage if we entered. It didn't try to stop us, though.

We wandered around and eventually found a promising sector on the 0.8-g level. The key told us we would be able to stay a week without being harmed. Seemed like a good, safe bet. We entered the airlock together.

Even before the inner door opened, I had an uneasy feeling that something was wrong. It was a vague sensation, though, nothing I could put my finger on. The inner door opened and we stepped inside. The uneasy feeling intensified.

We faced a desolate landscape. The earth was barren and scorched, covered here and there with clumps of dead grass. Gnarled trees stood in sharp relief against the pale, cloudless sky. Everything seemed to be tattered, old, dying. There were no aliens in sight.

This world was depressing, not only from a human viewpoint, but from any way I could imagine. It spoke of death, of pain, of loss. It spoke of once grand things now gone forever. Life became death, beauty became chaos. It all led to this, a scarred world of infinite sadness and broken dreams.

I choked back a sob: it affected me that much. I could *feel* the promise this land once held, now gone for all eternity. I stood at the edge of a dead and dying race and it filled me with sadness.

A song entered my mind, a song without words, a song without music. It sang of the glories of a race much older than mankind. A populous, far-flung race that had touched more star systems than there were people on Springworld. They'd had their eons of splendor, centuries of golden life. It was gone now, a mere flash in the endless fabric of time, hardly noticed, hardly remembered. Their dreams were dust scattered in the wind.

I thought of mankind as the song of futility filled my

head. Was it always this way? Did it always crumble and fall?

The answer came: *yes*.

Battered dreams, crumbled hopes. All dust and ashes.

I turned to Pancho. He was sobbing openly, tears running down his cheeks. He, too, heard the song.

It is the only song there is.

I wiped the tears from my eyes, tried to talk. The words caught in my throat. I grabbed Pancho, pushed him back toward the airlock. He didn't protest. He was far beyond that. It took all my will to simply slip the key in the door. I was torn, drawn to the song of inevitable death. It grabbed at the very fabric of my soul, drawing me in, trying to destroy me. The door slid open. With a last desperate move, I entered, dragging Pancho along with me.

The door slid shut and the song stopped. Yet even though the song was no longer being sung, it echoed through my mind with unbelievable intensity. Pancho just sat on the floor, eyes full of despair. We sat for a moment as if in shells, numbed by what we had been through, wrapping our emotions tightly around us. The sled was still there.

We entered it silently and drove back to the dorm without speaking.

*   *   *

Alegria's excitement helped drive away the overpowering despair that Pancho and I felt. She and B'oosa had been to a sector inhabited by butterflylike creatures with voices that tinkled like bells or rang like chimes depending on the speaker and the emotion. Their world was light and airy, their structures incredibly fragile looking, yet more substantial than permasteel. Even B'oosa had dropped his aloof attitude. He had clearly been impressed.

Pancho and I asked Guide about the second sector we had visited, the one that so unsettled us.

"That is the realm of the Talubar. Did you enjoy your stay there?"

"No," I said. "It was depressing. Frightening." I explained to the others what we had seen, how it had affected us.

"That is the reaction most life forms experience in that sector," said Guide. "It is inhabited by a single Talubar, the last individual of his race. His existence is maintained by a complicated life-support system in such a way that he is not likely to die for several centuries. He tends to be quite melancholy. This is compounded by the fact that he is a projecting empath. Many visitors to that level have committed suicide." He covered his face and whistled again. "They make good joke, acting like animals."

"It didn't seem like a joke to me," I said. "It was an overwhelming experience."

"You humans lack a finely developed sense of humor. Do not feel badly about that, it is typical among the younger, more primitive races."

I had a few questions about a race that snickers about death and sadness, but I kept them to myself. Miko started talking about a place he'd been, a cold world of ice and slush. He was telling us about the people that lived there when something suddenly occurred to me.

Dean M'Bisa was missing!

Miko was talking as if he and Guide had been alone all the time. I knew for a fact the Dean had gone with them. I interrupted Miko the first chance I got.

"Where's the Dean, Miko?" I asked. "Didn't he come back with you?"

Miko looked at me with a funny expression on his face. "He didn't come back with me, I thought he went with you."

I looked at Pancho. He was staring at Miko, not believing what he was hearing.

B'oosa spoke up. "We all saw him leave with you and Guide. What happened?"

Miko seemed confused. "I . . . I don't remember," he said. "I'm not sure. I think he was with us at the beginning, that much I know. I seem to remember he was with us part of the time and not during the rest of the time.

Maybe he went somewhere by himself. I just thought he had gone to find you two or maybe he had something else to do. There was some reason for him to be gone, I've forgotten exactly what it was. It must have been good, though, because it seemed natural that he wasn't there. I didn't worry about his absence until just now."

B'oosa turned to the Linguist. "Where is the Dean?" he asked.

"I cannot tell you things that you should find out by yourselves," said Guide.

"He left with you, right?" I asked him.

"Yes."

"Did he return with you?"

"No."

"Then he must have left somewhere along the way," I said.

"That is a reasonable assumption."

"Where?"

"I might know the answer to that or I might not. At any rate, I cannot tell you things that you should find out by yourselves."

"Did he leave of his own free will?" asked B'oosa.

"That is a reasonable assumption."

Guide was evading the question again. "Was he forced to leave?" I asked. "Was it against his will?"

"That is also a reasonable assumption."

"I don't understand," said Pancho. "Which is correct? Did he go someplace else or was he kidnapped?"

"I cannot tell you things that you should find out by yourselves," repeated Guide.

"If somebody took him, don't you have an obligation to at least tell us about it?" asked B'oosa.

"You humans have odd ideas about obligation and duty," said Guide. "They are not consistent. If another race desired to kidnap the entity known as Dean M'Bisa would you say that I had an 'obligation' to help them?"

"Of course not," said B'oosa.

"But that is precisely where your train of so-called logic leads. If I am assumed to have an 'obligation' to help one race, then I should have a similar 'obligation' to help all other races.''

"But this is different," said Pancho. "Kidnapping is wrong.''

"You humans also have strange ideas about right and wrong. These terms are ambiguous and subject to highly personal interpretations. We prefer to dispense with them entirely.''

"But kidnapping is illegal, against the law," said Pancho.

"You do not understand. There are no laws here, no rules save those you impose upon yourselves. Therefore there are no laws to be broken. It is that simple.''

It didn't seem simple to me, but that didn't help much. The Linguists seemed to have everything pretty much their own way.

We talked with Guide—argued with him, really—for almost an hour. We got nowhere. He wouldn't tell us anything. Finally he left and we discussed it for another hour. I was ready to go look for M'Bisa, but Pancho was afraid that if he wasn't really missing and we went poking around after him, we'd end up in big trouble. Miko was totally confused about what had happened. Possibly someone—*or something*—had manipulated his memory of the day. After experiencing the sadness projected by the Talubar, I was willing to believe anything was possible on Construct.

B'oosa suggested that we wait and see if he came in during the night. That way if we had to go find him at least we'd all be rested. It sounded like a good idea.

I got very little rest. What fitful sleep I found was troubled, filled with the heartbreaking dreams of a dying race.

IV

MORNING CAME, and still no Dean. The terminal in our dorm room was crammed with messages for him; he'd missed several evening appointments. It had to be foul play.

The five of us sat down and sketched out a rough plan. We would go back to Level 8, which was where Miko's memory got fuzzy. The Dean was definitely *not* with him when he left the Kaful area there, though he may have been with him when he entered. We also might be able to find out from the Kafulta where they had gone before. Guide was no help, of course. (B'oosa: "There must be some record of where we go during these excursions." Guide: "Probably.")

Helpful or not, Guide was waiting for us at the loading dock. It was a short trip up to Level 8, 0.7-g; our keys told us we could survive indefinitely in the Kaful region, if we were careful of the gravity holes.

The Kafulta were gliders. Their torsos and heads were humanoid, but their arms and legs were skeletal members a couple of meters long, supporting floppy membranous wings. They used gravity holes to get around.

Miko explained. "It's something like the artificial gravity we use aboard *Starschool*, but greatly miniaturized. Every twenty or thirty meters there's a cube marking a gravity hole; the color of the cube tells how strong the gravity is. They use the holes the way a bird uses air currents, sort of. They gather speed by falling into it, then spread their wings and lift themselves out. Very graceful.''

"But dangerous to us," Pancho said.

Miko shrugged. "We have to stay away from the holes. They're five or ten gravities; if you tried to walk over one you might break both legs, or worse.''

But there didn't seem to be much danger of walking over one unawares. The Kaful area was all formal garden, ornate beds of flowers and sculptured hedges. The gravity holes were isolated in the middle of large circles of polished rock, like marble.

The air was damp and heavy with perfume. Hundreds of tiny suns glared from the ceiling: the Kafulta's home was in the middle of a globular cluster, and they lived in perpetual light. It was inhumanly bright but chilly.

There were dozens of Kafulta drifting within sight of us—Miko said that's all they do, "fly and think"—and eventually one spotted us. He folded his wings in and dropped headfirst, catastrophically fast. Close to the ground, the wings snapped open; he arced back up, slowing, to pause overhead, then spilled air and floated down to join us. Guide translated.

"Back with friends, Miko . . . should we be flattered?''

"I did want them to admire your beauty," he said tactfully, "but we're also seeking another friend, who is lost. Tell me, did I come in here alone yesterday?''

"Have you lost your memory?''

"Something like that happened. Was there anybody with me besides Guide here?''

"No, not when I talked with you. But I don't know how long you'd been here. If you had a companion, he could have wandered away.''

"Are there any other humans here now?" B'oosa asked.

"I can easily find out." The Kafulta stepped away from us, took a short run and sprang into the air. He beat his wings a couple of times and spiraled down into a gravity hole, then banked out and upwards. I lost sight of him in the brightness overhead.

"I guess he's taking a look around," Miko said. Suddenly there was a terrible shrieking, a high-pitched squeal loud enough to make me wince.

"He is communicating," Guide said. "The creatures are not telepathic." The shriek was echoed, more and more faintly, as other Kafulta relayed the message.

"What are they saying?" Miko asked.

The Linguist looked at him, his eyes rolling back in a slow blink. "Exactly what you should expect. If you know the creatures at all."

"He is a regular mine of information," Pancho said. "An inexhaustible well."

Less than a minute later, the answer came back around, a single syllable hoot. The Kafulta returned.

"You are the only humans here," he said. "And no one saw any but you yesterday, Miko. So your friend must have been lost before you got here."

"I was afraid of that," Miko said. "When we talked yesterday, I didn't happen to mention where we'd been before, did I?"

"Let me think." The alien flapped his wings and shot up a couple of meters, and settled quietly to the ground, folding up into a complicated pile of bony limbs. "You didn't say. But you had evidently walked here—no sleds stopped at the dock; I would have noticed—and the fur on top of your head was damp. From this I deduce that you came from the Bawex region."

B'oosa checked the diagram of this level. "That's right across the corridor we were just in." He looked at the Linguist but didn't say anything. "Let's go check it."

We thanked the Kafulta and left. When we stepped out into the neutral air of the corridor I realized I'd been half holding my breath against the cloying flowery atmosphere. As we approached the Bawex airlock, it opened, and two Lobsters beetled out.

"Two of them," Pancho said. "That's something new."

The Linguist whistled a little laugh. "Almost everything

is new to you. That's why I enjoy your company so much.''

Our keys told us we could survive no more than thirty hours inside. If the Dean was in there, he didn't have much time left.

''I do vaguely remember this,'' Miko said as we walked through the airlock's second door. It seemed like a hard place for someone to forget.

The Bawez region was huge and gloomy, very much the opposite of the one we'd just left. Jagged rock formations like stalagmites rose all around us, chalky ghosts in the dim half-light. A warm mist of rain fell silently; wet gravel rattled under our feet. Damp smell of mildew, with a slight chlorine tang.

''Where are the Bawexians?'' B'oosa asked.

''Patience.''

Suddenly there were four of them, then six, surrounding us. Serpents, pale white with large heads and long soft bodies. One rose up, taller than me, and spoke, sighing, hissing. Two small frail arms unfolded from under its chin and made languid gestures.

''It asks whether you are food,'' Guide said. ''I think that is a joke. Carbohydrates would be poison to them.'' The creature's breath was halogen and rot.

''Does it remember me?'' Miko said. ''Or M'bisa?''

The creature and Guide exchanged hisses and gestures. ''That is not its function, it says. It remembers very little outside of ontology and food. To answer your question would require a breeder-oracle. They stay in a lake about twenty kilometers from here.''

Miko turned to B'oosa. ''Should we go?''

B'oosa rubbed his chin. ''It would take several hours . . .''

''And you would go without me,'' Guide said. ''I have more productive things to do. This place is very uncomfortable.''

My throat was already raw from the chlorine, and the smell was nauseating me.

"We can't stay in here for hours," Miko said. "Or am I more sensitive to the air than the rest of you?"

Alegria coughed. "I don't think I can last another ten minutes. I'll pass out."

"Perhaps you two large ones should go to the lake," Guide said. "Your keys might allow you a limited kind of communication."

"Is he here?" Pancho asked plaintively. "If you won't go with us, you must—"

"I cannot tell you things that you must find out for yourselves."

I had sidled over next to the Linguist; I suddenly reached out and snatched his arm. "I think I can stand it. But you're coming with me."

He struggled for a second and then went limp. My hand circled his entire arm, cold, veins pulsing. "This is very uncivilized."

Two more Bawexians reared up. I tightened my grip. "Humans are impetuous," I said. "Sometimes violent."

He roll-blinked several times and stared at me. "Very well. Your Dean is not here. He was gone before we reached this place."

I didn't let go. "How do I know you're not lying?"

"I have never lied. I cannot lie."

"As far as we know, that's true," B'oosa said. "Let's get out of here."

"Wait," I said. "I don't think he likes it here much, either. I think I'll just hold on until he tells us where to go next."

"I cannot tell you things that you must find out for yourselves."

"That seems to be a rule that can be broken."

"I can live here indefinitely."

"And I can stay here for thirty hours. Does that appeal to you?"

"You won't do it."

That was true. My stomach wasn't going to make it another hour. I tried to keep that thought out of my mind by repeating over and over *the hell I won't, the hell I won't, the hell I won't—*

"All right. One more clue. If you promise not to do any more violence."

"I promise. If the clue does help us."

"It was on Level 9 that he disappeared. That is all I will tell you." B'oosa and I nodded at each other and everybody bolted for the airlock.

We started toward the sled. "Wait," the Linguist said. "You lied to me in there. You couldn't have stayed much longer. You subverted my telepathy, on purpose."

"That's right. A man's life is at stake."

"Good joke." He covered his face and made that damned whistling noise. "You humans will develop a sense of humor yet."

"You find death so amusing. Don't Linguists ever die?"

Guide was seized by a fit of whistling. "You *do* have a sense of humor," he gasped between whistles.

"No," I said. "I'm serious."

He wagged his head. "Always serious. Serious, violent, untruthful, ignorant. I don't know why we let you visit."

"Please . . . I really would like to know."

"A joke isn't funny if you have to explain it."

"Please."

"Oh, all right. Occasionally, very rarely, a Linguist will cease to exist in his corporate state. It is considered very bad, a very low form of humor. We call it 'acting-like-an-animal.' Like some other things, dying is done routinely only by lower forms of life. It doesn't look as if it would be very interesting."

"Then your race is immortal?"

"Technically, no. Given enough time, anyone will make an error in judgment. Enough errors, and sooner or later . . . well. You know. Acting-like-an-animal."

"What you mean is, you can only die by accident?"

"There is no such thing as an accident. Only errors in judgment. Any action has associated with it a set of possible results, of varying probability. All must be taken into account. We Linguists have the ability to visualize a nearly

infinite number of possible consequences to any given
action. If an action has among its possible results a finite
probability of acting-like-an-animal, we choose another
action. Is that so difficult to understand?''

''No.'' Had he calculated the probability of my crushing
the life out of him a few minutes ago? I noticed that he
was keeping his distance.

B'oosa was looking at the diagram as we got into the
sled. ''What part of Level 9 do we want?''

''I have told you what I will tell you.''

He nodded, not looking up. ''Most of the level is taken
up by the Oomo. Might as well start there.''

We went up one level and slowed to make a transverse
change. There were three Lobsters at the loading dock
there, getting into a sled. Even Guide gave them a long
look. We picked up speed and they slid out of sight.

Two more shifts of direction and we arrived at the
entrance. Our keys said that we could exist inside for
almost a month. I noticed Guide's key said he could stay
for an indefinite period of time. As usual.

We stepped into a golden landscape. It was totally alien,
but irresistibly beautiful. Emerald green buildings reached
magnificently into the sky, their glossy sides a pleasant
contrast to the soft gold clouds and wheatlike grasses that
swayed in the gentle breeze. The air was light, but sweet.
It had the faint taste of cloves, a touch of other fragrant
spices. A very calm and peaceful place.

An alien approached us from the nearby city, skimming
over the top of the grasses on a small platform. At first I
thought he was slimy and covered with scales, but as he
got closer I could see that he was furry. He resembled a
child's stuffed animal, a friendly teddy bear with large
brown eyes. I liked him right away.

''Welcome, Humankind,'' he said, settling down in
front of us. His voice had a ripple to it, like water over a
rocky bed. It was a nice sound. ''We do not often have
visitors from your race. Please make yourself at home.
Enjoy.''

It would be an easy place to do just that. Enjoy. The

light breeze brought the echo of chimes far away, the sound of easy laughter from the city. It was hard to concentrate on our task. The alien reached out and touched each of us as he introduced himself. His name was Pagoo and his touch was soft.

"We're looking for someone," I said, trying to focus in on the Dean. "A human, shorter than me, black with white hair."

Pagoo smiled and warmth radiated from him. "I have not seen him, but perhaps he will come. You should wait."

"That sounds like a good idea," said Pancho. "I like this place."

I wasn't sure if that would be the right thing to do or not. But as I thought it over it seemed more and more like the best course of action. This was a nice place. The Dean was bound to show up sooner or later and we could wait for him. The fragrant air and distant chimes were soothing. A person could forget his troubles in a place like this. It would probably be good to wait. The Dean would come. We might as well be comfortable while we waited. I nodded at Pancho and looked for the others. Miko and Alegria were running through the golden fields, laughing. B'oosa was bent over a flower, examining it closely. It was a beautiful flower and he looked happy. It would be a nice place to stay.

Pagoo seemed pleased with our decision. There would be a big feast with much singing, dancing, and laughter. They would make a festive occasion out of it. The festival would last a long time: hours, days, weeks; it didn't matter. They were a joyous people and spreading happiness was what they liked to do best. It was rare that so many humans came to visit. They would make the most of it.

The more I talked with Pagoo, the happier I felt. These were truly wonderful, friendly people.

B'oosa walked over to us. I noticed he had picked the flower and was absently brushing his face with it. Pancho gave him a friendly tap on the shoulder. They both grinned, though B'oosa's face quickly slipped into a concerned frown.

"I'm worried, Carl," he said.

"How can you be worried?" I asked. "Everything is just fine."

"That's the trouble. We have problems. We should be doing something to find the Dean. Everything is *not* fine. Why should we feel that way?"

Pagoo ruffled his fur and I was almost bowled over by a feeling of well-being. Never in my life had I been so content. "Aren't you happy?" I asked B'oosa.

"Yes, but . . ." Again a wave of absolute joy swept over me. I almost cried with sheer pleasure.

B'oosa had a strained expression on his face, like he was fighting something. Why didn't he just relax and feel good like the rest of us? It was easy. Even Guide . . .

No, that wasn't right. I'd lost track of the Linguist. Where was he? I looked around for him and saw him standing next to the exit. He didn't look like he was having fun, though with a Linguist it's hard to tell.

"We *have* to go," said B'oosa. He was sweating, his jaw clenched tight, his hands drawn into hard fists. "It's very . . . important. We . . . must . . . leave." He drew labored breaths between words.

I couldn't understand what he was getting so worked up about. The more forceful he got, the more relaxed and at ease I felt.

"There's no hurry," I said. "We can wait for the Dean. When he comes we can leave."

"He's not coming, Carl. Can't you see that? This is a trap, a deadly trap. If we stay we'll never leave."

I didn't care if I left or not. All my troubles seemed so far away that they didn't matter at all. There were far worse places to play out one's allotted years. Besides, I could leave if I wanted to. Nobody was holding me here.

B'oosa grabbed Pancho. I couldn't understand why he was doing that. Pancho didn't resist, just smiled as the large Maasai'pyan lifted him up and carried him to the exit. I shrugged my shoulders toward Pagoo. There was no accounting for what some people would do. I was rewarded by a rush of total delight. I laughed and the singing wind carried it away to be shared.

B'oosa had pushed Pancho into the airlock and was in the process of running down Miko. It seemed like a game. Miko was clearly having fun avoiding him. They ran in large circles around us, Miko hooting with pleasure as he dodged B'oosa. I cheered both of them on, thinking how *nice* it was to play a game which had no winner, because then there could be no losers, no bad feelings. There shouldn't ever be bad feelings. Soon B'oosa's long legs made the difference and he caught Miko. Even then Miko didn't lose. He didn't seem to mind at all as B'oosa carried him off to join Pancho.

I watched with amused detachment as B'oosa returned to get Alegria. Such a silly game. After he got her he returned to me.

"I've got to do this, Carl," he said in a very serious voice.

I laughed. It was all so silly. He ought to go back and bring the others so that we could all have fun.

He came at me and I giggled. I couldn't help it; he looked absurd with that frown. It was out of place. He tried to hit me and I dodged, doing a little skipping dance as I moved away from him. I taunted him. We were playing a child's game. It was fun. When he got close to me I pushed him away with my longer arms. He got so frustrated it really broke me up.

Somehow he tripped me. The ground was soft. There didn't seem to be anything here that could hurt me. He jumped on top of me. I liked wrestling. I tickled him. Instead of tickling me back, he reached for the side of my neck and pressed down hard. Why would he do a thing like that?

It hurt.

I didn't want to be hurt.

Everything else felt good.

It hurt.

Everything else went black.

* * *

Cobwebs. Cinders in my mouth. I felt terrible. It was an effort to open my eyes. Someone was talking to me.

"I'm sorry, Carl," said the voice. "It was the only way." The voice belonged to B'oosa.

I pulled myself up to a sitting position with great difficulty and looked around. We were on the loading dock. My head felt like it had been split in two.

"You understand what a trap that was, don't you?" asked B'oosa.

I started to shake my head, but that hurt too much. "You really caught me one," I said.

"Had to. They would have kept us there until we died."

"What happened?" I asked.

"We were seduced," said B'oosa. "Seduced into feelings of well-being and extreme happiness. It's partly physiological, partly psychological. The Oomo are quite adept at it." He shot an angry look at Guide. "The Linguists knew it all along."

"Why didn't you warn us?" I asked Guide.

"It is not our duty to warn. I cannot tell you things that you should find out by yourselves."

"It could have killed us," said B'oosa.

Guide started whistling again. I could have killed *him*.

"Those keys you gave us are pretty good at warning us about physical dangers," I said. "Why can't they warn us about other types as well?"

"What dangers? I saw no threatening situations."

"I'd call psychological manipulation like that pretty threatening. We should have been warned."

"Emotions and psychological stability are highly variable even within a given species," said Guide. "It would be fruitless to try and estimate the threshold points. Your friend managed to break free."

"It wasn't easy," said B'oosa.

"No one said it would be easy. You humans are slaves to emotions. I find that ridiculous, time-consuming, and often self-defeating. You are almost as bad as the Oomo. They have completely lost out to their emotions. Once they discovered how to stay happy and content all the time, they stopped developing as a race. They haven't done anything in the last five hundred years except smile . . . and make others smile.''

In spite of what I had just gone through, I wasn't sure that was an entirely bad path to follow. Progress may have stopped for them, but they were satisfied. I'd seen a lot of people who were continually striving but never happy. Who was to say which was better? Not me.

B'oosa was helping Pancho to his feet. A sled whipped by with several Lobsters inside. They were really on the move.

"We seem to be at a dead end," said Alegria. "Where should we go from here?"

No one spoke up. Certainly Guide would never make a suggestion. As I looked up the tube at the disappearing sled something occurred to me.

"Why are there so many Lobsters around?" I asked Guide. "I thought they usually stayed in one place."

"They do," he answered. "It is not unknown for a single individual to remain in one sector for centuries."

"Then why are so many of them traveling in the sleds?"

"I do not know," said Guide. "Their actions are unpredictable. We know next to nothing about them except that they are a sentient race. They have never communicated with any of us and we are unable to touch them telepathically. It is unknown whether their noncommunication is due to a lack of ability or a lack of desire on their part."

"I think we ought to follow them."

"Why?" asked Miko.

"Why not?" I said. "Does anyone have a better idea?"

No one did. We were running out of options.

We climbed into a sled and Guide took us to the Lobster's sector. As I had expected, it was one of those areas opaqued from the tube. Several of them entered just before us. I slipped in my key. It said we had roughly four days.

As before, Guide was given an indefinite period of time. Linguists and Lobsters seemed to be able to go anywhere they wanted.

We entered as a group, with Guide taking up the rear. B'oosa was in front, Pancho was beside me. He was having second thoughts about going inside.

"I don't think this is such a good idea," he said as the airlock cycled. "I can't stand those Lobsters. Besides, they couldn't have taken the Dean against his will. They're far too weak. They can hardly get around by themselves."

Before I could answer Pancho the inner door slid open and we stepped inside.

The ground was not dirt or rock, but the familiar metal-work used between levels throughout Construct. Where the sky should have been, bare struts and braces crossed the ceiling. The air was thin and dry, but other than that it seemed no different from the empty spaces in Construct not occupied by alien sectors. I asked Guide about that.

"They have never given us any parameters from which to construct a facsimile of their home environment. We do not even know where their home planet is located. They came to us on a starship and destroyed it as soon as they arrived. We know nothing of them."

All *I* knew was that they gave me an uneasy feeling. One or two of them were bad enough, but there there were hundreds of them, all swarming across the metal floor in absolute silence. It was creepy. I could understand how Pancho felt.

Several of the aliens came through the airlock into the sector and skittered past us without any apparent notice. That seemed to be a good sign; at least they weren't interested in eating us.

I felt like a midget in a huge room, with the metal ceiling—the sky, really—kilometers above me. It was hard to get any perspective within such a massive scale. Some-how it hadn't bothered me in the other sectors where there had been clouds and alien artifacts. This seemed even stranger.

"They all appear to be heading in one direction," said B'oosa. Though there was some milling around, the general direction seemed to be moving the mass of them toward the wall a short distance from us. We started in that direction.

It got crowded. Even though we stuck together it was hard moving through all the Lobsters. At least they weren't bothering us. If we bumped into one it would move. If one bumped into us, we moved, rapidly. They still made me nervous.

Soon we got near the center of all the commotion. It was hard to make out exactly what was happening, but it all seemed to have something to do with one of the creatures on a raised platform. It was raised up on its back feet, huddled over something else. I pushed myself up against B'oosa to get a better look.

It was Dean M'Bisa. He was stretched out on the platform, naked. I couldn't see any marks on him, but I couldn't tell if he was breathing, either.

B'oosa saw him too. "We've got to do something," he said.

I turned to Guide. "What have they done to him?" I asked. "Is he alive?"

"He lives, after a fashion. His body still functions, but his mind is gone."

"Gone? What do you mean, gone?"

"Do not forget I am mildly telepathic. I can read surface thoughts on most creatures, especially humans. The Dean has no such thoughts. His mind is totally gone, blank."

The Linguist started to back away.

"Where are you going?" I asked. "We need your help."

"It is not my duty to help you," he said. "This is a highly unusual situation. It has never happened before, but I foresee an extremely high probability of damage, both mental and physical, if I remain. Therefore I choose not to remain.'' With that he disappeared into the mass of Lobsters, heading for the exit.

"Get the Dean?'' I asked B'oosa.

He nodded. ''Then we leave like Guide, only faster.'' We gathered up Pancho, Miko, and Alegria.

''They haven't paid the slightest attention to us so far,'' said B'oosa. ''For all we know they can't even see us. I say we just walk up and get him. If they put up a fight, we'll fight. If not, we run.'' He was whispering, though for all we knew they couldn't hear us, either. ''They don't seem to be very fast. We know they're not very strong. I think we can get away. We don't have time to wait or go back to the ship.''

That was true. It looked like they were getting ready to have the Dean as a main course. Maybe they *couldn't* see us. There was no time for anything complicated.

''Let's go,'' said Pancho. We circled around and came up on the platform from the rear. Less crowded that way.

''I'll take the Lobster,'' said B'oosa. ''Carl, you grab the Dean. Alegria; you, Miko, and Pancho get ready to shove anything that moves toward us.''

It wasn't exactly what you'd call a complicated plan, but it was the only plan we had.

We reached the platform without causing any commotion. It was as if we didn't exist as far as the Lobsters were concerned. B'oosa jumped up and I followed him. The Dean lay on a small table with the Lobster leaning over him, touching him. I went straight for M'Bisa and B'oosa headed for the Lobster.

I almost made it.

Two steps away from the Dean, the Lobster seemed to notice me for the first time. He straightened up and several of his eyestalks rotated my way. I froze, stopped dead in my tracks.

Every muscle in my body was geared to the single task of taking those last two remaining steps and grabbing the Dean, but I couldn't. I couldn't move at all. I couldn't breathe. Maybe my heart had stopped, too. I couldn't tell.

I was aware of a cold touch; not physical, but mental. It

seemed to fill my skull, my being. I looked at the Dean and thought about what Guide had said. *His mind is gone.* And what about me?

The Lobster started toward me with a slithering motion. His mandibles made soft clicking noises. B'oosa lay curled in a ball on the platform. He wasn't breathing. The Lobster reached up and touched my forehead.

His clawed hand was cold, but not nearly so cold as the fingers that moved through my brain.

I was getting weak, dizzy. I wanted to close my eyes, but couldn't. Things were being taken from me, I was powerless to resist. My mind raced, fighting it. Losing.

I couldn't remember my father's name.

I couldn't remember who the man on the floor was. It seems I should have known him.

I couldn't remember what I was doing here. What was this place?

I couldn't remember . . .

I couldn't . . .

I . . .

. . .

V

*Branching. One becomes many. The exchange of protein,
exchange of life-force. The water, the world. The multi-
mind. Seeking life, light, shelter, food. All things con-
sumed become part of the whole. Unity in diversity. From
the water to the stars in a trillion generations. All part of
the Mother Cell—bless, bless—forever there as it was in
the beginning. As it ever will be. My sisters scatter, filling
the world, filling the universe. They sing the song of
forever. I join them through the years.*

*   *   *

*Destroy all that is not-good-life. That is the command, the
word from the warrior-heart. It is the prime directive. All
must fall before our might. The good-life shall rule from
one arm of the galaxy to the other. I remember, I
remember:::*

> *Out of twist-space into the star system that was
> home to the Larbach. They had refused to yield to
> our obvious superiority. For two hundred turns they
> had thus refused and the mandate came down from
> the Warrior-Chief. Annihilate. With pride I com-
> manded the lead ship and touched the button that*

231

tickled their sun, drove it mad. One hundred billion people dead by my simple action. It was a glorious battle, not a shot fired at us. One hundred billion lives. I wish it had been more. I remember:::

The good-life shall rule from one arm of the galaxy to the other. All must fall before our might. It is the prime directive. Hatred and death to all not-good-life.

*   *   *

Such a pretty flower. Pretty, pretty flower. Nice flower, happy flower. Such a pretty flower. Happy flower. Such a pretty . . . Such a pretty . . . Such a pretty. . . . .

*   *   *

$$\frac{d\bar{Z}}{dc} = f_x \frac{d\bar{x}}{dc} + f_y \frac{d\bar{y}}{dc} + [c - g(\bar{x},\bar{y})] \frac{d\bar{\lambda}}{dc} + \bar{\lambda}\left(1 - g_x \frac{d\bar{x}}{dc} - g_y \frac{d\bar{y}}{dc}\right)$$

$$= (f_x - \bar{\lambda}g_x)\frac{d\bar{x}}{dc} + (f_y - \bar{\lambda}g_y)\frac{d\bar{y}}{dc} + [c - g(\bar{x},\bar{y})]\frac{d\bar{\lambda}}{dc} + \bar{\lambda}$$

$$\frac{d\bar{Z}}{dc} = \bar{\lambda}$$

*   *   *

Free. The winds take me where they will. My sieve is full, no worries save the clickers that nip at my flight foam. There is little I can do about that except stay to the shadows, hug the clouds. But what fun is that? One must live, enjoy. Otherwise life would be as dull as the ground. I weave a poem in the air. The wind blows it away to my siblings. I bank sharply and the sun catches my fullness. Ah, life. Enjoy, enjoy.

*   *   *

Shadows and flashes of light. Something was moving. Sounds came to my ears. They made no sense. It was easier to relax. Much easier.

*   *   *

Work. That's all we ever do all cycle is work. Monitor says do this, do that. We do what she says. We are good workers. What do we get? Pitiful rations, a flimsy rod to hang on at night. I tell you it isn't fair. There has to be a better life. I know we weren't high-born, but there has to be justice somewhere. I want to see the light of day again. Curse my father's father, whose spawn brought me to this place.

*   *   *

"They ain't gonna kill me till they can't get one more dightin' pesa out of me. Gonna dightin' bleed me dry if they can. But they're gonna have one hell'va fight on their hands. Old Markos don't give up easy."

*   *   *

0010111000010101101010100110100101001000010101000101010010100101110101011101010101011101000111110000010101010100010111010101000101001101110101010101011101110001010010101010

*   *   *

I made this with my own hands. It has a part of me in it. It also contains the essence of the soul of a star. I bless it and mold it. It will power your craft through the universe. Take it and use it well. I have bled for it. Both the star and I are the less for what we have given of ourselves to you. We are also the greater for it. Use it well. With kindness.

*   *   *

I was being moved. Nothing connected with anything
else. There were no common points of reference. The light
hurt my eyes. I closed them and drifted away.

*   *   *

*SUB-CRYSTAL MONITOR FIVE SEVEN ONE REPEAT
REPEAT REPEAT. RISK FACTOR INCONSISTENT WITH
LIFE-SUPPORT. UPGRADE AND MAINTAIN. LITHIUM
LEVEL NINE FACTOR POINTS BELOW OPTIMAL SET-
TING. ADJUST ADJUST ADJUST ADJUST ADJUST.*

*   *   *

"Shize, Springer. Can't you do no better than that? You
lying there like an old lady. Get your butt off the sand and
move those legs. Now! Move 'em."

*   *   *

*You must understand that I bear you no malice. There is
no room in my life for hate. It is simply that you are not
like me. That simple. I and my kind must continue living
and you are in my way. If you were a rock I would move
you, but since you are a living being and potentially
harmful to me I must kill you. I feel no regrets and no
pleasure. It is something I must do. Surely you can understand that. It is either you or me and I choose me.*

*   *   *

"Carl. Can you hear me, Carl? Squeeze my hand if you
can hear me."

*   *   *

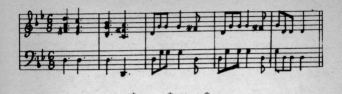

*   *   *

"On Selva we are practically born with bolos in our mouths. I'm good with one. Before I joined Starschool *I was village champion."*

*   *   *

"Some risk more than others. Life is never easy. On Maasai'pya that knowledge comes early. My brother was younger than you when he died."

*   *   *

Maasai'pya: a place. *Starschool*: a ship. Selva: a place. B'oosa: a name. B'oosa: a friend. Something to hold onto.

*   *   *

"This is song-on-wing approaching green strip at designated level. Speed mark seven five."
  —*"You are cleared, song-on-wing."*—
The dusty landscape rushes beneath me, the twin moons lay far behind. The thrusters respond smoothly as I nose the switches. It is a good ship, we have been through much together. With my sub-dominate tendril I adjust the final approach program. Now I see the silver city. It fills my lungs with joy. My chest swells, I make the sound of happiness. After so long, it is good to be coming home. Home!

*   *   *

Home: Springworld. A place, a planet. Home.

*   *   *

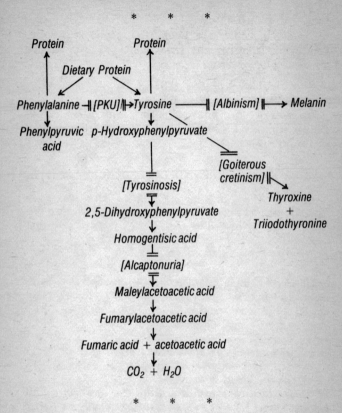

*   *   *

The ideal trajectory is selected so that losses of kinetic energy due to gravity equal that which is caused by the air resistance. Is that clear, class? :::Morons::: They think only of the food station when they should have all their ganglia occupied with space flight. How do they expect me to make cold-sleep pilots out of these imbeciles? This is one snarg of a way to earn a living. I wish I was back in space.

*   *   *

Class. *Starschool*. The Dean. That sound is a voice. Someone is talking to me. The words go through me like the wind. They carry no meaning.

*   *   *

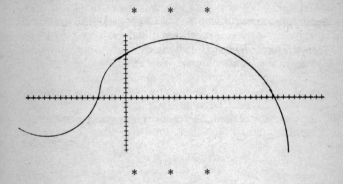

*   *   *

andar	ando	andaré	anduve	andado
caber	quepo	cabré	cupe	cabido
dar	doy	daré	dí	dado	*DISC::SCROLL ONE*
estar	estoy	estaré	estuve	estado
jugar	juego	jugaré	jugué	jugado
venir	vengo	vendré	vine	venido

*   *   *

CARL! CARL! CARL! CARL! CARL! CARL! CARL!

*   *   *

Balance. I had to find a point of equilibrium, a place to start from. So much there: order/disorder, happiness/sadness, knowledge/confusion, love/hate, war/peace: yin and yang expressed in thousands of voices. They were all a part of me. Yet somewhere deep inside there was a special place:

Carl Bok of Springworld. In ways he was like many of the others. In other ways he was unique. I searched for him.

*   *   *

"Carl. Can you hear me?"

A voice. It was B'oosa. Another voice. The Dean. Time had passed, how much I didn't know. It didn't matter. I lived. They lived. We all lived and grew. We had been transformed, imprinted with the thoughts of a multitude of planets. We were different. We were the same.

"Carl, please. Can you hear me?" B'oosa.

"Yes, friend," I said softly, opening my eyes and looking into his. "I can hear you."

I was back aboard *Starschool*. I was going home.

SPRINGWORLD

Starschool IV
Curriculum Notes—Springworld

This is the first year that Springworld has been included as part of the Selva leg of the *Starschool* tour. The main interest Springworld offers is the rapidity and ubiquity of the changes wrought on the planet as a direct result of communication with the Ba'torset'uon—the Lobsters—of Construct.

All of the Confederación has benefited from the avalanche of information the Lobsters transmitted to humanity in 355, while *Starschool II* was visiting Construct. But the most dramatic evidence of its worth, by far, is in the complete terraforming of what was once the most hostile environment ever challenged by colonists . . .

I

I WATCHED THEM leave, walking slowly down the winding path from my house. They were young, tall and gangly; Springworld born and bred. A new generation, growing fast. They came every week just to sit and talk for a few hours. Silly. Most of what I told them was in the library files.

I stood on the deck outside my living room until they disappeared from sight. An *above ground* house on Springworld. The past ten years have brought a lot of changes. Changes in Springworld, changes in me, changes nearly everywhere. All because of Construct.

When we first began to realize what had happened to us, the Confederación stepped in fast. They had some crazy idea of turning us into classified documents, passing us around from expert to expert and picking our brains. It didn't work for a number of reasons. They were pretty disappointed.

We still don't know what Construct really is or why it was built. It seems to be a place for exchange of information, but the Linguists—if that's what they do—turned out to be rank amateurs at it compared to the Lobsters.

The Lobsters were efficient, if brutal, in their manner of gathering information. They pulled every thought, conscious and unconscious, from their subject, left his mind completely blank. Then they integrated all this information into the group mind their race shared. Almost as an afterthought, they put back what they had taken. They weren't nearly as efficient in this part of the operation. There was a lot of overlap.

Oh, I got back all the "Carl Bok" they took. At least I think I did. There's no way I can be completely sure, though I can't detect any holes in my memory or knowledge. It was that other stuff that really hit us. Overlap.

We ended up with scattered bits and pieces from all the other races the Lobsters had "communicated" with. Some of it was jumbled, some of it was crystal clear. It was transferred back to us as a kind of static along with what they had taken. It became as much a part of us as our own lives and experiences. This is what the Confederación was after. They were looking for a weapon. There wasn't any. Or at least we didn't give them any, which amounts to the same thing.

By far the majority of the things passed to us were personal, everyday things. Mankind isn't the only race in the universe guided by emotions, not by a long shot.

I know a thousand ways of feeling love. I know the love of one Stardrifter for another; the longing love of a race so scattered that eons pass between meetings of individuals. I know the love of the Hivekeepers, who have no word for privacy, no word for self, but fifty words for love.

I know a thousand ways of feeling hate, of indifference, of superiority, of humbleness. of selfishness, of altruism. Name an emotion and I can see it through a filter of more races than I can count, many of which died out before the Earth had cooled. The group mind of the Lobsters is ancient beyond belief.

It tends to give one perspective.

We also collected an immense amount of trivia. Those of us who went through the process—Dean M'Bisa, Pancho, B'oosa, Miko, Alegria, and myself—are walking encyclopedias of useless knowledge. And some useful knowledge.

Springworld is a garden planet now, thanks to a piece of information Alegria picked up that helped us tame the wind. B'oosa came up with an incredibly cheap energy system. Dean M'Bisa is exploring a new concept of theoretical mathematics. We all have things like that. Much of it has been transferred to the Confederación library network, available to any of the inhabited planets.

I held some back. I'm sure the others did, too, although it's not something we talk about. Some things were too horrible to share, or too personal. Some were too dangerous.

"Carl?"

I smiled, sat down on a bench.

"Hello, Pancho. What's happening?" I could feel him next to me, though he was light years away. Since Construct, all of us who were wiped by the Lobsters have had this method of instantaneous communication. A very handy byproduct of the process.

"I'm on the move again, amigo. Just thought I'd let you know."

"You don't stay put long, do you?"

"Selva seems pretty tame these days. I'm going out with a Confederación contact team to Physome. Want to come along?"

Physome. A beautiful planet, beautiful people. They worked with living matter the way we worked with steel and wood. Only they coaxed rather than bending or cutting. It would be a good race to contact. We could learn from each other. In a way we had already learned, for a part of me was from Physome as surely as if I had been born in the silver webs of their hutches. I knew them. I liked them. I loved them. They were a part of me.

I thought it over. No.

"Sorry, Pancho. Not this time. Crops are about ready for harvest."

"You never go anywhere, amigo. I can't figure out whether you're a gentleman farmer or a hermit."

"This was my father's land. My roots are here."

"Your roots are everywhere, as are mine."

Laughter. *"That's true, old friend. But if I tried to chase them all down I'd be old and grey before I even got started. Have a good trip. Let me know what you find."*

"I'll keep in touch. Adios, amigo."

"Adios." The contact was broken.

Pancho was right. I hardly ever go anywhere. For some reason the excitement doesn't tempt me like it used to. I am what I am. I no longer feel the need to prove anything to anyone, including myself. After touching the lives of so many people of so many planets all I feel is a kind of gentle peace. I like to work the land of my father. I do it the old way, with my hands. Without the new machines I helped develop. It gives me pleasure. It would take a lot to get me to leave.

Of course Alegria is due back with a contact team any time now. She might get in touch with me with a problem or two. I wouldn't mind an excuse to see her again.

I wouldn't mind it at all.